W9-ABL-964

Walking Naked

by the same author

Walking Naked

Nina Bawden

ASBURY PARK PUBLIC LIBRARY
ASBURY PARK, NEW JERSEY

St. Martin's Press
New York

Copyright © 1981 by Nina Bawden
For information, write: St. Martin's Press,
175 Fifth Avenue, New York, N.Y. 10010
Manufactured in the United States of America

Library of Congress Cataloging in Publication Data

Bawden, Nina, 1925-
Walking naked.

I. Title.
PR6052.A84W3   1982   823'.914   81-16713
ISBN 0-312-85456-0   AACR2

*The author and publisher gratefully acknowledge
the kind permission of Michael and Anne Yeats to
reproduce 'A Coat' from* Collected Poems
of W. B. Yeats.

I made my song a coat
Covered with embroideries
Out of old mythologies
From heel to throat;
But the fools caught it,
Wore it in the world's eyes
As though they'd wrought it.
Song, let them take it,
For there's more enterprise
In walking naked.

William Butler Yeats
'A Coat'

For Virginia and Alec Waugh

PART ONE

The Game

'I really don't know what to wear,' Andrew said, just before eight o'clock on that Saturday morning.

Or I assume that he said it. Since I was asleep at the time I can't know for certain. I can only say that when I heard him make this remark a few minutes later (five past eight by my watch, the gold watch that he gave me for my fortieth birthday) it sounded like a repeat performance.

Novelists have to make some assumptions. We can't be awake all the time, nor present at every event. You have to take some things on trust, as Bishop Berkeley might have answered himself when he enquired about the continuing existence of a particular tree when he was not there to see it.

So you must believe what I tell you. (If you don't, we have no future together and you might as well abandon this narrative and go and play golf or croquet.) At about eight o'clock on a Saturday morning in March, Andrew, my husband, stood naked in front of his open clothes closet, scratching the mole on his left buttock, frowning at the rack of his suits, at the polished shoes placed beneath, at the neat piles of ironed shirts in the good hardwood shelves that had been custom built to receive them, and debated aloud what he should put on.

If he was irritated because I did not respond, he would have realised at once that I was still heavily sleeping, the deep, drowned sleep that comes on me just before dawn when I have had a bad night. Andrew knows about my bad nights and worries about them more than I do.

Another assumption. But I have been married to Andrew for sixteen years now and am entitled to make it. He knows his own pain and can bear it. He suffers more as an observer. I have seen the look on his face when one of his children is hurt or unhappy

9

and I know that my night fears trouble him in the depth of his soul even though (or perhaps because) he does not understand them.

Andrew is the boy on the burning deck, the brave lad with his hand in the gap in the dyke, the soldier who holds the pass. He wants to keep us all safe. That is quite a burden to carry.

When I wake at four in the morning, I am afraid the house will fall down. The bulge in the ceiling will swell like a boil and burst open, showering down plaster; the staircase will come away from the wall. I worry about the cost of the repairs and the difficulty of getting a builder we can rely on. I fear for Andrew and the children, for the au pair girl, for our dog and two cats, crushed and broken, smothered with cement dust, poisoned with fumes from the boiler. I lie awake in the dark and listen to creaks, small shifting and settling sounds, as our poor house struggles to keep us warm and dry under its rooftop. It is, of course, always worse when there is a storm.

Once, in the middle of the night, in a storm, something did happen. I could hear the big trees round the house cracking and groaning like sails. And then another sound; harder and drier. Explosive. Metallic. I got out of bed to look out of the window and saw that a corrugated iron structure that had been erected over the roof of a house on the opposite side of the street had come adrift in the gale. Huge sheets of corrugated iron were breaking loose from the scaffolding and being tossed in the air like dead leaves, floating up and down the street as if they weighed nothing, crashing down on parked cars. They could slice a man's head off like a guillotine, those sharp sheets of iron, but while I watched I saw people, my neighbours, foolish friends and acquaintances, running out of their houses in their night clothes to move their cars out of danger.

But that is something that happened quite recently, after the events about which I am writing and, curiously, while it was happening, I was not particularly frightened. My house fears go much further back. Perhaps to the time I heard my father weeping because my mother, while he was away at sea, had arranged to buy (at twenty-eight shillings a week) the house they were renting. This was in the thirties, in the Depression. I stood on the other side of a closed door and heard him say, 'Suppose the roof leaks, or a chimney blows off, who will pay for it?' Or the war. A London child, hearing the flying bombs cut out over my head and counting the seconds before the explosion. More likely, since I am more affected by fiction than I am by Bishop Berkeley's 'reality', it was a film I remember, towards the end or just after the war (or maybe later than that, an old black and white film on television) in which a staircase came away from the wall and the people who were standing upon it (queuing outside a theatrical agent's office, I think) fell to their deaths, screaming.

Or perhaps, as Andrew says, what I suffer from is a vague and indiscriminate dread (only he calls it anxiety) fastened on something real, to make it more bearable.

Perhaps Andrew is right. But explaining things doesn't cure them.

The house fear is not too bad, really. Or so I tell myself in the daylight. It is familiar now, and the familiar cannot be frightening. Although the house that I inhabit at four in the morning is not like any house I have ever lived in, I know it intimately, as if I had been born there. It has a large entrance hall with black and white tiles on the floor and a staircase that is sometimes plain wood, sometimes carpeted, that rises to a broad upper landing where there is a round window. A door on the left of the hall leads into a long room that is usually full of people sitting at a table and laughing and talking. There is wine on the table, and food, and the walls are either lined with books or have dark, gold-framed pictures upon them. That room is sound and all that is alarming about it is that I know (as the laughing people do not) that the rest of the house is crumbling about it. In the attic, for example, the floor boards are rotten and the water tank has an evil smell because a corpse, a bird with draggled feathers or a small animal, is floating on top of it. Sometimes – but not always – I can see the sky through the rafters. Apart from the occupied room, the happy room, there is no furniture in the house, only a bath tub, stained yellow and blue under a dripping tap, and an old, broken oven in the derelict kitchen. But

II

the worst room of all is the room on the right of the hall that is always kept locked. Sometimes I have a key to the door, sometimes not. Even when I do have a key, I don't always use it – it seems I can choose, most of the time, whether I do so or not. (Andrew would make something of this, I dare say, if I told him.) When I do use the key, unlock the door and look in, this room is always the same. The ceiling is hanging down in one corner, the walls bulge and the boards squeak and splinter under my feet. And where the ceiling is sagging, in the far corner, beyond the cracked, greasy window, a slow ooze of dark slime creeps down as I watch.

It is usually worse when I have been drinking. That is, when I have had something to drink; sherry before dinner and a couple of glasses of wine – half a bottle, perhaps – with the meal. I don't drink all that much any longer.

And I know how to deal with it now. It is a matter of conscious effort. I *will not* be trapped; taken over and terrified! It would be easier if I could put the light on and read but when I wake to these horrors I know that Andrew has probably only just gone to sleep and the light will disturb him. I welcome sleep, snuggling down with anticipatory pleasure almost as soon as I get into bed, but he lies awake for hours, reading or listening to the radio. (Perhaps the fact that our sleeping patterns do not fit has a psychological cause, perhaps not.) I try to tell myself that when I wake in the night it can be a creative time. I can think of the day ahead, of the weeks; the meals we will eat, the parties we will go to and give, the arrangements to be made for the children, the book I am working on. If none of these things divert me from the rotting timbers of my nightmare house, I force myself to relax physically, to breathe deeply and slowly, at the same pace as my sleeping husband beside me, and, in springtime and summer, wait for the first birds to start singing. Lately, I have found that the persistent hum of the traffic on the new motorway at the foot of the hill, half a mile or so from our house, is remarkably soothing. This long, straight, beautiful and friendly road, arched with slender and elegant bridges and planted on its banks with poplars and birches, speeds between London and the south west of England, Land's

End. It comforts me to think of it as life rushing past, childhood at one end, old age at the other, and myself lying here in the middle, looking forward and backward, seeing my end in my beginning, facing both ways. And sometimes, when I get to this point, sleep will come; the sweet, safe, consoling sleep before dawn.

When I woke this particular morning, Andrew was standing in front of his open clothes closet, naked except for a pair of dark purple socks. Seen from the back he is quite elegantly shaped; slender, tapered legs and a flat, neat bottom from which his almost waistless torso rises to sloping, well-padded shoulders. He has a head of thick, dark, fine hair that grows in a Vee down the back of his neck (he washes his hair every day and has it cut, at an expensive, Unisex hairdresser, every six weeks) and a triangular wedge of dark hair between his shoulder blades. He was scratching the mole on his left buttock and whistling under his breath very softly, not to wake me, perhaps, although it was time I woke up.

I looked at my watch and said, 'Andy.' He stopped whistling and looked over his shoulder.

'Oh, you've decided to face the world at last, have you?'

'It's not too late, is it?'

'No. Not really. You had a good sleep, though.'

This was said with lightly measured reproof. He was glad I had slept. On the other hand, *he* had been awake for hours. Honour satisfied, he padded to the bed, sat on the edge, jangling the springs (he has got thinner recently but at that time, which is four years ago now, he weighed more than he should) and touched my cheek with his hand. The tips of his fingers were cold. 'Help me, Laura,' he said. 'I don't know what to wear.'

I could see by the sly glint in his eyes that he had worked on this line. A joke to ease us into a difficult day.

I yawned and stretched, bracing my feet against his firm thigh. 'What's it like out?'

'Sunny and cold at the moment. Clouding up later and getting colder. That's the forecast, though of course you can't trust it. And it's not the point, anyway. I mean – what suit? Shirt and tie? There won't be any chance to change, will there?'

My husband worries about his appearance. Well, most people do, but some men affect not to care. I feel tender towards Andrew because he admits it, though sometimes I am annoyed when he insists I choose his clothes for him, seeing it as laziness on his part, an unimportant decision to be left to a wife. Now he smiled, looking anxious. 'You must admit, it is a *dilemma*! How should one appear for all these different occasions? Sombre or sporty? Formal or casual? Not easy, is it?'

I said, dodging the issue, 'I don't know what to wear either.'

'That shouldn't be difficult. You can put a plain coat over a pretty dress. A scarf and some yellow beads in your handbag. It's easier for a woman than it is for a man.' He picked up my hand and pretended to examine the lines on my palm. Then he looked at me. His eyes shone as he went on with the little speech he had been rehearsing while I was sleeping. 'I mean – *honestly*, Laura – what does a respectable Englishman wear to play in a tennis match, go to a Boat Race party, visit his son in prison and his father-in-law on his death bed?'

'We don't know that he really is dying,' I said, addressing myself to what seemed the easiest problem. 'If he is, he won't care what we're wearing. And what made you think of *yellow beads*? I haven't got any.'

'My mother had some yellow beads, I think. I don't know . . .' Andrew pulled down his upper lip and pressed it against his teeth with his forefinger. A nervous habit. 'I was only trying to make you laugh. An ordinary day in the life of an ordinary family.' He smiled, and sighed. 'Lord above, Laura! How did we get into this *mess*?'

'By living,' I said. 'By not being born dead.'

I was pleased with this answer. It had a tough, gallant ring to it. A note of cheerful stoicism, which is what I aspire to. The more honest reply to the question, that we are both obsessional about obligations, would have been in a lower and less inspirational key.

I can always make myself brave with words, drawing them on

14

like a comforting garment against the cold weather. I tell myself that this facility makes me tougher than Andrew, as my foolish night fears (at least, they seem foolish in daylight) give me more strength for disaster. Since nothing could be so dreadful as my imaginings, I am prepared for anything.

So I tell myself, knowing I lie. The truth is, life frightens me; I am always afraid. Perhaps everyone is afraid; the trick is to learn how to deal with it. I write because I am afraid of life, I think sometimes.

But I am such a coward, *really*! Travelling to lecture or read from my novels as I am often invited to do (the appetite people have for sitting in cold halls and listening to writers when they could be at home by the fire and reading in comfort is a constant amazement to me), I am beset with neurotic terrors. When I was younger I used to be afraid of losing my way, being unable to speak the language, having no money. Now it is the state of my bowels that worries me, and the crowns on my teeth. Humiliation of some kind, or failure. Suppose I should lose my notes, or both pairs of reading glasses? I see myself standing helpless and silent in front of all those expectant strangers. Desperately smiling. A rictus of fear.

I said, 'You can take a change of clothes in the car. Not that clothes matter. Honestly, darling, we'll get through somehow. We don't have to go to the party if you're too tired after the match. Or if you don't want to. There won't be time to come home before we go to the prison, but we could have lunch in a pub. Beer and sandwiches. Take it all *calmly*, that's the main thing. It's not such a mess, really.'

Lying again. Most of life is a mess and a muddle; all chance and luck. Perhaps you can look back years later and say, well, *this* happened, or *that*, and then it will all fall into place, cause and effect, straightforward and logical. That is the business of fiction, to put things in order.

Andrew said, 'The party would cheer you up, wouldn't it? That's what I thought, anyway. A bit of a boost for you, after the boredom of watching me play. I'm sorry about it, but as I told you, we've got this man from Boston, on a sort of state visit, and the Chairman has been laying things on for him. He's a keen young chap, so Old Pussy says, and he thought it would be a good thing if I could show him Hampton Court and give him a game. I couldn't really say no . . .'

'Did you want to?' I said.

The Game (called Real Tennis in England, Court Tennis in America, and Royal Tennis in Australia) is important to Andrew. The competition, the intellectual excitement, and keeping fit. There are also (though this is not why Andrew is fond of it) professional advantages for him. There are only about sixteen courts where you can play this unusual game in this country, three in Australia, seven in America, and two in regular use in France. The fact that Andrew is able to offer this select form of entertainment to visiting bankers is unlikely to secure him a partnership in the bank that he works for because it is a family business and he is not one of the Family, but it has given him a marginal advantage over the other managing directors. It means that his name will be favourably mentioned in the Partner's Room at the monthly lunches of smoked salmon, steak and kidney pudding, followed by Cabinet Pudding or Angels on Horseback. This menu never changes – certainly it has never changed in the twenty years Andrew has been there and there is no reason, short of political or financial catastrophe, to suppose that it ever will. It is said that a distant cousin, new to the bank, once suggested that soup should be served instead of smoked salmon at one of these lunches. He was reprimanded, and a few weeks later (a civilised interval) asked to resign. This may be an apocryphal story. Andrew is inclined to think it is true. When he first heard it, he laughed. He still laughs, though more cautiously, and he does not like me to repeat it at parties. It is the way the game is played and business conducted and Andrew, growing older, with a wife and children, a stepson in prison, does not wish, cannot afford now, to question it.

I am not mocking him. I understand the importance of games and the ritual that goes with them; it is just that the ones that I know are so different. From the moment that Andrew was born he was destined (or to be more exact, *forced* by his terrible parents) to play the right games, the games that fitted the system. He went to his pre-preparatory school at four years old, equipped with running shoes, rugger shorts, gymnastic gear, boxing gloves. From that moment the games that he played were organised and competitive and applauded by adults.

The games that you play in the street are not like that. No adult is watching, and though there are rules, no one teaches them to you except other children.

Where I lived, in the East End of London, I knew my street like I knew my own hand; the front doors, the door knockers, every crack in the paving stones. There were 'Safe Games' like Hopscotch, and Touch, and Farmer, Farmer, May We Cross Your Golden River, and 'Almost Safe Games' like Last Across (played on the busy main road) and What's The Time, Mr Wolf? This was not really a Danger Game, but when I was small, around eight, it was the game that frightened me most, following another child, dancing behind, trembling with fear for the moment when a transformed and horrible face, slavering fangs and glittering eyes, would turn on me and shout, 'Dinner Time!' My two youngest children, Henry and Isobel, were seven and five when I played this game with them, twisting round with a savage growl halfway down our long garden and laughing as they ran screaming. Coming home early one afternoon, and catching me at it, Andrew was shocked. It would give them bad dreams, he said.

Andrew has never played in the street. When we have children's parties he organises races and team games and quizzes. Losers and winners and prizes.

When I was thirteen, we played a War Game. This was in 1942. My school, evacuated from London in 1939, had returned now the worst of the bombing seemed to be over, and the big bomb site, several streets away from my house, had become a good, secret playground. A row of small houses had fallen; the mounds of tumbled brick and timber and broken baths and lavatory pans were overgrown in the summer with willow herb and brambles. The site was boarded up but we found a way in and were private there, playing Jews and Germans, or Nazis and Resistance Fighters, which were really elaborate Hide and Seek games, childish in origin but elevated in our eyes to an adult seriousness by their topical nature. If we were Resistance or Jews and were caught, we were 'tortured', until we revealed where our friends were hiding. The physical torture was ritual, self-inflicted, and fairly harmless. We burned our own finger tips with matches while our captors counted the seconds, rubbed our legs and arms with stinging nettles or thistles for as long as we could bear to, climbed as high as we dared in what was left of the shattered houses, creeping up broken stairways, walking the fragile boards of such upper floors as remained. The rules were that while a hostage was occupied in this way, burning or stinging himself, or climbing the ruins (once he stopped moving he was deemed to have 'lost his nerve' and 'given in') the other Resistance Fighters or Jews were free to 'escape' to the one house at the end of the row that was still moderately intact; home and safety.

After a while, how long I can't now remember, we grew bored with these naive exploits and worked out a more ingenious method of extracting 'confessions'. The game began in the same way; the victims were allowed five minutes to conceal themselves at one end of the site before they started to make their dodging, crouching journey through the carefully deployed lines of the enemy to the safe house at the other. The first to be intercepted was blindfolded and verbally threatened. Teeth were to be pulled out with pincers, sharp sticks thrust up fingernails, ears twisted off, nettles pushed up our bottoms. (One rude boy said 'arse-holes' but that was ruled out of order.) These trials were, for the timid and imaginative, harsh tests of courage, and those who gave way the quickest were (for the same reason presumably) the most inventive tormentors. A Jewish girl, a refugee whom my school had 'sponsored' when she left Germany in 1938, Hilde, my 'best friend', a black-eyed, sharp-featured beauty, was the child I feared most – and could frighten most easily. I suppose this was why we chose to be on opposite sides; knowing each other's weaknesses we were excited by the prospect of giving and receiving real cruelty, finding in it, perhaps, a curious, half-sexual pleasure. (It was the 'torture' aspect of this game, I realise now, that made it so addictive; once someone had been caught, both sides gathered round to watch, the chase was abandoned.)

Hilde would stand blindfold before me and my heart would begin to thump. 'Dirty Jew. Hitler would know what to do with you. You think you're safe, don't you? Well, you're not. The Germans are winning the war, he'll be coming to get you, and you know what will happen then, don't you?'

I had no real understanding of what I was saying. I did not know about the death camps then; only that Hilde's family, left behind in Berlin, were in some vague kind of danger. I mention this, not to excuse myself, but as a matter of historical interest. Some of the working classes who had seen Oswald Mosley and his bully boys in action knew what was happening in Germany, as did the intelligentsia and most of the upper classes (their attitudes either approving or deeply ashamed), but a great many middle class and lower middle class British were either totally ignorant, or held the opinion that whatever Hitler was doing to the Jews, they had 'probably asked for it'.

Hilde knew more than I did, of course. She would tremble and swallow; the blood would drain from her cheeks and lips, which developed a blueish tinge, and she would always 'give in' before the five minutes which was the time she was allowed if she was to save her companions. When I snatched off her bandage in triumph, she would grin at me shakily; a pleading, sickened grin that sometimes gave me a twinge of uneasiness. But more often not. After all, it would be her turn next time . . .

She had a soft, prettily accented voice with a slight hesitation that when I was in darkness held an extraordinary menace. 'Rats,' that soft voice would say. 'You don't like rats, do you, Laura? I have a rat here, a thin, savage rat with red eyes. A hungry rat with poisoned teeth, sharp as needles. It's coming toward you, creeping along, closer and closer, in a minute, you'll feel its stinky breath on your ankle.' And although I knew it was only Hilde, crouching in front of me, about to blow on my leg, this knowledge was useless. 'Beast,' I would shout, tearing off my own blindfold, 'Oh, you rotten beast, oh, I *hate* you . . .'

And she would look at me, bubbling with laughter. Sweet Hilde, my friend.

(How could we do this to each other? Why did we? We shared our sweet ration, our stamp collection, helped each other with homework, giggled at boys, dressed alike, wore our hair the same way, the same colour of hair ribbon, planned our futures – if we could marry twin brothers, we thought, we would never be separated.)

Well, of course it was only a game. And only that summer.

Towards the end of it, after the school holidays, in the September, we discovered that someone was living in the only house that still stood on the bomb site. An old woman, bombed out from some other part of the city, perhaps, or a tramp, taking shelter. Hilde and I had not been to the site for several weeks (we had been on a school camp in the Cotswolds) and when we did go, just the two of us (to smoke cigarettes privately) the old woman was already well settled, living in the basement kitchen. She had mended the window with cardboard and staked out an area round the house with a rough fence of wooden planks and barbed wire. Perhaps if this fence had not enclosed a blackberry patch we might have left her alone but the site had been our private domain for a long time and the berries were ripe. Hilde and I stood outside the fence and watched her, hobbling round her pathetic garden, watering a few small things she had planted with an old saucepan; a skinny ancient in rags, hardly human. We watched her and giggled whenever she farted, which was almost continuously, and saw, with horrified disgust, that there were brown marks of excreta on her bare legs. We went back the next day with two boys from our class, a lanky fourteen-year-old, known, for some reason, as Turtle, and his friend, Dickie, smaller and plumper, who had bright orange hair and an enviable crop of warts on his fingers. (Why I envied these warts, I cannot explain now. Any more than I can explain why my second child – Jeremy's sister, my daughter, Claudia – chose to tattoo her wrists when she was thirteen, making small incisions with a razor blade and rubbing in chalk and ink. At certain ages people do certain things and afterwards forget why.)

All I can do is set down the facts. Which are that the four of us, Hilde and me, Turtle and Dickie, ordinarily kindly and decent young people, broke down an old woman's feeble fence, invading her territory at first to pick the sweet, dusty black-berries (she had no more right to them than we had, we considered) and later, when the berries were finished, to tease and torment her, because when she saw us she flew into such extraordinary rages, waving her stick and screaming at us with wild, incomprehensible cries. I think now that she may have been dumb. At the time she simply seemed wonderfully and entrancingly mad. We had no intention of harming her (we would have been mortified if anyone had told us we were being cruel), only of provoking her into one of her theatrical displays. To hang round the house until she hobbled out, to see her contorted face, her shit-stained legs, hear her unintelligible shrieks, was an enduring excitement. It endured until one afternoon when she was waiting for us with a shot gun. She didn't take aim, just brandished it threateningly, as if it were only a stick, keeping up a shrill, high, mournful wailing like an air raid siren. We all turned and ran except Dickie, brave, foolish Dickie, who sped to take the gun from her. She dropped it as he reached her and from some hidden pocket in her filthy clothes produced another weapon. A meat knife, Dickie said afterwards, though he could hardly have had time to see before she sprang at him. Whatever it was, it was sharp; when he twisted away and staggered to where we were waiting outside the broken fence, blood was streaming from a long cut in his arm. Once he had reached us he began to cry, bawling (with fear more than pain) all the way to the hospital, but for a long time he was my hero. I was proud when he cut his warts and bled them on to my hand.

We never went back to the bomb site and we never saw the old woman again. Perhaps she was taken away to a mad house. The police came to take a statement from Dickie while he was being stitched up in Casualty. Or perhaps (this was Hilde's suggestion) she blew her brains out with the shotgun.

*   *   *

There are so many unfinished stories. This one shocks Andrew. And rightly. His children – our children, Henry and Isobel – have been taught not to tease the old and unfortunate, the disabled, the mad. Quite right too, but sometimes I think that their lives lack excitement. They have always been fetched from school, guarded and cherished, never (as far as I know) played Last Across. There are no wild places in our pleasant suburb except an acre of common land up by the station and Andrew will never let them play there because of the rapists and murderers that his mother was always so frightened of, although he doesn't admit that his caution has anything to do with those hysterical, old lady fears, saying only that they might cut their feet on the broken bottles and empty beer cans that litter the undergrowth. (Not that I would wish Henry or Isobel to encounter a rapist or a murderer, naturally, or even to come home with cut feet: my attitude in this, as in many things, is somewhat ambiguous.) Nor is Andrew against a certain amount of Imaginative Play. He is amused when the children play Monsters, growling at night in the bedroom, but he would disapprove of their latest game which they call Bloody Axe-Murderers. So far, fortunately, he knows nothing about it and probably never will know. Henry and Isobel understand perfectly well what they may and may not do when their father is in the house, within earshot. They are intelligent and circumspect children.

As Jeremy was at their age. And on the day about which I am writing, he was in prison. His half brother and sister did not know this, of course, nor did Beatrice, our au pair, nor my mother and father, nor Andrew's mother, nor most of our friends whom we were likely to meet at the party, nor the American banker with whom Andrew was to play a game of Real Tennis at Hampton Court.

Henry and Isobel, in fact, sitting in the sunny kitchen, drinking freshly squeezed orange juice and eating high fibre cereal, knew, on that morning, very little about anything. By the end of the day they were to know a bit more, although we didn't know that, or we would never have left them.

We explained what was going to happen (what we thought was going to happen) while we ate breakfast. Beatrice would look after them in the morning and Granny (Andrew's mother) would come to lunch and stay for the rest of the day while Beatrice went to a language class and out with her friends for the evening.

'Is Granny going to put us to bed? I don't want her to put us to bed,' Isobel said. 'She makes us drink hot milk with skin. It makes Henry sick.'

Henry screwed up his face and made vomiting noises.

'Ask her if you can leave it. Be good and ask her *politely*,' Andrew said coaxingly. His mother was fond of the children – 'Her babies', she called them, in a proprietary manner that always annoyed me – but they were at their worst with her, whining and demanding sweets and refusing to drink their milk or eat their green vegetables; worn out, by the time she left, by the endless games she made them play, draughts, and ludo, and snap. A gameswoman herself, a tireless bridge player, she knew no other way to amuse them.

'I want to play in the airing cupboard,' Isobel said. 'Granny won't let us play in the airing cupboard because she thinks we take off our knickers.'

Henry giggled.

'It's a bit warm for the airing cupboard, isn't it?' Andrew said.

Neither child answered. They exchanged secret glances.

Henry covered his mouth with his hand and laughed, spluttering orange juice and spit through his fingers.

'I like Seaside Granny best,' Isobel said, pouting plumply, deliberately retreating to babyhood. 'I want Seaside Granny to come.'

'She has to stay with Granpa,' I said. 'Granpa is ill. That's why we're going to see them.'

'I want to come with you,' Henry said. 'If Granpa is dying, that would be interesting. I've never seen anyone die.'

'My hamster died,' Isobel said. 'It was full of maggots.'

Henry turned white.

'Fat maggots,' Isobel said, smiling evilly.

Henry slid off his chair and ran to his father, hiding his face in his jacket.

'Isobel!' Andrew said, frowning at her.

'He started it, didn't he?'

'Never mind.' Andrew picked Henry up and cuddled him. Isobel glared. Andrew said, in response to the glare, 'He's younger than you, pettikins. Don't tease him.'

Andrew hates maggots and snails and white things turned up under stones. Being grown up he cannot admit it, but he can protect Henry.

'You'll have to look after him today, Isobel,' Andrew said. 'You're in charge.' He smiled at our au pair girl, a cheerful, adult-to-adult smile, to show he was not trying to undermine her authority. 'Isobel will have to help Beatrice and Granny to look after Henry.'

Andrew is fair and kind and punctilious. He respects other people, particularly if they are older or younger or poorer or less successful than he is, behaving in most situations with a patrician grace that is quite without condescension. Being socially inept myself, I find this ease admirable, even though I know what it sometimes costs him to put the show on the road, how he works at remembering names and family backgrounds (whose old parent is ill, whose child is about to get married or take an examination) and how he worries over what clothes he should wear.

He decided, this day, on a mid-grey mohair suit, a pale green shirt, and his black and orange Tennis Club tie, putting a darker shirt and a tweed jacket in the back of the car to change into after the party, before we went to the prison; an old raincoat to protect these clothes if we had a puncture and he had to change the wheel; and, of course, the tennis gear he would be wearing at Hampton Court to play the Chairman's 'keen young chap', the American banker.

He was not so young, after all. Andrew was, then, forty-seven. The banker looked slightly older, although he may not have been. He had one of those lined, lean, eager faces that change very little between forty and seventy. His wife, who was with him, was also lined and lean and beautifully dressed in the kind of good, American clothes that never seem to need ironing, emerging fresh and creaseless after long weeks of travel. They both had a robust but refined appearance, energetic smiles and excellent teeth.

The wife's name was Irma. While the men went to change, we walked round the gardens.

Once, I would have been bored with this situation, being left with a wife while our husbands were more interestingly occupied. When I was young, except for my close friends, Hilde and Rosie, other young women bored me. It seemed to me that men had more important things to talk about and that listening to them raised my own status, but now it does not seem like that. Perhaps women have changed, or perhaps the change is in me. Settling into my middle age (my prime, Andrew calls it, thinking to console me) I no longer look for sexual flattery.

Older women pay each other compliments in compensation. I complimented Irma on her pleated white skirt that swung elegantly from her thin hips, and on her low-heeled, tan shoes. She thanked me, smiling calmly. I said (overdoing it, gushing as usual), 'You have such wonderful clothes in America,' and she looked surprised. 'But you have lovely things here,' she said. 'I bought this skirt and sweater in London. I always buy my woollens in England.'

Andrew's mother used to have a friend (a rich widow, dead now) who had a house in Limerick. We stayed with her for a couple of nights early on in our marriage and she told us that she had bought the house because it was so convenient for shopping. I asked her what she meant (Limerick being hardly the kind of shopping centre it seemed she might patronise) and she said, with apparent astonishment, 'But so close to Shannon Airport, dear! To Paris, and New York.'

I wondered if I should tell this story to Irma and decided against it. She might not find it amusing. She might even think it a critical comment on her innocent remark about woollens. That I was a Communist, perhaps, sneering at rich people's habits! I did not want to let Andrew down by making a remark that was open to misinterpretation. I know I often let him down, out of clumsiness. So I said, 'I do hope your husband will enjoy this funny game. It's not at all the same thing as lawn tennis.'

'Oh, but Ed plays it at home,' Irma said. 'We have a court in Boston.' She beamed, showing white, even teeth. 'Ed has been so looking forward to playing at Hampton Court. It really is most kind of your husband.'

We walked back to the court, our feet crunching on the pale, weedless gravel. We had discussed Hampton Court, American clothes, and the weather – still fine, but the clouds were beginning to gather. Now we spoke of our children. Irma told me about her son at Harvard, her daughter at Cornell. I replied with anecdotes about Henry and Isobel. To mention the children of my first marriage seemed to require too much explanation. Particularly with Jeremy in his present predicament! All the same, as we went into the gallery (quaintly called the *dedans*) from which we were to watch our men playing, I felt I was being dishonest. Not, of course, that Irma would wish to hear my whole history. But was I hiding it out of vanity; a wish to appear, speaking of my young children, younger than Irma? She would think me odd, certainly, if Andrew should bring up the subject of his stepchildren later. With luck, he would not have the opportunity . . .

We took our seats. I apologised for the chill in the *dedans* (for economy reasons the court was only heated for four months in the winter) and for the fact that Andrew and I could not take our American visitors out to lunch afterwards. If we had not had a previous engagement we would have done, naturally; it seemed dreadful to have dragged them all this way out of London just for a *game*; most inhospitable; I hoped they would not feel too abandoned . . .

'Well, no,' Irma said – kindly cutting me short before I fell to the floor and lay at her feet, grovelling. As it happened, she and Ed were lunching with the Chairman and his wife who were coming to Hampton Court to collect them. 'It would have been so very nice,' Irma said, sincerely and courteously, 'if you could have joined us.'

As we could have done. Had we been asked. (Perhaps

Andrew had been asked, and not told me?) Or if we had not been due at the prison at three o'clock. There was time enough for us to go to William and Rosie's big annual party because we could leave when we liked, but not time enough for a leisurely expense account lunch with the Chairman. (If Andrew had been asked, what excuse had he given?)

I said, 'I'm sorry we can't. It's just that we had already accepted this invitation. It's the Boat Race today, and these friends of ours have a house that looks over the river. Our oldest friends, really . . .'

But old friends would have understood if we had to change our plans, surely?

I explained about the Boat Race between Oxford and Cambridge, on the Thames river, four miles from Putney to Mortlake. A bit longer, perhaps. I wasn't sure of the exact length of the course, but I did know that the first race had been in June 1829, and that since then Cambridge had won more often than Oxford.

Irma nodded. She had heard of the Boat Race. In fact, her brother had been at Magdalen just after the war and had rowed for Oxford. She told me this with a charmingly diffident smile. Feeling foolish, I asked if there was any equivalent sporting fixture in America that everyone in the country would know about. When I was quite a small child, the Boat Race had been an important event in my calendar. At my school, we wore favours, dark blue or pale blue rosettes, and fought for our teams in the playground, passionate advocates of one side or the other, even though it was most unlikely that any of us were connected with either of these old universities. Oxford and Cambridge were just names to us. We were slum children at a slum school in the East End of London, I told Irma – and wondered, at once, why I had proffered this information. What was I trying to prove? That I had risen from humble beginnings? Was she supposed to applaud me?

The Army and Navy Football Game, Irma suggested, as our husbands began to knock up on the court. This was sometimes played at Annapolis, sometimes at West Point, occasionally, she thought, in New York. It was the only thing she could think of that was in any way similar in its general appeal to our **Boat Race**. She frowned as if she were giving this unimportant matter her entire attention but her eyes were on her husband, brown and slenderly muscular in his white shorts and shirt, an elastic bandage on his right elbow, winding up athletically, a series of shadow overhead passes with the racket singing through the air, to deliver his first ball to Andrew.

The Court at Hampton Court, in Tennis Court Lane (as any of the members will tell you at the drop of a racket) is the oldest in play in the world. It dates from 1530. The game, the origin of modern tennis (more properly Lawn Tennis: this game is Tennis) as of rackets and squash, is much older. It was originally, as its French name *Jeu de Paume* suggests, a hand and ball game, probably played by monks in their monasteries and knights in their castles. It is played in an enclosed, walled court which has a sloping penthouse on three sides and a stone floor. The ball is played both off the walls and over a net and the players, either two or four, stand on opposite sides of the net. The court (which is longer and wider than a lawn tennis court) also has galleries, an angled buttress which is called the *tambour* and a large gallery behind the server (you only serve from one side) called the *dedans*. This is where spectators usually sit, protected by thick net from the fast, solid balls. The scoring is that on which modern tennis is based; there are four points to a game and they are known as 15, 30, 40, with deuce being 40 all. A set is won by the player who first wins six games.

There are two main points of distinction between Real Tennis and its Wimbledon grandchild. First, the Chase, which is an element of great subtlety, being both a point in suspense and the only means whereby service changes. Second, the ball. At first sight it looks like a modern tennis ball but it is heavy and very hard and hand-made. The core is a tight circle of small pieces of cloth compressed to make the spherical shape and then bound by string in a close, elegant and symmetrical pattern. The whole is then covered with white flannel and sewn, so that it appears, to a casual, untutored eye, much like an ordinary rubber and air tennis ball.

The Chase (for a non-player and anti-sportswoman) is harder to describe. In essence, it is where a ball in Real Tennis bounces for the second time without being struck and may not be dead. That position is then marked 'Worse than Last Gallery; Better than Two; Half a Yard.' When either there are two Chases outstanding, or the score is within one point of the game, the players reverse positions and play off the Chase, or Chases. The object is to beat the Chase laid by your opponent. The best Chase on the service side is 'Better than Half a Yard' and that is nearest to the back, *dedans* wall. The nearer to the net, the worse the Chase. But only by means of a Chase does service change.

Andrew has often explained these rules to me and I think that I understand them (though perhaps not the finer points) even if I find it boring to be a spectator. But, bored or not, I do know when the game is played well, and after the men had been knocking up for five minutes, the ball crossing the net at a variety of speeds, angles and heights, accompanied by polite cries of 'sorry!' and 'were you ready?', I could see that Ed who was serving (guests of the club were always given first service) was what Andrew calls a 'useful player'. And if this was apparent to me, it must have been even more apparent to Andrew, on the far, hazard side of the net, and to the marker who had just called out, 'Ready gentlemen? Three six-game sets to decide the winner. Love all.'

By the time Andrew had gained service he was four games down and forty-love against him in the fifth game. 'Good set to win,' he shouted in his cheeriest voice, hitching up his long white flannels, his back now to the *dedans*, conscious of the women behind him. The wives. The attractive American with her handsome dark eyes and neat breasts jutting under her sweater, watching with some interest, probably, he feared, with some knowledge. He had been playing badly, even for him. He had only managed to change ends because he had been able to pick up the one loose ball Ed had served, and crack it into the last gallery. There was little chance of winning the point, the game, or, for that matter, the set. He needed to concentrate and change tactics. Instead, he was thinking of the women and the impression he was making. His own Laura, somewhat fuller in the chest, getting on towards the heavy-dugged end of the spectrum, would be bored by the game (she had never really understood either the finer points of the rules or why he was fascinated by the improbable blend of chess-like thinking ahead and the hard, fast-moving, spin-taking ball) and she would be trying, probably without pleasure of any kind, to be polite to the stranger beside her. He served, a useless 'railroad' that stood up and waited to be hit. Ed forced it fast to the corner of the *dedans*. Andrew was wrong-footed, had no chance of reaching it, and could feel Laura wince, not at his losing the point, but in straight fear as the ball crashed full toss into the safety net an inch or two in front of her face.

He served again, it was a new game, the set almost lost without his winning more than a token point; it was luckily a sly rather flat 'cherry-bob' that barely touched the penthouse, curved into the corner, and died in the nick. 'Too good,' shouted Ed. 'Could do with some more of those,' Andrew laughed – and began to mean it.

For some reason that now eluded him, he had not geared himself up to play seriously. It had been a surprise, in the changing room, to find his opponent was not the novice he had somehow expected. Andrew had discussed it beforehand with the professional and they had planned a suitable handicap, to give Ed some games, making a good rabbit's competition of it, to encourage him. Not to let him win the match, of course, that would be daft, but to put him in a good mood for the Chairman. For lunch with Sir Boniface Pusey. Old Pussy. Did he know he was called that? Well, he must do. Pussy by name, and Pussy by nature. A lazy big cat, leaving the stalking, the chase, to his pride of young lions, only stirring himself for the kill.

This was an affectionate metaphor. When Andrew had applied for a job in the bank, Pussy had asked him if banking had always been his ambition. Andrew had hesitated over his answer, settling for the truth, finally. He had hoped to work in the theatre, writing plays and directing. After four and a half years in a provincial repertory company he had known he would never be good enough. Not good enough to satisfy him-self, anyway. He had waited to be turned down. But Pussy had said, 'Good. *Very* good. Always distrust it when people say banking has always been the thing they have set their hearts on. Not natural in a young man.'

Ed returned the next ball but Andrew was in position and put it away convincingly. Thirty love. Two good length 'railroads' and Andrew had won a game; one-five. The next service was lax and Ed returned it to the forehand corner, beautifully cut and low over the net. Andrew dived for it and missed. 'Better than a yard,' called the marker and that, Andrew privately admitted, as he served another loose ball, was that. Well, if Ed was better than he was, the best he could hope for was not to lose to him too disgracefully. Of course, you could see it as losing to win, a tactful move in the larger strategy, the greater game. Was that what Pussy expected? You could never be certain, he was rarely predictable. Cunning old cat, Andrew thought, not the fool Laura thought him. Taken in by that aristocratic, epicene voice, the pale, almost lashless eyes, nervously blinking. Affronted because he had once spoken of her to Andrew as 'your clever little wife'. Andrew had told her this. Stupidly. 'Why *little?*' she had wanted to know. Scenting condescension from this rich man, this old baronet, her husband's employer.

Self-employed, answerable to no one, she resented the fact that Andrew was not his own man. Merchant banking, in her view, was a parasitic profession; modern pirates sucking blood from the 'workers'. Laura was belligerent about her working class origins, though they were not so working class really. Struggling lower-middles would be more accurate if you had to use these ridiculous terms. Her parents had bought their own house, pushed their bright daughter up the educational ladder, were proud that they owed nothing to nobody. That tough old bugger, her father. A lifetime of hard labour. Did he think now, at the end, it was worth it?

Changing ends to play off the Chase, advantage against him, Andrew rubbed his damp palms on his flannels, mopped the sweat from his brow with a slightly torn handkerchief, and remembered the man who had taught him to box, an elderly

31

pugilist, teaching in his prep school and boxing on his knees while the little boys aimed their wild, puny punches at his vast, solid chest where black hairs, like spider's legs, curled at the neck of his grimy singlet. The smell of lockers, of changing rooms, greasy showers, had disgusted finicky Andrew. Poor little Henry, he thought now, remembering Isobel and the upset over maggots at breakfast. Henry must never be taught to box. A vicious, uncivilised game. He had tried to stop Jeremy boxing when the boy left his father to live with them, but Jeremy had insisted on entering for the school tournament. Beaten in the first round but coming home proudly to show the purple bruise on his cheek; the honourable scar; the mark of his valour. How old had he been? Twelve? Thirteen? Already a masochist, preparing for his future role as one of life's losers.

It was the end of the set. Andrew had to beat better than half a yard and all he could think of was prison yards and his dearly loved stepson, but he put him out of his mind for the moment, or at least at the back of it. He took the service early, straight off the penthouse and forced the ball to the *dedans*, but Ed vollied it easily, almost lazily, and tucked it away. Six-one; first set. You have to force yourself to live life in separate compartments, pack up your troubles in your old kitbag, Andrew thought, re-membering himself, a boy in the Cadet Corps, OTC, JTC, or whatever it was called that year, marching along with full kit on his back, playing soldiers. He missed the next service com-pletely, a good underarm twist that span away from him and died; and then, with a sudden rush of blood and adrenalin he knew that he wanted to win. In an instant, nothing else mattered, except winning the next point, and the next, and the game.

And the next game . . .

Eye on the ball, until – *when* – it and the racket meet. Head down, racket and wrist cocked up, feet always moving, never still. Fifteen all. Thirty fifteen. Forty fifteen. Should he risk a Chase to win service? Luckily Ed serves a ball that goes round the corner of the penthouse. Andrew stands well back, moves in and cuts it into the backhand court: better than half a yard. He changes to the service end and Ed loses the Chase and the game.

Concentration now; no more thinking about children, parents, sexy wives, or even Old Pussy. Just the game. One love. Two love. Three love. Four love. Andrew is serving better now, accurately, consistently. Not every one an ace, but all of them needing to be treated with respect and this means that Ed has trouble getting them back and Andrew is ready to make a winner of the next return. A slight faltering in the fifth game, Andrew loses service, but Ed lays a lousy Chase of worse than second gallery, and Andrew wins the game with a decisive volley into the last gallery. With the gift of a hazard Chase, he returns to the service side, and after a game that went to two deuces, he wins the set. One set all.

On to a winning streak with his services, and moving much better round the court, Andrew wins the third set, six-one.

As he loses the soap for the third time in the shower (it is a small slither, anyway, and someone has broken the holder) Andrew feels such a sense of zestful well-being that he is able to disregard the sliminess underfoot. 'I expect you found the balls a bit heavy, Ed,' he finds himself saying, 'and you probably noticed how far they bounce off the back wall. Quite different to Boston.'

'No, Andy.' Ed smiled at him. 'I found it just wonderful, playing on Henry the Eighth's Court. I'm just sorry I couldn't give you a better game in the last two sets. But as you probably realised' – he rubbed his right elbow where the elastic bandage had been – 'I've had some elbow trouble and I think I'll need another course of hydrocortisone injections when we get back home. But thank you,' – vigorously towelling his hair, dark and sleek and close as a seal's – 'I've enjoyed it marvellously. It's made this visit to the U.K.'

Showered and dressed, scented with cologne, they joined the women in the chilly, stone-floored passage outside the *dedans*.

Laura was saying to Irma, 'I'm so sorry about lunch. Next time you come to England, you really must visit us. Stay a weekend, if you can spare the time. Or at least come to dinner.'

Over-hospitable, smiling too anxiously. Andrew grinned at her, trying to tell her that there was no need to worry. She had done what was expected, been polite to Irma for an hour or so, played her part adequately. But she had never understood, his Laura, the difference between necessary acquaintances and friends. A mixture of shyness and honesty made casual contact an ordeal. An interested look from a stranger, a kindly smile, threw her into a turmoil. How much should she tell, reveal of herself? To hold back seemed mean-spirited. People were either friends of the bosom to be loved and trusted with secrets or they were nothing. 'Next time you come,' she cried, valiantly eager, 'We really must try and fix something.'

Irma, who understood this game better, murmured that they would be delighted. She turned to Andrew, recognising, perhaps, a more experienced player, and said, 'Your wife has been so kind, we have had a most enjoyable morning.'

I always know when Andrew is sexually attracted to someone. He stands straighter, pulling his shoulders back, his eyes brighten with moisture, his lips swell and glisten. He never looks at me like that now. I do not expect him to, naturally; we have been married too long. Although we love warmly and truly, there is no aching lust any longer between us, no racing of pulses, no painful, beautiful anguish. But I resent it when I see that look on his face. Oh, how I resent it! Not out of fear – I am certain that Andrew will never leave me, and almost certain that he has not been unfaithful – nor common jealousy. The pain that I feel is the sadness of loss for a time that is past.

So I tell myself in my high-minded way. The truth may be somewhat less flattering. I wish to be admired all the time, to be seen, by my husband, especially, as superior in every way to all other women. Even my imperfections (as I have made Andrew reflect in the previous passage) are signs of rare sensitivity, of acute moral delicacy. (These slightly sneering – or over-conscientious – comments on my character are not essential to this story. I make them only to encourage you to trust my voice, accept me as an honest recorder.)

And, to be honest, they only occurred to me later. At the time, when Andrew put his hand under Irma's elbow to lead her from the stone-flagged, cold passage into the warmth of the outer air,

34

the fitful spring sunlight, all I really felt was a mild, childish grumpiness, a faint pique at the sight of him leering tenderly down at her as I followed behind with her husband. And then, as we walked to the car park, and saw the Chairman getting out of his Bentley, a familiar awkwardness. I am nervous of people with titles, partly because the English class system offends and embarrasses me (producing such degrading fawning and sycophancy) and partly because I never know how to address them. 'Sir Boniface' is a particularly uncomfortable mouthful. Andrew calls him 'Boney' to his face and 'Pussy' behind his back but I do not feel able to do that. This is why I am stiff with this affable, elderly man, not (as Andrew believes) because I dislike him.

Nor, I think, does he dislike me. In fact, as he advanced towards us, blinking shyly, apologising for being late, caught up in the traffic (the Boat Race, of course, all those cars jamming the roads to the river) it seemed that his light, pink-rimmed eyes rested upon me with a distinct, if somewhat quizzical, pleasure.

It may of course simply have been that he was glad to see me playing my part for once, a good Bank Wife, doing her duty instead of gadding about on her own concerns or staying at home to finish a chapter. But when we shook hands he held mine very firmly and continued to hold it, his dry, warm old fingers caressing mine gently, while he asked how the game had gone, and congratulated Andrew when he heard he had won it. (No hint that he would have preferred him to lose, I was pleased to see.) Then he said to me, 'I'm so glad you could manage to get here this morning. I know you are busy.' And, to Irma, 'Did you know Laura was a literary lady? We are all very proud of her.'

He let go my hand and smiled down at me (Andrew's dwarfish 'little wife') from his immense height. A fresh-faced, kindly old man, anxious to reassure me, sensing, perhaps, that I was not at my ease – though not, of course, knowing why. I noticed (for the first time) that he had a sweet mouth; not full, but curving almost youthfully upwards into the yellow folds either side of it, and that his pale lips were glistening. As Andrew's lips had glistened when he looked at Irma.

I wanted to laugh. Not at him, at myself. I tried to smile modestly.

He said, 'My wife saw you on television the other night. Last week, wasn't it? She said you were very good. I'm so sorry I missed you.'

They were all looking at me. Andrew grinning, Irma and Ed with more interest than they had shown up to now. As if I had suddenly become much more visible.

'It's rather a silly programme, that book programme,' I said, I meant to sound shyly deprecating but I think that I sounded severe. Condemning Lady Pusey for watching such rubbish.

'My wife enjoys it,' the Chairman said. Although his expression remained kind and humorous, his high voice had a crisper tone suddenly. A note of dismissal.

'Silly ass,' Andrew said, in the car.

'I'm sorry. You shouldn't take me out in polite company. I'm not fit. I didn't mean to be rude.'

'I know that, my baby. Pussy knows, too. He's not such a fool.'

'I never said he was, did I?'

'Not in so many words. But you have a look sometimes. Like when he called you a *literary lady*. Prim disgust!'

'Only embarrassment. I felt he was patting me on the head kindly. Like a child! Perhaps I wouldn't feel like that if I were taller. Taller and thinner. Like that woman, Irma. Long legs and neat little breasts. Do you think of me as *heavy-dugged*?'

Andrew looked at me with an astonished expression.

I said quickly, blushing, 'Oh, never mind.'

Andrew laughed. 'You know that I think you are beautiful. I like small, round women.'

'I shall go on a diet.'

'If you do, I shall leave you.'

We had had this conversation before. I have always felt that if I were half a stone lighter, my life would be different. But I will never go on a diet. I am too lazy and greedy, and Andrew knows it. We smiled at each other.

Andrew said, 'Pussy wasn't teasing you, darling. He really is impressed by your being a writer. It's a mystery to him, how people get round to it.'

'Not a serious occupation, though. Scribble, scribble, scribble, eh, Mr Gibbon? Of course books do make nice furniture.'

The walls of the Partner's Room at the Bank are lined with fake books. When I first saw this room I thought it was a real library, all those gold-tooled, leather spines, until Andrew opened a section to show me the drink cupboard behind it.

Andrew said earnestly, 'Pussy does read, you know. Not just *The Economist* and the *Financial Times*. He reads Trollope and Dickens.'

'Goodness me!' I said. 'Does he really?'

I wondered why I was being so grudging. Perhaps it was simply my distrust of 'business' in general. I understand occupations that produce something, or provide some obvious service – bricklaying, publishing, carpentry, medicine – but the sort of work that goes on in 'the city', in big banks, huge corporations, is as mysterious to me as my writing is to Sir Boniface Pusey. This distrust (which is ignorance, really) made me nervous for Andrew. I knew he worked hard, was no doubt still regarded by his employer as a 'keen young chap', reliable, meticulous, honourable, a good man to send abroad with his fluent German and French, his pleasant manners, his ability to get on with all sorts of people. But these qualities seemed to me imprecise qualifications, not readily marketable, and I sometimes feared Andrew was not wary enough. Pussy had favoured him generously, promoting him over the heads of older men who had worked for the Bank longer than he had, almost (Andrew said) as if he were one of the Family, and my husband's gratitude for this kindly patronage seemed to me dangerously innocent. Pussy had no sons of his own. What would happen when he retired, or had a stroke or a heart attack, handing over to a nephew or cousin or some other relation who did not share – or resented – his quasi-parental interest in Andrew?

Of course I never said this. It would have hurt Andrew to know that I feared for his future. And shocked him to think I was calculating his chances in this crude way, worrying in case his loyal affection for his elderly Chairman might turn out one day to be a black mark against him. Besides, as I said, I was (and am) ignorant of the game Andrew seemed to play so lightheartedly. Or perhaps only 'seemed'. Perhaps Andrew is really full of cunning and guile. All I can say is that I have never seen any evidence of it.

He said, in the car, clearing his throat, sounding defensive, 'You know, Laura, Pussy only meant to be kind. Trying to cheer you up. I suppose he thought you might need it. Wanted to let you know he was sorry.'

He looked at me apprehensively. One quick look and away. I said, 'Andy! You haven't told him about Jeremy, have you?'

Why did I ask? I knew the answer.

He took one hand from the wheel and rubbed his upper lip nervously, massaging his front teeth. He stared straight ahead, at the road, 'Well, yes, I'm afraid I did, actually. We were having a drink last night. The first time we'd had a chance for a private talk since I got back from Zurich. He asked how the children were. I showed him those photographs of Henry and Isobel. He asked about Claudia. I said she was married. Then he asked after Jeremy. I couldn't not tell him. He really is interested, it isn't just casual. I couldn't lie, could I?'

Little George Washington. I was shaking with anger. I locked my hands in my lap and looked out of the window. 'What did he say?'

'He said he was sorry.'

'Just that?'

'What else could he say?'

'He could have said, *fucking police*!'

'That's not his style, really. And I didn't go into too many details. It would have taken too long. I wanted to get home to you and the children.'

'Oh, for God's sake!'

He said, pleadingly, 'Don't be upset. It isn't important.'

'If it isn't important, why did you tell him? Or tell me you'd told him?'

He sighed, as if I were being unreasonable. I wanted to hit

him. Only he was driving and it would have been dangerous.

'Please don't quarrel,' he said. 'Not today. Laura. *Please.*'

The injustice of this appeal made my eyes sting. Was this how he saw our relationship? Reasonable Andrew, always the gentleman, hen-pecked by his harridan wife? So unfair! We don't quarrel all that much; when we do, the cause of the fight and the form it takes hardly varies. We fight about sex sometimes. We would both like it more frequently but one of us is, too often, 'too tired'. But mostly we quarrel, or at least I do, about the difficulties I face working at home, which are filed in my head under the general title, *Waiting For The Gasman.* It is all right for Andrew, he goes to an office, has secretaries to answer his telephone, fend off unwelcome callers, write his letters, book his air tickets, make his dentist appointments. I am left with the sick child, the au pair weeping in the kitchen because her boy friend has left her, or because she is suffering from premenstrual tension, the cat mess to be cleaned up, the clothes that must go to the cleaners (Andrew's clothes, mostly), the food to be ordered and cooked, the builder who may be coming to fix the leak in the gutter and if he doesn't come must be called and reminded, the window cleaner, the piano tuner, the Jehovah's Witnesses, the Mormons, the telephone call from my mother-in-law, the man from the Electricity Board to read the meter. I rage and scream, blaming Andrew for these interruptions to my working day, although none of them are his fault except that he shares the house with me and is equally responsible for it. This, of course, makes me even angrier; I wear myself out because I have no genuine grievance, complaining about one minor thing after another, and when I am quite exhausted, go·and cook a meal, fix a drink, or, if this attack of frustration erupts late in the evening, go quietly to bed and to sleep, even though I know that Andrew will not recover so quickly and will lie awake churning and suffering and blaming himself . . .

But this was quite different. For once, *he* was in the wrong. Spilling out, over a social drink, what should be kept private. For my sake, for Jeremy's . . .

'I don't agree,' Andrew said. 'How do you think he would feel if he thought we were hiding what's happened. As if we were ashamed of him. Of course there are some people who can't be told, obviously. Your parents, for example – they'd be too distressed – and there's no point in spreading it abroad for the sake of it. But those who won't be particularly hurt, but will *care*, who know him, and us – well, if they ask how he is, it seems right to tell them.'

I said, very stiffly, 'That's all very fine. I know what you think I suffer from. Secretiveness. A lace-curtain mind. But if you'd been brought up as I was, clinging by your fingernails on to the edge of respectability, you wouldn't find it so easy to be calm about your son being in prison.'

'I'm fed up with your bloody childhood,' Andrew said, through his teeth.

'Oh, I *am* sorry! I do beg your pardon for mentioning it.'

I heard myself being huffy and whining and spiteful and was ashamed as I often am when I quarrel with Andrew who never (or very rarely) descends to the level of infantile malice with which I attack him, but shame didn't stop me, only set me off on another tack. 'All right, then. You're not ashamed of Jeremy, nor am I – I'm only scared *for* him, terrified witless – but I know that if I were you, I wouldn't go bragging about it to my employer. Okay, he said he was *sorry*, well, I daresay he was when you told him, why shouldn't he be? I mean, he's *polite*, for God's sake. You wouldn't expect him not to be, would you? But later on, when it *sinks in* that his precious protégé, his blue-eyed boy, has a son who's a jail bird, he may look on you rather differently. I can't think it'll do you much good.'

'I wasn't trying to do myself good,' Andrew said. 'I was just telling the truth to an old man I'm fond of. Who's been good to me. Fatherly.'

He sounded husky, as if his throat had dried up. When Andrew says 'fatherly' in that hushed and awed way it really means something; a tribute to a kind of affection he has never known.

Andrew's father was a sadist. A thug. An Australian who married late, in his forties, a rich, younger woman, the daughter of a well-heeled Melbourne family. He brought her to England in the early twenties and started, with his wife's money, a factory in the Midlands that made suitcases out of waste paper. They had a boy who died before his third birthday; then Andrew, born a year later. From Andrew's account of the way his father behaved to him, his brother might well have been murdered – battered babies didn't make the headlines then, as they do now, particularly if they belonged to prosperous families.

Andrew's father beat him. He beat him when he wet his bed. He beat him if he didn't eat his dinner. When he was four years old he beat him because he found him in his mother's bed one night (he had crawled in for comfort after a nightmare) and later, when he was eleven and twelve, searched his sheets every morning for the stains of wet dreams and beat him if he found any. But mostly he beat him for what he saw as failure.

He sent Andrew to expensive schools – buying his son's way in to the kind of upper middle class British society he felt himself to be excluded from by his cheap suitcases, his Australian accent – and he beat him to protect his investment. If Andrew came second in class, he beat him if he didn't come top; he beat him if he didn't come first in at least a couple of races on the summer sports day. He beat him with a cane, with a strap, with his fists, until Andrew was seventeen. On his seventeenth birthday they had a political row. It was the 1945 General Election and Andrew had been canvassing for a friend's father who was the local Labour candidate. 'Bloody traitor,' Andrew's father had called him. He struck Andrew in the face and Andrew knocked him down. After that his father never touched him, nor spoke to him directly again. When he had something to say, he addressed his son through his mother. 'Tell that bastard to get out of my sight', was his final instruction, the night that he died of pneumonia and Andrew came to his bedroom to help his mother lift him up on the pillows to ease him.

'Why didn't your mother leave?' I asked Andrew, but he couldn't answer me. Perhaps she was too afraid, or too ashamed, or too stupid. She didn't know, Andrew insisted loyally, how bad the beatings had been. She was usually out of the house, shopping or playing bridge, when his father attacked him, and Andrew didn't confide in her, hiding, once he was old enough, his tears and his bruises. Or perhaps she saw nothing so terribly wrong in what her husband was doing. 'Your father only wants you to be successful,' she told Andrew once, and perhaps she believed this. It was what she wanted too, after all, and her methods of training, though less obviously brutal, were hardly less damaging.

The first time I met her she showed me Andrew's school reports tied up with ribbon and the silver cups he had won, playing squash and in boxing tournaments. These trophies were sacred objects to her but although she showed them to me with pride she had never, so Andrew said, congratulated him at the time, only compared him unfavourably with other boys, his Australian cousins, his friends, who had in some way done better, conducting throughout his boyhood and adolescence a campaign of denigration that persisted into his adult life. When he was made a managing director of the Bank all she said was, 'Well, that's about as far as you'll get, I suppose,' and launched into a song of praise about a neighbour's son who had been chosen to play golf for England.

She did not mean to hurt Andrew. Although she still put him down when she could (more out of habit by this time than in order to urge him on to try harder, climb the next hill) she was not doing so on this occasion. Competitive sport was her religion. She was an addict, a junkie; most afternoons, when she was not playing bridge, found her in her darkened living room, getting her daily fix from the television. To be selected for the English golf team was an infinitely greater success than Andrew's promotion. If we had questioned this judgement she would have turned spiteful, thrust out her pudgy jaw and said, with thin sarcasm (the only way she knew how to argue), 'Well, I won't say that most people agree with me, I know that won't wash with you, since you think you're so clever. All I can say is that I think to be asked to play for your country is a great honour. In my humble opinion.'

She was proud of her humble – or honest – opinion. 'I always say what I think. My friends can rely on me, they know that I'll give it them straight from the shoulder. My *honest opinion*!'

As I write this, I can hear her voice speaking, see the thrust of her jaw, the belligerent spark in her large, slightly protuberant eyes. So pleased with herself, so delighted; quite unaware that what might once have been youthful openness, charming candour, had changed, as she and her bridge-playing cronies aged, into an unpleasing frankness. ('You are going bald,' is a less agreeable statement than, 'How thick your hair is!')

It astonished me that Andrew still loved her. Well, no, it didn't astonish me. I merely wished that he didn't. And not just because I know (though I do fight against it) that I am jealous by nature. I would have been happier, more at ease with myself anyway, if I could have liked her, and I would have tried harder to like her if I had known Andrew was free of her, that he no longer had this painful, useless desire to win her approval.

Not that he was deluded. He knew what she'd done to him. When he made that crack about my 'bloody childhood' he wasn't getting at me, only saying that compared to his childhood, mine had been paradise.

I suppose I do complain sometimes. Who doesn't? We all know (or believe secretly) that when we were children we were happy and trusting and hopeful and good and that we would still be all these pleasant things if sometime, somewhere, somehow, we had not been betrayed.

For the record. My father was a seaman, an engineer on an ocean liner, my mother a teacher. They were decent intelligent people, not poor in any fundamental way (they had clothes, food and shelter) but they had started from nothing, *with* nothing except self-respect and what used to be called 'character', and walked a tightrope across an abyss all their hard working lives. They both came from large, closely knit, secretive families that closed doors against strangers, asked nothing from nobody, supported their old people, did their best for their children. In the war, when my school came back to

London, my mother did not question that she should return too, from the farm in Dorset where she had been staying with my little sister, in order that I should go on with my education. She had left Cora, my sister, in the care of the farmer's wife and, teaching jobs being scarce, went to work in a munitions factory. She worked shifts, and long hours; I 'minded' the house, went to school, did the shopping, ran the streets, played the War Game with Hilde. If it had not been for Aunt Milly, who was not an aunt, really, but my father's third cousin, we would have been happy.

(Or, at least, I would have been happy. I didn't miss my father who had been at sea all my life except for brief holidays, and to be without five-year-old Cora, whom I had resented since she was born for the way she took my mother's attention, was heaven.)

Aunt Milly used to run a café for working men in the Mile End Road. She had been bombed out just before my mother and I came back to London and now she lived in our small front room with her bad legs, her sour smell, and her suspicious mind that had nothing to occupy it except endless grievances.

She complained. She complained about her bad legs that made it impossible for her to get out. She complained about the neighbours, thumping on the wall when they turned up the wireless too loud, until they complained about her. She complained about the wartime shortage of food, about the weather (always either too hot or too cold or too wet or too 'heavy') and about the way my mother's tiresome cough kept her awake at night. She complained about me.

'Want, want, want,' I heard her say to my mother, raising her voice so that I could hear from where I was, in the kitchen. 'Want, want, want, gimme, gimme, gimme. That's all I hear from that girl of yours.'

I remember this occasion. My mother had taken Milly a tray of tea and biscuits and asked her if she had any spare clothing coupons. We had used ours and I was growing fast, my school skirt barely covered my bottom (an indecent length at that time), my black wool stockings were nothing but cobbly darns and I could barely button my blouses. My mother must have said something, explaining the fix I was in, because Aunt Milly answered, still loudly, 'Eats too much, that's her trouble, stuffing her face, stuff, stuff, stuff, soon as she gets in from that posh school she goes to. She thinks I don't know what she's up to but I sit here with my door a bit open and I can hear her rootling around in the larder. What's happened to my butter ration this week, that's what I'd like to know? I've not seen it! What you do with yours is none of my business. If you want to go without, starve yourself to fatten her up, then that's up to you, but I've a right to what's due to me, I've worked for it, let me tell you. That great lazy girl doesn't know what work is, nose in a book all the time. At her age I knew all right, I was earning my living the hard way, down on my knees scrubbing floors, scrub, scrub, scrub, that keeps you thin, I can tell you!'

And so on and so forth. This is a fair example of Aunt Milly's conversational art – and quite enough, too! I think I have recalled this particular soliloquy with tolerable accuracy, partly because the insistent rhythms of Aunt Milly's speech patterns still moan in my head, unforgettable as an old popular tune, but largely because, on this afternoon, when my mother came back to the kitchen, her face was so full of such wicked glee, such bright and beautiful laughter, that although I had boiled with rage as I listened to the rude and unpleasant things Aunt Milly had been saying about me, I no longer cared. My mother had been looking so tired and now she was merry and joyful and sharing a joke with me.

For Aunt Milly was fat. She was so fat that she had to eat standing up. If she had tried to sit down and lean forward over a table like ordinary people, there would have been no room for her stomach. 'Poor thing, we shouldn't laugh,' my mother whispered, pushing the kitchen door shut behind her, but laughter was spilling out of her like happy rain, washing away all her weariness, making her young again. I said, 'I never touched her butter ration, honestly, Mum,' and she put her arms round me, hugging me, still laughing softly. 'I know that, my duckie, pay no attention. She's an awful old mean-mouth but we're stuck with her, aren't we, no one else will look after her.' She held me away and touched my cheek gently. 'She's old

45

and she's miserable and that makes her spiteful. Just try to think of her as a sad and silly old woman.'

Well, perhaps. I think my mother was over charitable. But certainly Aunt Milly would have done me no harm, except for the occasional minor hurt, eased at once by the way it drew my mother and me together, if my mother had not fallen ill. Her cough became worse, keeping me awake as well as Aunt Milly. And, at the same time, the farmer's wife wrote to say that Cora was pining.

My mother said, 'Just a couple of weeks, you'll be all right, won't you? Time enough to show that poor baby I haven't abandoned her, and give me a bit of a rest from the factory. I know Milly's tiresome, but she'll get her own dinner if she knows that she's got to, as long as you can keep the house clean and manage the shopping.'

Quite soon after she had arrived at the farm, she began to cough blood. I went to see her in the sanatorium several weeks later. She had left housekeeping money in a brown envelope tucked behind the tea caddy on the kitchen mantelpiece and I used the last of it for the train fare. I remember that envelope with my finger tips; the slightly soggy, creased feel of the paper, and the hard, comforting edges of the coins in one corner. If I make an effort of memory, I can remember the journey – standing in the corridor of a train crowded with soldiers and kitbags, and the long, leg-aching walk up the hill to the hospital – but remembering what my mother looked like when I got there requires no effort at all.

She lay propped up on pillows covered with striped mattress ticking, on a high, iron bed that had been wheeled out of the ward on to the terrace. There was a red blanket over her and she wore a red dressing gown and her cheeks were red, too; tight and shiny as apples. Her hands were brown from lying there in the clear, autumn sun, and the heavy wedding ring that had belonged to my father's grandmother was loose on her finger. When she opened her bag to give me some money to re-fill the brown envelope, the ring slipped off, and she gave a tired, fretful sigh and passed the bag to me. She said, 'Find it for me, love, will you?'

I found the ring and put it back on her finger. I held her thin brown hand and said, 'Milly and I are managing, so you don't have to worry, Mum. We're managing fine.'

My mother coughed. She hawked, with a disgusting, liquid noise that made me feel sick, and spat into a mug on the locker beside her. She covered the mug with a lid and looked at me with apology. 'Sorry, duckie. Better out than in, that's what they tell us. I'll be all right in a bit, I feel so much better already, but you ought to go and have an X-ray. If you go to the doctor and tell him, he'll give you a note for the hospital.'

Aunt Milly said, when I got back, 'If she doesn't get better my girl, you can blame yourself, I can tell you! If it hadn't been for you and your *education*' – she pronounced this word with a hiss of contempt that any old-style theatrical dame might have envied – 'she wouldn't be where she is now.' She gave me a triumphant glance from her eyes that were submerged in her cellar-pale flesh like shrivelled prunes in a dough cake and added, in case I had missed the point, 'You and your Grammar School! If it hadn't been for that, she'd never have come back to London and got stuck, working all hours, in that factory!'

'And you'd have had no one to run errands, would you?' I said. I still had some fighting spirit left then, though it was to grow weaker.

For a while, several months, we were evenly matched; settled into a kind of phoney war, each of us entrenched, fairly cosily, behind fixed battle lines. I shopped for Aunt Milly, kept the accounts, did some sketchy cleaning, carried the coals for her fire, and, since it was impossible for her to get upstairs to the lavatory, emptied her commode. In return, she dragged her huge, heavy body into the kitchen to wash and iron my clothes and cook my tea when I came home from school in the evening. Though she kept up her resentful whining, she did not attack me directly.

Then, sometime that winter (I forget the exact date but I know it was cold: either late that autumn or the next year's early spring) her nephew, Bob, came to stay on ten days leave from the Army. He slept upstairs in Cora's room, next to mine, and it was natural for Aunt Milly to suspect we were having a sexual orgy. She would have suspected it even if there had been nothing between us, but as there was something (and at my instigation) it gave her a fine chance to take the offensive.

Bob was in his twenties, old to my eyes, but good looking enough to practise on. I made up my face with Pink Pearl lipstick and powder and dabbed Evening in Paris behind my ears, confident that I knew how to deal with the passions that might be aroused. Hilde and I (lacking adult instruction) had worked out our own set of rules for the sex game. Kissing was all right, even with tongues, as long as neither party had a bad cold, and gentle breast-fondling through the clothes was all right too, though not squeezing because (this was Hilde's theory) it could give you cancer. But if you allowed the game to go further, let a boy *do it*, you might have a baby, so you must never let him get his hand in your knickers.

It didn't occur to me (or if it did, I put it out of my mind for convenience) that Bob, being an older man, might try to play the game differently. When he came into my room one night, a bit drunk, and lunged at me, damp-mouthed, breathing heavily, I wasn't at all alarmed, only embarrased. He fell on the bed and the springs creaked. I fought him off, giggling. 'Silly fool, go away, Aunt Milly will hear you!'

That was enough. He knew Aunt Milly as well as I did. But of course she had heard him, lumbering about over her head. She said nothing while he was there; biding her time until he had gone back to his unit and I was alone, at her mercy.

'I know what went on while I lay helpless downstairs, don't think I didn't, don't expect me to feel sorry for you if something should happen! I saw you, waddling your bum, waving your chest about, tempting him! You needn't expect me to stick up for you if your mother and father find out about it, in fact, I'm not sure it isn't my duty to tell them . . .'

Etcetera, etcetera. This kind of monologue (running on sometimes for a good twenty minutes) was repeated so often, growing more lurid and threatening with each repetition, that although at first I tried not to pay too much attention, her persistence not only humiliated me, but produced such doubt in my mind that by the time my father appeared, unexpectedly, one rainy evening, I was no longer completely sure what had actually happened between Bob and me. As I kissed my father, hung up his wet naval raincoat, and went to make tea, I was afraid that Aunt Milly would give him her version.

This fear obsessed me all the time he was there, which was only an hour, between trains; he was on a short leave from his ship, docked on the Clyde, and passing through London to Dorset to visit my mother and sister. And it quite overshadowed the news he was bringing me. Cora had been taken into the sanatorium. She had a patch of tuberculosis on one of her lungs. My father made light of it. Perhaps he was anxious not to alarm me.

'It's not really necessary to put her in hospital, but of course they want to make certain. And, besides, there are other children on the farm to consider. You've had an X-ray, haven't you, Laura?'

I said that I had, and he smiled with relief and asked if I would like to go with him to Dorset. Company for him in the evenings, and a nice surprise for my mother. It wouldn't matter if I missed a few days from school.

Aunt Milly was watching me with her squashed-up, prune eyes, and all I could think of was my terror that she was about to betray me; give my father a hair-raisingly vulgar account of my sexual behaviour. I rushed to placate her. 'Oh, I can't, Dad. I can't leave Aunt Milly.'

My father stared with surprise. He had blue eyes with very clear whites and black, bushy eyebrows above them. Though he was in his fifties then (this was his second World War) he was still very handsome. He raised one of his thick eyebrows and looked at me questioningly. But I couldn't explain.

It wasn't only fear of Aunt Milly, I realised bleakly. I really didn't see how I could leave her. She couldn't go to bed unless I was there to help her unfasten her corset, take off her stockings. And worse – she couldn't empty her own commode! How could

I speak of this intimate problem to my father, whom I had not seen for nearly two years? He was a stranger to me.

I said, 'You'll just have to give them my love. I really am sorry. Tell Mum that I miss her.'

Later that evening, Aunt Milly said, 'You hurt him, refusing to go. I suppose you and that Hilde have got some arrangement or other you don't want to break but you might have thought of your mother and father and your poor little sister. I'm sure I never knew a girl who put herself first like you do. Me, me, me – all the time!'

'I,' I corrected her. 'It should be *I,I,I*. That's grammar, Aunt Milly.'

But she had won. She had beaten me. Perhaps what she did was only an extreme example of what many mothers do to their daughters, preparing them for a subservient role by chipping away at their proper and healthy self-regard, making them feel they are selfish, have let someone down, are always at fault, in the wrong.

I had hurt my father. It was my fault my mother was ill. She would be hurt because I had not come to see her and Cora. And I had turned down the last chance I would ever have in this world to see my small sister.

Although when Cora died, Aunt Milly did not actually blame me (there were some depths of malice even she could not stoop to) she did say, 'To think that you couldn't spare the time to go with your Daddy and say goodbye to her.'

She was a stupid and silly old woman, a laughing stock, but she weighed me down with a load of guilt I have only recently crawled out from under.

On the other hand, on the whole, when I look at it now, I got off fairly lightly. Compared with Andrew's mother and father, Aunt Milly is nothing much to complain of. I didn't, after all, *love* her, and because I didn't love her, I could endure her; escape from her, out of the house; giggle about her with Hilde.

I was thinking these bracing thoughts in the car as we drove between Hampton Court and the substantial house on the river that belongs to William and Rosie, who were giving a party.

I looked at Andrew, whose profile was glum, and said, 'I'm so glad you won your game, darling.'

PART TWO

The Party

William and Rosie give wonderful parties. If there is an art in it, theirs is the art that conceals art. It is my belief that Rosie has a natural gift for friendship and hospitality and that William, who is less open and easy, has worked at his host's role, perfecting it over the years, but if he has (and it may be, as I will explain in a minute, that this is invention on my part) it is never apparent. To arrive at one of their parties is an exhilarating experience. Although you know that it must have been prepared beforehand, invitations sent out, drinks bought, flowers arranged, it always has the feel of a spontaneous occasion – as if all these nice people happened to drop by at this particular moment to find wine and food and old friends waiting for them. Or, if that is what they are looking for, sexual partners. (I said they were 'our' oldest friends because it was at one of their parties that I met Andrew.)

And yet, these last years, on the way to their house, I have often felt vaguely uneasy. To be exact, to be honest, ever since I wrote that novel about them. My Women's Lib novel (every woman has one of *those* in her), only I wrote mine at the end of the fifties before the movement got started. I wrote it because after I left my first husband I was, for a long time, very sour about marriage and I suppose I 'used' William and Rosie because they seemed to me irritatingly happy, and I wanted to prove to myself they were not.

Of course – well, not *of course*, but to explain to those of my readers who are not novelists – the book was not 'about' Rosie and William in the sense that they were in any way recognisable. Certainly not physically. Rosie is tiny, skin and bone, and William is thin as a stick; long, agile legs, short body, small head. Richard and Elizabeth, the pair in my novel, were both large, heavy people; they had two sons instead of Rosie and William's two daughters; the husband was a teacher instead of an accountant, which is William's profession, and the wife was an unsatisfied housewife with political ambitions, not a successful family physician, like Rosie. My fictional characters were travelling through Morocco, through the desert which was what their life had become (*using symbol without pretentiousness* one kindly reviewer said of this device) and Rosie and William have never been to North Africa. They do not care for travelling for the sake of it and would never have contemplated the kind of rigorous journey (heat, flies and dysentery) that I described. It is not that they are afraid of discomfort. They cannot be bothered with planning for holidays, scorning (though of course never saying so) the shifts that most of us go to, searching the brochures for good package deals, booking cheap fares in advance. When they feel like it, they go to a cottage in Provence owned by a rich publisher friend who lends it to them as payment in kind for the annual audit William does for him for nothing. Tax avoidance, I call this, taking a prim view because it is my publisher to whom the cottage belongs and he has never offered it to me instead of paying me royalties, but to Rosie and William it is simply good housekeeping from which their friends benefit, because with the money they save (or steal from the taxpayer) they are very generous, and not only with parties. Their house by the river is always full of guests – itinerant young, elderly uncles and aunts, acquaintances down on their luck.

Sometimes, at night, when I find myself in my dream house, it seems that the happy room, where people are laughing and talking, is a little like Rosie's big dining room that has book-lined walls and a fine view of the river.

But that should not make me uneasy. Nor should the fact that when Rosie had finished this novel she rang up and said, 'My God, darling, I know it was all about you and that *ghastly* time you must have had with Pete in Morocco, but once or twice – I know it sounds *totally* stupid, but I simply must tell you – I found myself identifying with that poor downtrodden woman and thinking, good *heavens*, how on earth does Laura know all those things about me?'

After all, I had plenty of letters that said much the same thing. Letters from women I didn't know; from other sisters under the skin. There was no real observable relationship between Rosie and William and my hero and heroine. Perhaps it is only because I was thinking of my dear friends and their so-happy marriage when I started writing, slyly boosting my spirits by imagining small signs and incidents that could show that all was not quite well between them, that a tiny sense of guilt occasionally nags me . . .

On the way to the party that Saturday morning, I had quarrelled with Andrew. Complaining (unfairly, untruly) that he had accused me of having a 'lace-curtain' mind. In my novel, Elizabeth, who is the narrator, says this about Richard.

When I told Andrew (making amends for my evil temper) he chuckled. 'I thought I'd read it somewhere. You are always so economical. Can't bear to waste anything. Not even an adjective.'

'Do you think it's the sort of thing Rosie might say?'

'Why Rosie?'

'I don't know. I just wondered.'

'Well, it doesn't sound strikingly like her. But you often use things that *I've* said. Not that I can think of anything off the cuff, at the moment, and not that I mind. After all, I married you, didn't I? With all my wordly goods I thee endowed. I suppose that includes my good phrases.'

'It's a compliment, in a way.'

'Yes, of course.' He took my hand and held it on his knee. Now we were friends again, his face was smoothed out and smiling. 'And, of course, you do make up some things yourself!' He snorted with laughter.

'Thank you.'

'Not at all. You managed to write that particular book without my help, didn't you?'

He pressed my hand gently; a loving reminder. He had just finished reading it the first time we met. Rosie had lent it to him.

She hadn't been match-making; it was her habit to brief people about each other before she introduced them. Otherwise they 'fiddle-arsed about' – this *is* one of Rosie's remarks – wasting time finding out, when they could be more enjoyably occupied. Not that she would have presented Andrew with my book to read as a *duty*. What she might have said was, 'Poor Laura, she's had such a *vile* time just lately. She's lost confidence and it makes her seem a tiny bit shy and mousey, but she isn't really, not *underneath*, as you'll see if you have time to look at her novel. She can be quite sharp and funny.'

I said, 'What did Rosie say about me? When she gave you my book?'

'She didn't give it to me. I picked it out of her bookshelf.' He grinned, teasing me. 'I thought it had a nice cover.'

'You mean Rosie didn't say *anything*?'

'Don't think so. I suppose she must have said you were a friend of hers. But nothing else. Nothing personal!'

Tactful Rosie! After all, Andrew might have disliked the book. If he had, she wouldn't have asked us to the same party. And she would never have called me 'poor' Laura! Too condescending. Rosie's heart aches when her friends are unhappy (which is whenever she thinks they are not absolutely as happy as she is) but she never speaks about anyone in a diminishing way.

I said, 'Can you remember what you thought when you read it? I don't mean, did you enjoy it. Did the characters remind you of anyone?'

'You and Pete, in the desert.'

'But you hadn't met me then.'

'No, that's true. Who should I have recognised? It has to be someone we both knew, doesn't it, if I'm not allowed hindsight? Nobody, I think, unless you mean Rosie and William. But you only used their Christian names, not their surnames, and they only made one appearance. As Rose and Will Potter.'

He glanced at me. Mildly interested. Quizzical. Wondering why this little game should amuse me.

I said, 'How ridiculous!'

'Why?'

'Because I don't think I realised.'

This was true. I had used the names, Rose and Will, without thinking, for two minor characters, and afterwards forgotten that I had done so.

I said, 'Oh, how silly. I suppose I must have realised at the time. Though not necessarily. They were just a couple of walk-on parts, not important. But you would have thought, even if it was quite unconscious at the time, that I would have picked it up later. Correcting the proofs. Not that it matters. I wonder if Rosie noticed. She never said anything.'

Had I really used their names 'without thinking'? Or had it been a cunning red herring to divert Rosie's attention from what I had feared I was doing?

'I don't know,' I said. I shook my head; sighed and laughed. 'There are so many layers.'

Not all of them, Andrew thought, equally interesting. He didn't know how to value her novels; he was too close to them. He hated it when she got lukewarm notices, feeling quite violent sometimes towards a careless or a grudging reviewer. Even when they praised, it was never generous enough to satisfy him, he felt so protective towards her, a pain in his guts. But although he might be fascinated by the way her mind worked, digging down like an archaeologist through her personal history (after all even indifferent art must be based on life, and her life concerned him because she was his Laura) others might find the cracked shards she threw up somewhat irrelevant, even, occasionally, boring. On the other hand, it was one way of keeping her occupied. Eventually she would make use of today's events, turn them to some account fictionally, in a way that he envied (would have envied more, he thought, if she had been a playwright and not a novelist) but in the meantime, before the curious process started to function, discarding, selecting, easing the pain by making a tale of it, her son was in prison, her father dying. Though he loved them both deeply, his role was peripheral, his job to comfort her. The mother, the daughter.

He hoped that the party would serve to distract her. He

hadn't been too keen himself, would have preferred a quiet lunch in a pub. He knew that William and Rosie, who knew what had happened to Jeremy (William, that good friend, had even come to court with them) would do their kindly and competent best, their sympathy carefully measured to be a support and not an additional burden – no anguished wringing of hands, just a steady assurance of continued concern. And yet he could not help wondering if they were quite the right people to turn to just now. Though who would be better? Some dreary down-and-out whose misery would make their situation seem easier? No, of course not. But *Rosie*, and *William*!

He was fond of them, naturally. He and William had done their National Service together in Germany just after the war; friendship growing out of a shared horror at the devastation about them, the bombed cities, the starving children living like rats in the cellars, the thin girls selling themselves for chocolate and cigarettes. They had all been shocked, all the young British soldiers, but it seemed to Andrew (although he recognised that this could be a form of self-flattery) that he and William were more deeply appalled, felt more guilty about what their country had done (in Dresden, in Berlin, in Hamburg) than any of their companions. Children during the war, they still felt responsible *personally*. But there was so little that they could do. William organised, through his parents, a system by which parcels were sent from their Kentish village to individual German families; cocoa and used clothing, tinned food and milk. Andrew had found it impossible to explain to William that his mother could not be persuaded to do something similar, that there was no point even in asking her, she would react with such bridling hostility. ('Who started the war, may I ask? They made their own bed, let them lie on it!') Instead, he told William that his mother was still too distraught by his father's sudden death from pneumonia to be asked to do anything, and William had 'understood' instantly. Like Andrew he was an only child, but unlike him, he was close to his parents. They were all three close to each other. William said, 'Your mother must be missing you dreadfully. I don't know how my mother would be able to bear it if my father died. She'd try and be brave for my sake, I know, but they have never spent a night apart in their whole married life.'

Hearing William speak of his parents like this, so innocently open about the love they had for each other (as if all families, everywhere, must love the same way) had made Andrew feel as if he had some shameful disease that could not be mentioned. He no longer felt much emotion about his father (any residual bitterness had been locked away in a kind of mental cold storage) and what he felt for his mother had more to do with the loyal link between two ex-prisoners who had suffered under the same savage jailer than affection between mother and son, but he was ashamed of the life they had led. And when he went home with William and met his father and mother, his own past seemed more than ever something that must be kept hidden; a poisonous secret.

William's mother was intelligent, and bright as a robin; his father a retired civil servant who read Greek for pleasure, grew roses in his walled country garden, and was cheerfully acquainting himself (since servants were no longer easy to find) with what he called 'the domestic arts'. The night William and Andrew arrived, he had cooked the dinner. He spoke of the difficulties of food rationing and smiled. 'A dish of herbs where love is,' he said ladling out rabbit stew with a fine, silver spoon, and Andrew, watching and listening at his friend's dinner table, seeing the polished candlesticks, the darned but still smoothly starched linen, the dusty bottle of good wine brought up from the cellar for the occasion, recognised that this was the world his parents had been so determined to flog him into joining; the old-style English Establishment, privately educated, gently mannered, money behind them, the kind of voices that expected to be heard.

He had not been envious, merely amused. And a bit condescending. After all, this old order was changing – as William's father, happily busy in the kitchen, seemed prepared to acknowledge. Now there was a good Labour Government to see everyone had a fair chance (although Andrew was a little vague about how this would be arranged, he was sure it would happen) the doors would be flung open to talent. Once his military service was over, he would go into the theatre and work his way up from stage hand to director, writing plays, perhaps, for his company. Poor William, destined to be an accountant (a job already waiting for him in an uncle's firm) had no such glittering prospect before him.

Of course, it hadn't worked out quite like that. He had failed in the theatre. And the privileged class that he had naively expected to disappear was still running the country, and probably ruining its economy by giving managerial jobs in its factories (and seats on the Boards of its merchants banks) to its incompetent children, nephews and cousins, hanging on to its money by clever tax dodges, putting it into numbered accounts in Switzerland, property and antiques, instead of investing in industry.

Not that William was in that league; his parents had merely been comfortable. It was Rosie's family that the money came from. Rich Rosie, Laura's old Oxford friend, guide and mentor. Laura's attitude towards their relationship puzzled him sometimes. There was a certain unsureness, as if she were over-anxious for Rosie's approval. And, from time to time, a little flare of jealous irritation that he found more understandable . . .

Andrew cannot bear to admit to emotions that he considers immature or unmanly. Jealousy is a feminine weakness, allowable in me because I am a woman. For him to be jealous of William would be despicable.

All the same, I am sure that he has, on occasion, been mildly resentful. Not of William's more assured social background; I may be foolishly inhibited by people with titles, but Andrew is free of such silliness. It is the lack of money that irks him – real money, that is; not income, but capital. Rosie and William are not ostentatiously wealthy. Although generous with friends, as I said, their own lives are modestly disciplined. They rarely buy expensive clothes or new motor cars and they seldom eat out alone or go to the theatre unless it is a very special celebration. But they bought their house on the river the same year we bought ours, and while we have a huge mortgage, theirs was paid for out of a family trust. And not only the house, but the carpets and curtains. They hardly needed to buy any furniture because William's parents had recently died (within two weeks of each other as so often happens with devoted old couples) and Rosie's widowed mother had just moved from her large house on the outskirts of Brighton into a small service flat. All the things that William and Rosie inherited were solid and service-able and some of them beautiful; when we came back from their house-warming party, our own house seemed bare. I remember that we stood, looking round our drawing room, and I made some wry remark (or just sighed, perhaps) and Andrew put his arm round my shoulders. He said, 'It's no good, my darling, we are the sort of people who have to buy their own heirlooms.'

He chuckled, as he always does at his own jokes, a habit I have always found sweetly endearing. I laughed with him and kissed him and we went to bed happy. But even as we made love, I wondered if he felt cheated. He had been brought up, after all, with some expectations, his father had always lived like a rich man, and it must have been a shock, when he died, to find he had only left enough money to buy his widow a small annuity. It had been barely enough, even then, to keep her in her bridge-playing comfort, and by the time Andrew and I bought our house, he was largely supporting her. Poor Andrew, I thought, as he collapsed on me, panting; a mother, wife, children, and now this terrible mortgage, how can he bear it?

Andrew has never complained of financial burdens and his affection for William seems unmarked by envy. Perhaps I only speculate in this way because it is natural to accuse (or suspect) other people of one's own failings. Though I have never been seriously jealous of Rosie, only angry when she appeared to be interfering between Hilde and me, and, more dangerously, wilfully, blindly, tried to organise Hilde's life into a con-ventional pattern, finding jobs for her, introducing her to suitable, unattached men . . . I wonder now (it seems curious that I have only just thought of this possibility) if it was Hilde she hoped Andrew would fall in love with and marry when she asked the three of us to her party! It would explain why she didn't discuss me or my novel with Andrew beforehand. 'You must meet,' she may have said, 'my beautiful Hilde.'

More speculation. But if it is true, and if Rosie's plan had succeeded and I had lost Andrew, would I have been jealous of *Hilde*?

As I write this, I understand how Andrew feels about this sour and destructive emotion. I cannot bear to think that my love for Hilde could have been tainted by it. Even though I am sure it was not, the idea makes my skin creep with shame and disgust. I want to hang my head and weep.

It was Hilde who rescued me from Aunt Milly.

This is hindsight. I was not aware at the time that I needed rescue. Although the situation had worsened, it had happened so slowly that I did not recognise how bad things had become. I could see that Aunt Milly was growing more helpless, that she needed assistance to get out of her chair and could no longer walk to the kitchen, but these signs of physical failure were accompanied by such harsh, spiteful grumbling that they seemed little more than new ways she had thought up for getting her own back on me. 'You can get your own tea. Why should I wait on you? Oh, I know you expect it, waited on hand and foot, that's what you'd like, isn't it? You wouldn't think there was a war on! Well there is, let me tell you, and I'm an old woman, time I was waited on a bit for a change. Instead of being a nursemaid to a girl of your age! If that's what your mother thought when she left us, then she's got another think coming! Seems to me, now she's out of that hospital, she ought to be back here, keeping an eye on her daughter. I can't do it now my legs have gone back on me, she ought to know that.'

I said, 'She's still not well, Milly. She's got to stay on the farm and have good food and fresh air. London's no good for someone who's ill. You just said yourself, there's a war on.'

A flying bomb fell at the end of our street. Our house was safe, but plaster came down from the ceiling in Aunt Milly's front room and that frightened her. She insisted that I move her big chair (in which she spent all her days now, and even some of her nights, legs propped up on another chair) into the broom

64

cupboard under the stairs. Once there, she refused to move, even to use her commode. She fouled herself and when I cleaned her up, said, 'Don't you pull that face my girl, dainty Lady Muck, you'll come to it one day, you'll learn all right, you'll find out.' All that night, lying in bed with my door open in case she called out for me, I could hear her complaining, not to me now, but to a whole range of invisible people who had in some way ill-used or neglected her – doctors, neighbours, dead husbands, my mother – 'I've worked all my life, never asked for a penny, nothing from no one, what's the use of it, all alone and who cares?' And then, sadly weeping, on and on, interspersed with deep sighs, 'Oh, poor Milly, poor Milly.'

I couldn't leave her. I suppose I should have sent for a doctor but we had no telephone and in any case I couldn't see what to say; it was only nursing she needed, not medicine. I stayed away from school – it was towards the end of the summer term, luckily, and I had just finished my matriculation exams. I looked after her as well as I could, fed her, changed her filthy clothes, tried to comfort her, though she didn't seem to know who I was any longer. 'Pity poor Milly,' she groaned, and I did pity her, I just didn't see what else I could do for her. I was trapped, by my own ignorance and by her fear and despair that infected me, so that at first, when Hilde came with Miss Loomis, the school teacher she lived with, I was afraid to let them in. The house smelt, my clothes smelt, and my hair; as they stood on the step – Hilde looking so clean in her school uniform, her flowered frock, white socks and round panama hat – I burst into tears with the shame of it and tried to shut the door in their faces.

Miss Loomis was stronger than I was. She pushed the door open. Aunt Milly was moaning in the broom cupboard and Miss Loomis went down the hall, leaving Hilde and me in the doorway. Hilde looked at me nervously, the colour rising up her white neck. 'I'm sorry', she said, 'but I thought I ought to do something.'

'You didn't have to tell Miss Loomis,' I sobbed, suddenly obsessed with sheer, selfish terror as I realised what was likely to happen. If Aunt Milly was 'taken away' they would never let me stay here, alone in the house. I would have to leave school, go and live on the farm with my mother . . .

Hilde said, 'It's all right, *she's* all right, Laura. Miss Loomis, I mean. She's really nice, honestly.'

She took my hand. We heard Miss Loomis talking to Milly, bent over with her head in the broom cupboard and her square behind sticking out. Her tweed skirt rode up at the back, revealing the elasticated legs of her pink, knee length drawers, a sight which, even in these circumstances, made Hilde and me grin at each other. She withdrew from the broom cupboard, twitched her skirt down, and advanced up the hall. The grave look on her broad, battered face (she had a lumpy, misshapen nose like an elderly boxer) made my legs tremble.

She said, 'I'm afraid your Aunt is very sick, Laura. I think you and Hilde should go away for a little, while I call an ambulance. You could walk in the park . . .' She paused, frowning – as I was to discover, Miss Loomis deplored waste of all kinds and although she wanted to spare us a painful experience, to walk without an object in view was a time-wasting activity. Her frown disappeared as she thought of a more useful alternative. 'You could go shopping for me, I'll write out a list for you.'

She removed her gloves and took an old envelope and the stub of a pencil out of her pocket. It was a long shopping list and when we came back to the house Aunt Milly was gone. Miss Loomis asked for a mop and a bucket and swabbed the linoleum in the hall and the kitchen while Hilde and I packed my suitcase.

I spent the night with them, sharing a comfortable bed in a large, airy bedroom with Hilde (Oh, the bliss of clean sheets, smelling of lavender!) and the next day Miss Loomis put me on a train down to Dorset. She had spoken to my mother (the farm had a telephone) and explained about Milly. 'Barking mad, dear,' she said when I timidly asked what was wrong with her. 'Don't worry, you did your best, but she's better off in a hospital. You've had a rough ride, now you must put it behind you and have a good holiday. Not a lazy one, though. Try and get in some regular reading. Two or three hours a day keeps the mind ticking over, stops the cogs getting rusty.'

She gave me Morley's *Life of Gladstone* in three heavy volumes, Conrad's *Heart of Darkness*, and an edition of *The Shropshire Lad*, bound in red leather. The novel and the poems went into my suitcase; she packed the Morley in a brown paper parcel and made a string handle covered with a thick piece of velvety plush. '*There* . . .' she said, letting out a long, satisfied breath as she always did when a job was well done. 'Now you won't hurt your fingers.'

At the time I thought she was being fussy; behind her broad back, Hilde and I pulled amused faces. Now, when I think of this small act of meticulous kindness, a lump comes up in my throat. Of all the things this good woman did for me (and she did a great many) this is the one that makes me want to cry.

I hoped my mother was pleased to see me. It was hard to tell. She kissed me when I arrived, she looked well, plumper than I had ever seen her and with a good colour, but she was so listless, all her old sparkle gone, that I felt awkward with her. We did things together, went for slow walks along the green, summer lanes and through the ripe cornfields, gathered blackberries, made jam, played bezique in the evenings and listened to the war news (very faint, on an old battery wireless) but occasionally I thought that she regarded me with a puzzled air. As if she wasn't quite sure what I was doing here with her.

She had a room on the first floor of the farm house and she spent a lot of time sitting in a chair looking out of the window with a strange, sad, unblinking gaze. There was a beautiful view from this window, blue hills rising on the far side of a wide, gentle valley, but it didn't seem to me that she saw it. Her eyes were turned inward, as I felt they were sometimes when she looked at me.

She was still mourning Cora, of course, and her grief was sharper because she had lived and her daughter had died; the guilty grief of the survivor. I understand this now. I didn't know it then. She never mentioned Cora and, to be honest, although once or twice I was briefly reminded (by an old teddy bear in a cupboard, a baby shoe under a pile of clothes in a drawer) I hardly thought of her. I had loved her (at least I supposed I had loved her) but she was dead and gone now and I was busy with my own concerns; how I should do my hair, the new clothes I hoped to persuade my mother to buy for me, the farmer's son, Bill, whose inexpert but energetic embraces (in the grain loft, behind the cow shed, in the dry, whiskery shelter of hay stacks) brought me to such a delicious pitch of excitement that I abandoned Hilde's rule and let him put his hand in my knickers. That was as far as I allowed him to go and perhaps it was as far as he wanted to go. Or dared, anyway – he was a year younger than I was. But the moment he touched me 'down there' a warning light flashed at once; not a moral restraint, but icily practical. If I got pregnant I would not be able to go back to school. And I wanted to go back to school very badly. I wanted to be in the Sixth Form with Hilde. I wanted to take my Higher School Certificate and, perhaps, go to college.

It may seem ridiculous that I didn't say this to my mother who had once been so anxious about my education, but she did not seem to care so much now, and I was afraid (shades of Aunt Milly!) that I was being selfish. Now Milly was in hospital, my mother would feel bound to come back to London and look after me. She might get ill as she had done before, and this time she might die. And, to be fair to myself, it wasn't only the crude fear of having her death on my conscience that made me keep silent. I wanted, longed achingly, with a pain that was almost physical, for her to be well and happy, laughing and gay as she used to be. Since our London house now seemed a grim prison (poisoned for ever for me by Aunt Milly) I was convinced that if my mother were condemned to live there she would never recover. Of course, if she were to suggest it herself (the muddled logic of this argument did not trouble me) that would be different. But she didn't suggest it. Even though she seemed pleased when I heard I had passed my Matric and done well, she said nothing about my future. I abandoned hope and sank into a rich and gloomy despair that was not altogether unpleasurable. I wrote to Hilde, a long, passionate letter full of fine, flowery phrases and virtuous self-abnegation. Besides my mother's 'comfort' – I chose that loaded word carefully – my education was quite unimportant. I was sorry my childhood was over, and I would miss Hilde, naturally, but I had no choice in the matter. 'Life makes its demands,' I wrote heroically, 'and we, who are only its toys, must accede to them.'

The mind has its sly, hidden corners. If I were telling a story about a fictional girl writing that letter, I would suggest (it would be unfashionable not to) that she knew more or less what response she was hoping for. But since I am feeling tender towards myself at this moment (or, rather, feeling tender towards the child I was then; fat, awkward, ignorant, vulnerable) I prefer to think that I had no expectations, no cunning idea at the back of my mind that Hilde might pass on my appeal to Miss Loomis. Certainly, when Miss Loomis wrote, inviting me to stay with her for the school term, I was almost as surprised as my mother.

'Is that what you want?' my mother said. 'It's very kind of her, but you don't have to stay on at school, you could leave if you like. You're nearly sixteen, after all.'

I think now that she may have been hoping I would stay on the farm and get a job locally. Cora was dead, my father at sea except for very brief visits; my presence would have been some small comfort. But perhaps I am wrong. Or perhaps, at that moment, she felt nothing very much about anything. What I said (trying to hold down my leaping joy because that too was 'selfish') that I would like, if I could, to go on with my education and live with Miss Loomis and Hilde, she hardly seemed interested. She said, in an absent voice, 'Well, of course, you must miss your friends, I know that.' And then, in a more alert tone, 'You'll miss Bill, too, won't you duckie?'

Her smile was tentative, a delicate invitation to confide in her, but I saw it (chose to see it, perhaps, because of what had seemed until now her lack of concern for me) as prying and prurient. I blushed with shame and vexation and said, 'Really, Mother, you're as bad as Aunt Milly.'

I said to Hilde, 'It was really disgusting. She looked at me with the eyes of a *brothel keeper*!'

Hilde laughed as she often did when I said something she thought was silly. I didn't mind; in fact I often said silly things, to encourage her. She had such a beautiful laugh; musically clear and so joyful that her whole face seemed to dance with it; dimples flashed in her cheeks, rosy lips gleamed and quivered, eyes shone like dark stars. She said, 'Have you ever seen a brothel keeper, Laura? Oh, you are dotty! I expect she was only interested.'

'Mothers shouldn't be interested in their daughters' sex lives,' I said haughtily. 'If they are, they should keep quiet about it. It's an embarrassing topic.'

'I don't think I'd mind, if it was my mother,' Hilde said. She spoke simply and thoughtfully, without any hint of reproach but the bright, dancing look had gone from her face and I knew I'd been tactless. Miss Loomis had warned me that Hilde had had no news of her family, her parents and her two little brothers. 'Let her talk about them if she wants to,' she said. 'But don't ask her.'

I said quickly, 'I mean it would be embarrasing from any old person, can you imagine Miss Loomis mentioning that sort of thing?' and was relieved to see Hilde's eyes shine again.

'She gave me a book,' she said. 'She gave me Aldous Huxley's *Science of Life*.'

We both laughed, though not unkindly. Miss Loomis was a source of affectionate amusement, and not only because of her innocent belief that everything one needed to know could be found in a book. The contrast between her prize fighter's appearance, shoulders broad as a man's and a face that looked as though it had been thumped into ruin by a heavy-weight champion, and her high-pitched, ladylike voice and fastidious manners (if she needed to blow her nose, she always retired to the bathroom) seemed to us especially comic. And there were her clothes! In the daytime she wore tweeds that looked (Hilde said wittily) as if they had tramped the Scottish Highlands with John Brown and Queen Victoria, but at night she put on lacy gowns frothing with pink maribou at the hem and round her stout, leathery neck. We knew her night attire intimately because when the land mines began to fall we all slept in the dining room; Hilde and me beneath the heavy oak table and Miss Loomis on top. 'An additional protection, my dears,' she said when we pointed out she would be just as safe, and more comfortable, in her own bed. 'I shall sleep better, knowing that I am shielding you with my body.'

She was a romantic woman, I think, dreaming in her secret heart of brave deeds and glory (a great general, perhaps, leading a cavalry charge) but she disciplined her romanticism into practical channels. She was an historian, an expert on mandated territories (she had written a pamphlet on this subject for the League of Nations), a Fabian Socialist and a passionate feminist. She believed that it was the masculine principle that had brought the world to the pass it was in, and that it was up to 'we women' to restore light and goodness and order. 'The price of liberty is eternal vigilance,' she informed us in her sweet, fluting, old-maidenly voice, 'and that means attention to minor details which is something all women have been trained to be good at. If the German Hausfrau had come out of the kitchen and taken an interest in politics, Hitler would never have come to power. It is up to you girls to see that such a thing never happens again in your lifetime. The future will be what you make it. Nothing is closed to you. It is my belief that your generation will see a woman Prime Minister.'

We smiled at this thought which seemed absurd to us then, but it was not absurd to Miss Loomis! The Oxford Union, at that time closed to women, was bound to open its doors once the war was over, and that would be one way for us to be noticed by the 'right people' and get into Parliament. With this end in view, she was coaching Hilde for her Oxford entrance, and she insisted that I study with her. When I protested that I was not as clever as Hilde (though I did not altogether believe this, I knew I was certainly lazier) she did not deny my mock-humble statement. 'Cleverness is not everything, dear, application can be as important. I know you have literary ambitions' – a faint smile suggested that she was recalling the over-blown prose of my letter to Hilde – 'but perhaps you would be wise to set them aside for a while and concentrate on your weak points, your Latin and French. Perseverance wins the crown, Laura. You are quite clever enough to do anything you set your heart on.'

It was the element of fantasy in her nature that made her faith so seductive. She might speak of discipline and endurance but beneath those harsh words we could hear trumpets blowing. We marched with her, to the same tune, believing as she did that a new world was coming and that it was our duty to prepare ourselves for it. We were proud to share Miss Loomis's ordered and dedicated life; going to school in the daytime, studying in the evening, and working (as the 1945 election approached) for the Labour Party, addressing envelopes, attending meetings, trudging round canvassing.

No moment was wasted. Even the parties Miss Loomis gave fitted into her plans for us. A dozen girls from our class would be invited for coffee and sandwiches on Sunday evenings; we would listen to classical music while we ate, and afterwards discuss some topical matter to give us practice in public speaking. *The Beveridge Report*; *Whither India?*; *The Social Consequences of Food Rationing*; *Class in British Society and its Effect on the Economy*; *The Future of Farm Subsidies*; *Whither South Africa?* *Europe and the American Presence.* These are some of the subjects Miss Loomis thought suitable and now, over thirty years later, that stretch of turbulent history is fixed in my mind by those solemn, schoolgirl debates.

They were not really 'parties', perhaps, those Sunday gatherings, but that was what Miss Loomis called them and the zest with which she used the word was infectious. We cut sandwiches and set out her pretty bone china with gleeful anticipation and were not disappointed. I can think of few social occasions that have given me such deep and involved enjoyment. Just to remember that book-lined sitting room, the shabby furnishing and chipped paint of wartime concealed by dim lighting that was partly economy, partly to give us the courage to speak out more boldly, the circle of girls on the floor and the square, solid figure of Miss Loomis presiding, intelligent eyes darting from one young face to another, nodding approval when a good point was made, interposing a quick sentence when the argument did not flow as it should, brings back a sweet sense of safety and happiness. I felt safe with Miss Loomis, and not only because she seemed fond of me; after Aunt Milly, the constant presence of a sharp and rational mind was wonderfully reassuring. Hilde and I might laugh at her some-times, but when we did we felt slyly irreverent – mischievous acolytes mocking a great clumsy goddess whose energy and moral power we relied upon absolutely. 'It sounds weird,' Hilde said once, 'but I always feel that as long as I'm with her, fate cannot harm me!'

Sad words. It seems extraordinary that I cannot remember exactly when it was that Hilde heard that her mother and father and brothers were dead. All I can be sure of is that it was after the war in Europe was over (we had gone with Miss Loomis to Buckingham Palace and shouted ourselves hoarse on Victory Night) and that it must have been term time, because I was with Miss Loomis, and a weekend, because Hilde was not. She had gone, as she occasionally did, to spend the Friday and Saturday nights with a couple in Brighton who had been among her sponsors when she first came to England and were still helping to pay for her education and maintenance. (They were Rosie's parents, in fact. I had not met Rosie then, but I can remember Miss Loomis saying, sometime or other, that it was nice for Hilde that these people had a girl who was roughly her age.)

I remember Miss Loomis weeping. I think that I was, to begin with, more horrified by the sight of her awesome collapse than I was by the cause of it. Although she wept with some restraint, hands covering her face, her whole body quivered and shook as if with some monstrous, internal earthquake. We sat in the kitchen, on opposite sides of the plain, scrubbed, deal table and I watched her, numb and appalled. Hours seemed to pass before she removed her hands from her wrecked face and mopped her red eyes. She looked at me and said, with a last, deep, shuddering sigh, 'I'm sorry, Laura, did I frighten you, dear? I shouldn't have given way, it's just that I have been afraid of this for so long. She must have been, too. That poor child, poor, brave, sweet child, what a torment to live with, how will she bear it? She doesn't know yet, they rang from Brighton to tell me they'd heard, but she's out at the moment, not back until lunch time.' Instinctively, we both looked at the kitchen clock. It was just before twelve. 'Time is terrible,' Miss Loomis said. 'It's terrible to think that at this very moment we *know*, and she doesn't . . .'

She spoke with a slow, wondering grief that brought the truth home to me as her tears had not done. I started to cry myself, weakly, and she stretched her large, competent hand across the table and took hold of mine. 'One good thing,' she said, 'at least she's with her own people at this dreadful time. They can comfort her better than we can, they have more right to.' I didn't understand what she meant and my bewilderment must have shown in my face because she went on at once, very gently, 'We are not Jewish, my dear. We can sympathise – oh, with all our hearts we can sympathise – but we can't really *share*. It would be impertinent even to try. There is nothing in your life or mine that can compare with what she has to accept and endure.'

This sentiment seemed to me a bit pious – the romantic rather than the rational Miss Loomis speaking – and I remember that I resented it. What cheek, I thought. Hilde was my *best friend*! This family in Brighton were only acquaintances! (In fact, as I was to discover, only Rosie's father was Jewish, and it was Rosie's mother who broke the news to poor Hilde. A gentile bosom she was drawn to, and invited to weep on.)

Not that Hilde did weep. (Not one tear, Rosie told me, years later.) She suffered the tender embrace for a courteous moment, then withdrew gently and thanked Rosie's mother for telling her. It was a relief to know the truth, even if it was not what she'd hoped for. And when Rosie's kind mother held out her arms again and urged her not to be stoical, to give way, to cry if she wanted to, she said she would be too ashamed. 'After all, it's they who've been murdered, not me. I'm the lucky one.'

She must have seemed genuinely calm. Otherwise they would never have allowed her to come home alone the same day. They telephoned Miss Loomis to say they were putting her on a train and that she had 'taken it remarkably well.' (If that stock phrase sounds cruelly insensitive now, you must remember that it was not, in those days, thought psychologically damaging to behave with dignity. Keeping a stiff upper lip in

74

the face of loss or adversity was not a comic cliché but a sign of true grit. Rosie's parents, who had lost two sons in the war, one in the Battle of Britain and one in a submarine, would have respected Hilde's wish to keep her grief private.)

Miss Loomis went to meet her at the station. They came home in a taxi. I flung the door open as soon as I heard it draw up, expecting to see my friend's face set in a tragic mask. Instead, she smiled at me brightly and said, 'You know, it rained *all weekend* in Brighton. I was telling Miss Loomis. It all looks so unspeakably *dreary*, all those huge rolls of barbed wire on the beach, and great rusty iron spikes sticking up to stop the German landing craft getting in. I suppose they'll get rid of them sometime, but maybe they won't, maybe no one will bother and they'll stay there for ever and ever until people have forgotten what they were *for*. They look so depressingly permanent. And what's even more depressing is all the *old people*, just sitting there in the shelters on the sea front and staring at all this barbed wire and the horrible, grey, heaving sea – as if they had nothing better to do, as if they were waiting to *die* . . .'

She rattled on in this way the rest of the evening, high as a kite, brilliant-eyed, cheeks pale as alabaster. She told us the details of every meal she had eaten in Brighton, the intricate plot of the film she had been to with Rosie (*Dead of Night*, with Michael Redgrave starring as a mad ventriloquist), the shops she had been to, searching for a pair of wooden-soled clogs that she wanted but had not been able to find in her size.

Her terror was plain to see. Pitiable to begin with, it slowly became irritating and hurtful. We loved her, didn't we? Surely she could have trusted us not to intrude on her sorrow? I was relieved when Miss Loomis stood up at last, getting up from her chair very slowly, as if all her bones ached, and said, 'You must be tired, Hilde. I think you should have a hot bath and go to bed now. Laura and I will clear away supper.'

We washed the dishes in silence. The kitchen clock ticked the time away. We heard the bath water run out. Miss Loomis looked up at the ceiling that shook very slightly as Hilde walked to the bedroom. She said, in an unusually humble voice, 'She may not have wanted to discuss it with me, Laura dear, but you are her age, she may talk to you. If she does, and you think there is anything I ought to know, that I could do for her, perhaps you will tell me.'

Hilde and I lay in the big double bed that had belonged to Miss Loomis's parents and that we shared, except for the nights we spent under the dining room table, all the time that we lived with her. The bed had a deliciously soft but rather uneven mattress made of goose down; we always rolled to the centre and lay entwined comfortably. (Innocently, too. Since Miss Loomis had never given us *The Well of Loneliness* to read it had presumably not occurred to her that lesbianism might have a place in a girl's education.) Tonight, as on other nights, we cuddled each other. Hilde was warm from her bath; I put my cold feet on her stomach and she gently stroked them. She whispered, breath warm on my cheek, 'Something's happened, Laura. I've got to tell you, only I don't know how . . .' She stopped, and I waited with a mixture of fear and shameful excitement (this was the first time real tragedy had come close to me and I wanted to know what it felt like) but she was only searching for the right circumlocution. She gave a sudden, sharp giggle. 'Laura,' she said, 'I've *been with* a man!'

I gasped and she giggled again; the soft flesh of her stomach quivered under my feet. I stretched my legs out and we lay side by side, the feather mattress billowing round us, snug as two puppies. She said, 'Shall I tell you?'

Rosie's parents had put her into a Ladies Only carriage at Brighton. They had wanted to wait until the train left but she asked them to go – 'They'd been so kind, I felt stifled,' she said – and when they had gone, a young man, a soldier passing by on the platform, had stopped to smile at her and pull a mock-sad face at the lettering on the window. He got into the adjacent compartment and when the train stopped at the next station, Hilde had joined him. By some strange chance this was an almost empty train and he was alone. He offered her a cigarette, they smoked and talked for a little, but not for long. There wasn't much time; any moment the train might stop at a station and someone open the door and surprise them. 'I was afraid he'd never get in,' Hilde said. 'It's supposed to be hard the first time, but he was ever so quick. I suppose he was scared like I was.'

There was a lot I wanted to know, but I was embarrassed to ask. 'But Hilde, it could have been dangerous. I mean he might have been a sex maniac. Or had some disease.'

'I think he was too young for that,' she said confidently. 'Quite young, anyway, and he looked nice and clean. That's why I decided. After all, I had to get it over with sometime.'

I shivered and she squeezed my hand. 'Don't worry. It only hurts a bit to begin with.'

'I'm not scared of *that*.' I wondered if I should mention my fear of pregnancy and decided that it was best not to worry her since she had already risked it. I said, 'I nearly did it with Bill. But that was different. I mean, he wasn't a stranger.'

Hilde was silent. Then she said, 'But that was it, don't you see, Laura? I couldn't have borne to do it with someone I knew.'

At the time the desolate implication of this remark did not strike me. In fact it seemed rather sensible. Losing one's virginity was obviously so unhygienic and messy that unless one was married (in which case it would be quite different) one was bound to be embarrassed afterwards. Perhaps the memory of love-making with Bill should have contradicted this theory but I was so convinced at the time of Hilde's superiority (she was not only more intelligent but more sensitive and civilised than I was) that our eager tumbling in hay lofts and orchards suddenly seemed shamefully gross to me, a lewd game played by two strong, rough children who should have known better.

I said, with a sigh of regret, 'I suppose you're right, Hilde,' and she laughed, deep in her throat, a full, happy chuckle, and put her arms round me.

'Only right for *me*, Laura darling. What's right for one person isn't necessarily right for another. So don't go and copy me now! Miss Loomis would never forgive me!'

I said, my voice muffled against her warm shoulder, 'Miss Loomis asked me to tell her if you said anything. Well. You know about what.'

'Don't,' she said. '*Please*' – and my heart contracted. What I felt for my friend at that moment was a kind of love that was new to me; a raw pain that I have only felt since for my children, when something has happened I cannot put right for them. The love that I feel for my oldest son, Jeremy, which is like an open wound, bleeding.

I pretended to misunderstand her. I said, with a wild, gasping laugh, 'Course I won't. I could hardly tell her *this*, could I?'

She was holding me so tight she was hurting me. She said, 'I can't talk about it. I'm so sorry, Laura, I shouldn't be like this with you, so sort of mean and dried up. After all, you know what it's like, you've lost your own *sister*.'

'That wasn't so bad,' I said gruffly, speaking the bleak, shameful truth. 'I mean, it was different.'

She let me go and lay still. Then sighed so sadly that I felt her pain twisting inside me. She said, '*It can't be.*'

I wasn't sure if this was in response to what I had said, or a more general statement. I waited, but that was all; she said nothing more. She slept quite soon after and I lay awake listening to her regular breathing, wishing that I could have thought of something to say that might have comforted her, something grand, elegiac, poetical, forming fine phrases and rejecting them because they did not measure up to the deep, helpless sorrow I truly felt for her. And, at the same time, with part of my mind, I was wondering if she felt any *different*, now she had 'been with' a man.

I didn't tell Miss Loomis about the soldier, of course. If I had done, it wouldn't have changed anything for her. That's what I tell myself, anyway.

Hilde will not be at Rosie's party, Laura is thinking, in the car, with her husband.

I said, 'Who'll be at the party, do you think, Andy?'

And he answered, as if he knew what was in my mind, 'The survivors, my darling,' and laughed. 'All the survivors.'

Rosie doesn't abandon the failures, the people who fall off the ladder. She was infinitely generous and sweet to me when

78

I left Pete, telephoning me daily, asking me to quiet dinners, just herself, William and me, or to tête-à-tête lunch time
sessions, feeding me delicious, small, invalid meals, pouring
gin down me – I have never drunk gin since, it has such dreary
associations – listening with alert patience to my repetitive
assessments and reassessments of my boringly commonplace
situation, responding with wisdom and tenderness. But she
didn't ask me to her parties until I was over the worst of my
self-absorption, partly because she believed that I needed her
undivided attention, and partly because people in trouble make
such unsuitable guests. Rosie's parties are celebrations and no
one can celebrate happily if some unfortunate is getting drunk
in a corner, or fixing innocent victims with an Ancient Mariner
eye and pouring out tales of woe.

I have sometimes thought (indeed, I was thinking it as we
drove along the wide, open road by the river) that it could be
alarming, knowing Rosie's kind and considerate habits, to
arrive at her house and find yourself the only guest. Even if
nothing seemed to be wrong in your life at the moment, you
might wonder, uneasily, if Rosie knew something you didn't, if
some disquieting rumour had reached her, if she had smelled
blood . . .

'What are you smiling at?' Andrew asked as we turned into
Rosie's driveway. I shook my head dismissively, laughing.
Because of course, after all my ungracious reflections, now we
were here at last, arriving at this welcoming house with its
windows open to the sun (and the chilly breeze, too, William
and Rosie being fresh air fanatics) and could see the party in full
swing already, familiar profiles and backs, and dear William
glancing out, watching slightly anxiously as Andrew parked our
Volvo Estate rather too close to a Bentley, I felt the usual uplift
of larky anticipation and energy. 'Amanda's here,' I said, as I
squeezed out of the passenger seat into the inadequate space
between my side of our car and the Bentley. 'Joe, too – that *is*
Joey, isn't it? He's got a lot balder. What's he doing now, Andy,
can you remember? You saw him when you were in San
Francisco last year, didn't you?'

'Teaching African History at some Californian college. New wife, and I think a young son,' Andrew said, briefing me rapidly, smoothing his thick, wind-blown hair, straightening his black and orange Tennis Club tie and waving to William whose eager, rubbery face was creasing into delighted smiles as he saw us. William waved back, disappeared from the window and reappeared at the open front door, long legs striding towards us, holding his hands out.

'Bless you, my dears,' he said, as he kissed me on both cheeks and thumped Andrew's shoulder with manly affection. 'I'm so glad you felt up to coming. I wondered if we ought to ring up this morning but Rosie said, better not, you might feel obliged to come and that wouldn't be fair . . .'

He mopped his brow with a large, red silk handkerchief, sweaty and beaming, and I knew that I had been right about William; he did worry over these social occasions, feared for his guests' comfort and happiness even as he smiled at them.

Rosie's welcome was graver. 'Oh, my darlings,' she said, with a searching look at our faces, not overdoing the sympathy, showing it only in the extra warmth of her embrace and the little sigh as she released us.

Dear Rosie. Forget all the snide things I have said about her. Goodness is always hard to describe (wicked people are much more amusing to write about) and so one searches for flaws. The only real flaw I can think of is that Rosie's loving kindness makes her assume rather too often a therapist's role. Though this is certainly quite unconscious on her part, springing naturally out of a true concern, a helpful intention, it has sometimes made me feel inferior. And perhaps there is a certain vanity in the way she has made no attempt at all to fight age; greying hair cropped short, no lipstick, no powder, no fuss about clothes. Today she was wearing a garment she might have borrowed from one of her daughters, a loose sack of fine Indian cotton printed in delicate colours and gathered round her tiny waist by a silver belt. When we were at Oxford, Rosie and I used to borrow each others dresses (or, more accurately, I borrowed Rosie's, her wardrobe being more extensive than mine) but this would not be possible now. While I have become what Andrew kindly calls rounder, she has grown skinny; a middle-aged forest sprite.

I said, 'Rosie, what a pretty dress, you look like a *girl*,' and her elfin face crinkled with laughter.

'Thank you, darling. But I must tell you a *funny* story! Last weekend, we took Mama to Scotland to visit some friends of hers, people she and Daddy used to stay with when he went salmon fishing. I met his old ghillie by chance in the village and we talked, and after a bit I asked him if he remembered me because it seemed that he didn't. And he looked at me for a minute and said, in that dry, Scottish way, *Aye, lass, but you've withered.*'

We laughed as she meant us to. She hadn't been asking for reassurance or compliments. Rosie is too honest for that kind of slyness; too sweetly accepting. (Or too complacent, perhaps? No. That's unfair.)

'Miserable sod,' Andrew said. 'Bloody nonsense.'

He kissed Rosie lightly on the top of her head and vanished with William, into the room, into the party.

Rosie took my arm, drawing me close. A pinkish glow fell upon her from the tinted glass cupola above the stair well; in its kindly light she looked young again, gentle and serious. She said, 'Darling, are you *really* all right? You don't have to cope with that crowd if you don't feel quite up to it. If you'd rather just sit down and be quiet with a drink and some food in my study.'

I shook my head, smiling. She nodded, still very serious; soft, troubled, brown eyes holding mine. 'How *is* Jeremy, darling?'

'Fine.'

She pressed my hand. Something more was clearly expected from me. I smiled again. 'He said when he wrote that it was really no worse than boarding school. I suppose that's bravado.'

'Of course, he hated boarding school, didn't he?' Rosie reminded me.

'He lived through it. He'll live through this, I dare say.' I heard myself, sounding callous. But I couldn't bear to be comforted. I said, in a vivacious voice, 'Amanda's here, isn't she? It'll be so nice to see her!'

Rosie looked surprised – with some reason. She knows that although Amanda amuses me, and counts (since we have known each other so long) as a friend, that I can only endure her in very small doses. At Oxford she was a big, flamboyant, gipsy-ish girl who edited *Isis*; now she is a stout, cigar-smoking hoyden with a boy and girl of her own (their father long vanished) and a varying number of 'difficult' foster children whom she takes on when the local authority have despaired of finding homes for them. She earns her living (and theirs) by firebrand journalism; writing about aspects of social injustice that my generation have known about for a long time as indignantly as if they were new to her. Which cannot be true, since she is the same age as we are.

I said, 'You know that story about Trevelyan, the Cambridge historian? When he was told that the attendance at Chapel was rising, he said he thought they had settled *that* argument years ago. Or some such remark. It's how I feel when I read Amanda. How can she bear to go on, fighting all those old battles?'

'Other people don't know about them, love, do they? There's always a new generation coming up that needs to be *told*,' Rosie said. 'I must say, I feel rather as you do, but one has to admire her, don't you think? I mean, all the *energy*!' She smiled at me mischievously and I thought, for an uncomfortable moment, that she was going to accuse me of professional jealousy, but it was only my guilty mind. (Amanda has what the Americans call High Visibility. She is much better known than I am; everyone – that is, everyone in *our* world has heard of her, and of course I am jealous!) All Rosie said was, 'Do you know Joey's here?'

'I thought I saw him. Just his back, through the window. I haven't seen him for ages. Several years, anyway. Has he lost *all* his hair?'

'Most of it.' Rosie had changed her tone and expression to fit in with mine. 'An improvement in some ways. It's solved his dandruff problem!'

We both giggled, like two silly girls. Rosie said, 'He was due to fly back to America yesterday but he changed his mind when he heard you were coming. He's longing to see you again, it's quite touching!'

She looked at me with innocent delight. Had she planned this, I wondered? A mild, romantic diversion, a little 'treat' for poor Laura on this anxious day. But although my body responded as perhaps she had hoped – heart lifting, pulse fluttering – in my mind I was hurt suddenly, almost to tears. A mawkish reaction that was my fault, not Rosie's. I smiled at her fiercely.

Nostalgia is a disease of age and when you are wide open to its infection you can never be sure how and when it will strike. It is always the unexpected attacks that are the most painful. I had learned to steel myself recently against obviously poignant reminders – pictures of Jeremy as a little boy, sad, childish letters from the school that he hated – but it had never occurred to me that I might have to arm myself against someone like Joey. Although what caused this particular seizure (a pain which I could locate, physically, as an aching hollow, not unlike indigestion, just behind my breast bone) wasn't Joey, not the balding, middle-aged man I had glimpsed through the window, nor even the memory of a much younger Joey, my unregretted, long ago love, who had once had a pale, dry haystack of hair and a problem with dandruff.

Joey was only a trigger. A key.

I could write: *Hilde and I were so happy our first year at Oxford*. But that is a portmanteau phrase, really; a kind of cheap suitcase containing so many different emotions that it is impossible to select one of them and label it 'happiness'. We were young and excited, free for the first time from the shackles of childhood and drunk with this freedom, kicking up our heels like colts let loose in a meadow, testing our muscles, our untried opinions, expectant and hopeful and trusting. Perhaps it wasn't so much that we were consciously happy; more that happiness, then, seemed a natural condition of life.

I am embarrassed, reading this paragraph. Nostalgia at its

worst; sentimental words drenched in the unreal, rosy glow through which forgetful people choose to look back at the sunny days of their youth. And indeed, taking an objective view, it seems almost perverse. It was an austere time, that immediate post war period, full of industrial unrest, political bitterness and a widespread resentment at the decline of British power in the world. We had fought a long, draining war, and were now worse off than the losers. But Hilde and I had been trained by Miss Loomis, that noble optimist, and these miserable assessments of the state of the nation passed over our heads like the tedious grumbling of tired or peevish grown-ups. It was clear to us that the National Health Service, the National Insurance Act – the whole founding of the Welfare State – were signposts on a brave road that was leading us all to the new Jerusalem, to a future as golden as Miss Loomis had said it would be, and one in which we as educated young women would have parts to play. They would be distinguished parts, naturally, even if they might not be the ones Miss Loomis had hoped for. In spite of her plans for us (which had not been as absurdly vainglorious as we had thought: although we didn't know it, the first British woman Prime Minister had gone down from Oxford the year we went up) neither Hilde nor I had any real political ambitions. In deference to Miss Loomis we joined the Labour Club and sat through long debates that were cosily reminiscent of her Sunday evenings – *Marxist Theory and Democratic Socialism*; *Whither India?*; *Can the Monarchy Survive the Death of Bourgeois Society?* – but our hearts were not in them. Though we didn't admit it (perhaps didn't know it) our interests and needs were romantic and sexual. We had been starved of male company; we were ready and looking for love. And, since we were looking, we found it.

Joey and me. Hilde and Fritz. It saddens me that I can remember so little of how happy we were. Perhaps happiness is never memorable, or, because it presupposes ignorance of what the future might bring, is embarrassing to look back upon. Or perhaps my profession inhibits me. Happy love is best celebrated by poets, not by workaday novelists. Whatever the reason, I can only summon up incidents, glimpses. The four of us skating on Port Meadow one winter night; the thin ice of the flooded field squeaking under our skates; Joey coughing with the cold between bouts of laughter at our joint incompetence as we clung and staggered together; Fritz (as always) taking the exercise much more seriously, trying to teach Hilde to strike out and glide; Hilde's face, darkly radiant in the bright moon, and laughing. And a summer ball. A punt on the river in the magical, blue, chilly dawn; Joey poling, wearing a borrowed dinner jacket that was too short in the arms, his face pale with exhaustion under his wild shock of pale hair; Fritz in a blue velvet suit; Hilde in a dress of a paler blue lying beside him, her head on his shoulder, a smile on her half-asleep face. She had grown slightly plumper and the extra weight suited her, rounding her breasts and arms, softening her strong, bony face, turning her from a striking girl into a beauty. Fritz was looking down at her with an expression I couldn't identify; a faint, twisted smile, a faint sadness. Then he looked up at me and after a brief moment in which he regarded me analytically as if I were a specimen under a microscope (this intent inspection was a cultivated affectation, meant to impress, but in fact it made him look like a supercilious schoolboy), smiled at me fully.

He said, 'Are you happy, dear girl?' I nodded and he said, 'Good. I think that makes four of us. Quite an achievement for one's first year, don't you think?' And I had the odd feeling that he had drawn a line under it.

That we had both found our 'men' at the same time seemed to Hilde and me a piece of remarkable luck. We were so close, closer than sisters. We told each other that if only one of us had 'met her fate' – though I put these words in quotation marks now, at the time we used them only half-jokingly – she would have given him up. As it was, we imposed on Joey and Fritz our childish desire to marry two brothers. It was at our instigation that we went out so much together; though Fritz and Joey were at the same college, their backgrounds were too different for them to be natural companions. And when we did spend evenings apart, Hilde and I always met afterwards, in her room or mine, for the pleasure of dissecting our lovers.

Joey, Hilde pronounced, was 'terribly sweet and nice, so straightforward'. Fritz, 'much more dark and complicated'. More interesting than Joey, I guessed that she meant, but I didn't resent it. I didn't want complications. I had had a drab growing up and I think, without realising it, I was afraid of maturity, trying to slip back in time, recover my lost adolescence. Joey came from a grammar school, as I did, from the same kind of family (a little lower in the social scale, actually, since his father was a bus driver) and I didn't have to explain myself to him. He was very bright, very funny, a marvellous mimic. We laughed a lot, kissed and sighed, talked about sex (in solemn tones for a solemn subject) but we never made love. There were no sweaty fumblings of the kind I had gone in for with the farmer's son, Bill. 'All or nothing' was what we decided in our earnest discussions. We would enjoy it all the more when we finally 'got round to it' at an unspecified time in the future. 'There is a lot to be said for anticipation,' Joey said gravely, 'and although I long for your body, it is a much greater step for a woman than it is for a man and I don't want you to be hurt. I want you to feel safe with me. That's more important than satisfying my sexual hunger.'

I didn't report this speech to Hilde. Nowadays, I suppose, I might have wondered if Joey were a closet queen (I am sure my daughter, Claudia, would have assumed it) but I had never heard of the term. I only feared that Hilde might laugh and suggest that Joey was unnaturally timid with women, and it would have seemed unsophisticated to argue that I thought (as I did) that he was being protective and manly. Whatever the truth, which lay, I imagine, somewhere in between, the limits Joey had set to our relationship gave me a sense of marvellous freedom. I was happy, for the moment, to be playing at love.

Hilde would not have laughed. What I was really afraid of, though this, too, was unlikely, was that she would repeat it to Fritz. And though I would have died rather than said so, Fritz often alarmed me. He was the son of a well known Labour politician and he had been to Eton; two things that placed him, for me, in a world that was as far removed from the one I knew as outer space. His family were, so he said, 'disgustingly rich'.

But what really frightened me was his apparent assurance. He had very correct, rather old-fashioned manners that made him seem, sometimes, like an old man playing at being a young one, a certain thin-lipped precision of speech and a calculating and faintly scornful expression when other people were talking that made me especially jumpy. If I became conscious of that look while I was speaking, it would stop me mid-sentence, convinced that what I was saying was so utterly foolish that only his excellent manners prevented him from laughing out loud. Neither Joey nor Hilde seemed affected this way but I think now (perhaps I realised it then in some subliminal way, and this was the cause of my nervousness with him) that while the three of us were cheerfully and unselfconsciously enjoying each other's company, Fritz was amusing himself with us deliberately, as an adult might play with children. And perhaps (again without really 'knowing' it, or at least not admitting it) I was aware that he was playing with us only because he and Hilde went to bed together, that he would never have wasted his time with us otherwise. I didn't ask Hilde, of course. I didn't even ask myself – held back by some deep, inner prurience. Since I was happy enough to discuss sex in the abstract, I cannot explain this, only record that when I was faced with the fact, I tried to ignore it.

That night on Port Meadow. Fritz had suggested the skating expedition when the river flooded and began to ice over. He had his own skates and promised to borrow three other pairs. This would take time and trouble but we never questioned that he should organise this sort of detail. It was always Fritz who booked punts, theatre tickets, decided where we should eat; part of the adult role that he had assumed naturally but that he may have resented. When his plans didn't work out as he meant them to, when one of us didn't enjoy the play, or the film, or let him down in some other way, he grew touchy.

We had dined at an Indian restaurant and by the time we got to Port Meadow it was a little before ten o'clock. The setting was perfect, a full, round, pearly moon, a dry, tingling night; Hilde's performance was not. Fritz was physically very graceful, and she had always been clumsy. Although she was

87

obviously intensely happy, laughing with joy, quite untroubled
by her own incompetence as she stumbled and clutched Fritz's
arm, her inability to learn even the simplest step baffled and
finally maddened him, ruining the vision he had had of this
occasion, of the two of them sailing the ice, in perfect step with
each other.

At some point she fell. Fritz stood over her, hauling her up.
Joey and I were some distance away (we had removed ourselves, tactfully, when Fritz's instructions to her had begun to
grow irritated) but the air was so still we could hear his voice
clearly. 'Get up, for God's sake, I've had enough if you haven't.'
And then, in a different tone, slightly softer, but in a queer way,
more brutal, 'I can think of a better way to get bruises. It's all
right for you, but if we fool around here much longer, I'll be too
tired and you'll be sorry then, won't you?'

Joey coughed, loud and long. He had had catarrh most of
that winter but this bout of coughing seemed somewhat exces-
sive. When he had recovered he looked at me shyly and slyly.
He waited – for me to say something, I think – and when I
didn't, he said, 'Poor old Fritz, he can't bear it when people
don't measure up to what he expects of them.'

My heart was bumping. I whispered, 'I can't bear it when
he's rude to her.'

'Oh, well, I don't think . . .' Joey stopped, and sighed. Then
he took off his long scarf and wrapped it round my neck. 'It's not
our business,' he said. 'Come on, you'll get cold.'

We walked back to my college, unusually silent. At the gates,
he unwound his scarf from my neck and kissed me. I looked
down the empty road. 'Where's Hilde?' I said. 'I thought they
were following.'

Joey said nothing.

I said, 'It's eleven fifteen, the gates will be locked in a
minute.'

Since Joey was aware of this college rule, this was a pointless
remark. I went on, equally pointlessly, denying what I knew out
of idiotic, mysterious delicacy, but wanting it confirmed, all the
same. 'She'll have to climb in again, what on earth is she *doing*?'

But Joey didn't answer, only kissed me again. Though

he was rougher this time, pushing his tongue in my mouth, he was careful to hold the lower part of his body away from mine to conceal his erection.

'Do you ever see Fritz?' I asked this bald, cheerful, plump man who had just kissed me in welcome (continental fashion, first on one cheek, then on the other) and with whom I now stood, crushed by the party, belly to belly; closer in this forced and false intimacy than we had been on that far away evening in Oxford. His jacket looked (as Joey's clothes always had done) as if he had slept in it, or rolled in a ditch, and smelled (which was new) of some repulsive herbal tobacco. I resisted an impulse to remove a blob of cheese dip from his tie, and thought he looked younger than when I'd last seen him, eight years ago.

I knew it was eight years because it was just after Isobel's birth. Joey's wife, his first wife, was dying of cancer. They had flown home from Africa where Joey had been doing some kind of field work, and she was in hospital. He had telephoned from a call box and I had left Isobel with Andrew's mother and driven to London. We sat in a pub, drinking malt whisky. I had missed one of Isobel's feeds, and when Joey wept, the milk flowed painfully into my breasts as if in sympathy with him. He apologised for dragging me away from my baby, but he had been out of the country so long and I was the only person he could think of, that he could bear to talk to, he said. His wife had suffered so much, such a cruel illness; he was lined with the agony of it and blaming himself. If only he had brought her home earlier! But he had been absorbed in his work and she had made light of her symptoms. Though I wept with him, it was not for his wife whom I barely knew (we had only met a couple of times when they had been on leave in London) but for my poor Joey. He looked, to my shocked eyes, terribly aged; grey-faced and so thin that his skin hung baggily on him, like one of his ill-fitting suits.

Now time and food and contentment had filled his face out again. He looked rosy and wise and benevolent; a kindly gnome in a child's picture book. The new young wife, of course, the new baby . . .

'Fritz?' he said. 'No, I haven't seen Fritz – oh, I don't know how long. Since my parents died, I don't come to London much, and I'm lazy, you know how bad I am about letters. I ring Rosie when I'm here sometimes. She gives me the news. And I read your books. I'd have sent you mine, only I fear they would bore you. You look so nice, Laura. It's lovely to see you.'

I smiled at him comfortably. I felt so at ease with him, I had to remind myself he was really a stranger. All I knew about the last eight years of his life was what Andrew had told me when he came back from San Francisco. Perhaps I could have written but like Joey I am lazy about letters, about keeping in touch. When I travel, though I mean to look up old friends, when the moment comes I procrastinate. They may have moved, or died, or they may not want to see me, why should they? (Andrew has no such doubts. As soon as he has arrived in a city, booked into his hotel, showered and arranged his business appointments, he settles down with his address book and the telephone. Energetic, methodical Andrew! He says that friends are important to him because he was an only child. When I remind him that my only sister died young, he says, *Ah, but you had Hilde!*)

I had not even known that Joey's parents were dead. I said I was sorry. He asked after mine. I told him that my father was not very well at the moment. Then, quickly, before Joey could ask what was wrong (this was only a polite exchange, after all, at a party) I said that I had been so glad to hear he had married again. How old was the baby, what was he like? Joey was delighted to tell me. The small boy was unusually advanced for his age; quite remarkably active and clever. Joey explained how remarkable he was at some length and I nodded and smiled, not really listening (though I suppose if he had said the child had six toes or green hair I would have heard him and commented), only watching his face, pleased by his pleasure, if a little surprised by how solemnly he seemed to be taking it. He had always been sweetly grave, but his gravity had been lightened by a nice sense of the ridiculous; he had been ready to laugh at himself. Perhaps the American wife had changed him. Or the baby. I have often noticed that men who have children late in life become very serious fathers.

Joey was saying that Ellen would have liked to come on this trip to Europe (he had been giving a series of university lectures) but had decided against it for the baby's sake. Eighteen months was a bit old to be lugged about without disturbing his schedule, and probably too young to be left without psychological damage. Ellen's mother would have been happy to move into the house and look after him, and he had a good relationship with her, but Ellen had been afraid he might feel abandoned if both his parents suddenly vanished, feel they had left him for ever . . .

At this point Joey stopped, rather abruptly. I wondered why; then saw the guilt on his face and thought I knew what had caused it. That word, *abandoned*! He had just remembered who he was talking to; he had remembered my two older children. What age had they been when they had been abandoned by me? He laughed nervously, hoping I hadn't made the connection, hadn't taken it personally.

I said, 'I didn't abandon Jeremy and Claudia. I just gave them back to their father.'

I wasn't really angry with Joey. Though I didn't mind letting him know he had been insensitive, the irritation he had sparked off in me was more general. How *smug* parents are when their children are little; how sickeningly certain that they will avoid the mistakes other people, their older friends, their own parents, have foolishly or ignorantly made. *They* will manage much better! *Their* sons and daughters will never drop out, take to drugs or some strange religion, become homosexual, land up in prison . . .

'Of course you didn't abandon them,' Joey said. 'You know that was different.'

Someone pushed past him, jogging the glass in his hand. It was still almost full (he had been too busy extolling his son's astonishing physical and mental capacities to drink from it) and wine spattered the sleeve of my dress. He said, 'Oh, I say, I'm most awfully sorry,' in an unnaturally high, anguished voice, fumbled a grubby handkerchief out of his pocket with his free hand and dabbed at me awkwardly. 'Oh God, I'm just making it worse, shouldn't you put some salt on it, or something?' He looked wildly round as if hoping a drum of salt might materialise out of the air; then gave up, shook his head, sighed, and said in a lower but still distraught tone, 'I'm so bloody clumsy. But I must say, I hope you don't mind, I was so sorry to hear about Jeremy.'

This was unexpected. I said, shocked, 'Did Rosie tell you?'

'No. It was Pete. I saw Pete in London.' He was watching my face. He added hastily, 'Quite by *chance*, you know' – as if I might think he had been disloyal, seeking out my first husband. 'We ran into each other in the Tate Gallery. We had a drink and he told me. Poor old Pete.'

'Why *poor*?' I asked, interested. It was usually very young women who were sorry for Pete. (As I had once been.)

'Oh, I don't know. He seemed so upset, I suppose. So disappointed. His only son, after all . . .' Joey grinned at me suddenly, like the old Joey, *my* Joey, the young man I remembered. 'It was just at the time,' he said. 'While we were talking. Though even then I thought he was making rather a meal of it, as if it was worse for him than for Jeremy. But you know how it is. How *he* is, I mean.'

'Well, yes. Yes, I do.'

'Of course. Sorry.' The impish, boy's grin reappeared. 'Like a good actor in a rotten play. You're taken in while you're there, in the theatre. It's only afterwards that you see what a sham it was really.'

I laughed, and he looked abashed. He said, 'Perhaps that's not fair.'

'Oh, it is. Perfectly fair.'

'Well, maybe. You know better than I do. What I meant was, I shouldn't have said it, since I can't be expected to be fair to Pete, can I?' He hesitated, his eyes resting on me with a kind of rueful, amused, affectionate regret. There was no need to be more explicit, but perhaps years of teaching half-listening students had taught him to be. He said, with a little laugh to show he was not really serious, no longer resentful, 'Since he swiped my girl off me and treated her badly.'

* * *

I have wondered if I should tell the next stage of the story through Joey's eyes. He is generous and he once loved me; I would like to appear in these pages as a lovable person. Joey could say (or I could make him say) pleasant things that it would be embarrassing for me to write in the first person. He would certainly be fairer to me than I am likely to be myself. Of all my past selves, the girl I was at nineteen and twenty is the one I like least. I am ashamed of her callow behaviour, her silly pride, her maddening pretence that she did not understand what was going on, her refusal to be her age, to grow up into a sensible, articulate adult.

But to give Joey a chunk of this narrative would not advance it. A different viewpoint can be illuminating but I have a fancy that, for my purposes, Joey's memory is too dismissive and tidy. As far as he is concerned our love affair ended when Pete 'swiped' his girl. I must admit, when he said this, I felt aggrieved for a moment – how dare he reduce an important chapter of my life to one simple sentence! But it was too late to put the record straight; too much time lay between us, too much emotional distance. So I simply smiled, somewhat mysteriously (no doubt injecting a certain wistful tenderness into this Mona Lisa response to suggest I was sorry I had used Joey so badly) and then excused myself in order to do something about the wine he had splashed on my dress. After all, I had to wear it for the rest of the day. I hadn't, like Andrew, brought a change of clothes with me.

As to what happened. There can be no objectively factual account, only what I remember. Or what *she* remembers – my nineteen-year-old self who, I must warn you, is not to be trusted. In fact, when I contemplate that tiresome young person, I feel rather like a serious spiritualist being forced to use a fake medium, knowing that she is going to falsify truth with her little pretences, her pathetic, transparent attempts to put on a good show, terrified she will be found out and humiliated. But there is no one else, so I have to put up with her. Perhaps she will come up with something . . .

What she offers first, is an image. A stone thrown into a pond, a startling, heavy splash, quickly over; then a slow, steady widening of ripples. (Just the sort of corny thing *that* Laura would think of, but let it lie, let it lie. She is only a tyro performer.)

The stone in the pond is the letter from Fritz that Hilde found in her pigeon hole the first day of the autumn term, her second year up at Oxford.

She had not seen Fritz in the summer vacation. Except for a week when she and I had gone walking in Wales, staying at youth hostels, she had divided her time between Rosie's parents in Brighton and Miss Loomis in London. Fritz had been on holiday with his parents in France, then with an uncle in Scotland. He had sent Hilde a postcard. She had written back. Fritz had not answered.

I don't know when she told me this. Surely, if it had been in the train, while we were travelling to Oxford together, I would remember? We were used to picking over the entrails of love; I would have seized on Fritz's silence as a dread portent. Perhaps this was why Hilde said nothing. Or perhaps she was too sure of Fritz to be nervous. Certainly, though she didn't speak much, she seemed happy, sitting in a corner seat, looking out of the window and occasionally, dreamily, smiling. I remember that I talked about the new clothes my mother had bought me (I was obsessed with clothes at that time; a substitute for sex, I imagine) and I remember what Hilde was wearing: a cream silk shirt and a full, New Look skirt in fine wool; a demurely expensive outfit that I rather envied.

When we arrived at the college, we went straight to our pigeon holes. In mine, there was a rose and a note from Joey, *I hope there's no worm in this bud*; and in Hilde's, a letter. She blushed, red as the rose I was holding, and opened it. Then (another terrible image but I am not responsible for it) the blood ebbed from her cheeks like wine drained from a glass and sank to her neck. Her throat burned sullenly dark beneath her white face. She gave me the letter.

Fritz had chucked her. It was a painful letter (and, being fair to Fritz now, as I couldn't be then) it must have been painful to write. He was ending their affair as gently as such a cruel thing could be done; *alas and alack, woe is me!* was the general tone. He and Hilde had had a wonderful year, wonderful for him, anyway, but now, alas, it was over. His father had been in touch with his tutor and what he had heard had displeased him. He had presented Fritz with an ultimatum. Either he got down to work, or he left Oxford. Fritz's father was 'one of those stern, old-fashioned Quakers who only say anything once', so there was no doubt in Fritz's mind that he meant it. If his feelings for Hilde had been more light hearted, he might have been able to compromise. As it was, she was too serious a distraction, so it had to be all or nothing. There was a little more crying woe, quite elegantly phrased, and then a brisk coda, saying that since he was resigning from the various clubs that they both belonged to, Hilde need not fear any 'social embarrassment.'

Hilde said, 'What I find quite intolerable is that the little rat puts it all on his father. So bloody cowardly.'

Her colour had returned; she was bright and blazing with contemptuous fury. I held the letter out, timidly, and she said, 'Do me a favour, Laura. Wipe your arse with it.' She swept from the entrance hall and when I followed her to her room, I found the door locked. I tapped, called her name, waited. She didn't answer.

She came late to dinner, entering after grace had been said and we were all seated. She bowed her formal apology to the dons at High Table, tall and statuesque in a long, closely fitting, red dress. As she came to sit beside me, in the place I had saved for her, she looked so intimidatingly calm and beautiful that the comforting phrases I had been preparing seemed almost insultingly naive. And unnecessary. She said, 'Don't look so anxious, darling, it's over and finished with.'

She really did not seem to care. Not only that evening, in the first flush of anger, but afterwards. She worked in the day time, long hours in the library; in the evenings she went out, with different men, hardly ever with me. I missed her company badly. I had always felt she was more exotic than I was, more interesting, and I was dull without her. Although she hadn't cut herself off, was still her old, lively self when we were together, nothing hectic or hysterical or in any way alarming in her behaviour, I told myself I was worried.

I took my 'worry' to Rosie, Hilde's only other close woman friend. Rosie had moved out of college into rooms in Walton Street, rented from a kindly, old-fashioned, university landlady who still provided old-fashioned service; bed-making, cleaning, bringing up afternoon tea on a tray. This Rosie had not yet met William and there was not (as far as I knew) any man in her life. She had come up to Oxford, a spoilt, pretty, fluttery girl with a wardrobe of extravagant clothes, most of which I had borrowed at one time or another. Now, in her second year, she had decided to abandon this image. A collection of human bones was arranged along the top shelf of her bookcase; she wore tweeds, ribbed stockings, and a pair of excessively heavy-rimmed spectacles. She prefaced a good many of her remarks with 'Medically speaking . . .'

Sitting on Rosie's floor, by her fire, eating her landlady's home-made, buttered scones, I suggested (shyly, obliquely) that if Hilde had not been so free with her favours, Fritz would not have tired of her. 'Men don't always respect girls for it. I know that sounds terribly out of date and frightfully crude, and it's desperately unfair, of course, but it could be true, couldn't it?'

Rosie looked at me, her soft, brown eyes magnified, by her ridiculous spectacles, into huge, liquid, cow's orbs. 'Fritz is *ambitious*, Laura. Love affairs take up time, and we're all here to work. I know I had a lot of fun my first year, but I mean to work *now*. Really, you know, if one is a *serious person*, one should realise that one is tremendously privileged to be here at all! And, after all, medically speaking, a lot of creative energy is used up in sex that at some periods of one's life ought to be more productively utilised.'

'Hilde seems to be managing all ways round at the moment. I mean, she is working, too.'

Rosie smiled sagely. 'Hilde is very mature for her age. My mother says she makes me seem like a little girl still! I suppose she has mature appetites. Perhaps Fritz found them too exhausting. Or perhaps he simply didn't want to get too involved.

Marry a Jewess, I mean. My father says a lot of upper class English people are still basically anti-Semitic. They wouldn't admit it, such *bad taste* after what happened in Germany, but they still make their stupid jokes.'

I was shocked. This had never occurred to me. But Rosie was half Jewish, of course.

Joey said, 'No, for God's sake, all that sort of thing's *over*. I mean, there may be a few ancient people lurking in the Home Counties. But Fritz is *our age*! Honestly, Laura! I think he simply meant what he wrote to Hilde. I did ask him – well, not *ask* him, exactly – we sort of talked round the subject – and it seemed clear that he really is keen on getting a First, that it really does matter to him. And Hilde, well, you know I think that she's marvellous, a marvellous person, but I think she could be *demanding* . . .'

I said bravely, 'Sexually demanding, you mean?'

'Well, no. Though I suppose she could be. But what I meant was, she puts so much into everything, she expects it back, so to speak. And Fritz isn't exactly an emotional power house. Not enough current to feed all the circuits so if he wants the old brain to tick over full blast something else has to go.'

He grinned, a bit sheepishly. I said, 'Don't try to be *funny* about it! He's hurt Hilde terribly – all the more, probably, because she doesn't show it.'

'Not necessarily. It's just possible that if she doesn't seem to be hurt, then she isn't. Not all that much, anyway.'

'Joey! Oh, *Joey*, don't you know her better than that? Don't you remember how happy she was, all last year? How happy we all were . . .?'

My vision blurred; Joey's concerned face swam before me. He kissed me, on my mouth, on the tip of my nose; then licked the tears off the ends of my lashes. 'Come on, silly, don't cry.' He held me at arm's length, half smiling, half frowning. 'Look – of course it was *nice*, going round in a foursome, and of course I enjoyed it, but it's the sort of thing you grow out of.'

'I haven't.'

'No. I know. But you will.'

I said, like a sullen child, 'No choice it seems, have I? But that isn't the point. Hilde's the point. We're her friends, we should try to do something for her.'

'What sort of thing?'

'Try and see more of her. Show her that even if Fritz has let her down, we're still here when she wants us. I mean, the kind of people she's running round with. . . .'

'*Men*, you mean, don't you?' Joey grinned suddenly. 'Why say *people*, when you mean *men*?'

'I was talking about friendship, not sex.' I pushed Joey away and glared at him. 'And none of these *men* – if you must be pernickety – mean anything to her. If she goes out with one of them more than three times, it's a record! She needs her friends, Joey. People she can be close to.'

'I don't know that she does,' Joey said slowly. 'I've got the feeling that except for you – and Fritz, possibly – getting too close frightens her.'

I was too personally wounded by this conversation to wonder if he might be right. I had always felt threatened when people I longed to be sure of did not agree with me totally. For me, Joey and I, as a couple, had been defined by Hilde and Fritz and I was angry when Joey did not seem to understand how much and how deeply the break up of our quartet had distressed me. I didn't reproach him (if he couldn't *see* I was hurt, I could hardly tell him; after all, it was *Hilde*'s unhappiness I had invited him to join me in mourning) but I sulked inwardly.

We began to see less of each other. This wasn't deliberate, simply that Fritz was no longer around to play nanny and organise our amusements. Joey's impulses were all velleities. He might decide we should go to the theatre, or on the river, but he seldom got round to booking the tickets, or making sure there was a free college punt. (I could have done these things, I suppose, but it was the custom in those sexist days for the man to make the arrangements and I was diffident.) Joey remembered appointments ten minutes after he should have kept them; was late for tutorials, lectures; expected me to know, without being told, that we had been asked to a party.

His irresolute behaviour, that I had once thought rather charming, a pleasant contrast to Fritz's fussy insistence on planning, began to seem merely feckless, a kind of uncaring laziness, like his untidy clothes, his dandruff, his constant colds. And my interest in politics, so central to his life, was waning. I still belonged to the Labour Club and went to its meetings with Joey, but I was beginning to recognise boredom (though ashamed of it, naturally, when I thought of Miss Loomis) and to discover other diversions more to my taste. Among them was Lord David Cecil who sometimes spoke at a literary society I belonged to and at whose feet I regularly and reverently sat, entranced by his delicate, quivering features, his rapid speech, like spattering gun shot, and by the passionate joy with which novels and poetry filled him. I don't think he ever noticed me, I was too shy to speak to him, but he opened doors in my mind I had not known existed.

I met Pete at one of those evenings. Though I knew him by sight because we attended the same philosophy lectures, I was surprised when he smiled at me across the room and came to sit by me. He was one of the ex-servicemen who had flooded into Oxford after the war, wearing naval bridge coats and old British Warms like decorations, and seeming to those of us who had come up straight from school, alarmingly grown up and purposeful. I was flattered to be sought out by this mature, handsome man (he was very good-looking in a slightly fleshy, full-lipped, high-coloured way) but as we walked back to my college it was the fact that he seemed to be deeply unhappy that gave him, in my eyes, an awesome, romantic attraction.

I can't remember how he introduced the subject of his unhappiness that particular evening. It seemed that one minute we were talking about the novels we had read recently (since Joey affected to find fiction 'irrelevant' this was a pleasure for me) and the next he was speaking about his 'troubled spirit' and the difficulties of 'finding oneself' in civilian life after the excitements of war, contriving to suggest by the rueful tone of his voice and the little sighs that broke up his monologue, that although other ex-servicemen might feel a similar sense of displacement, his suffering sprang from deeper and more sensitive roots, a rare kind of soul sickness that made him doubt if he would ever feel at home anywhere.

He smiled at me sadly and apologised for burdening me. I had been so sweetly receptive, he had forgotten how young I was. Too young to understand.

I denied this indignantly. I had not 'found myself', either. I had hoped for so much when I came up to Oxford but had been disappointed. The work was a dull extension of school, not the intellectual freedom, the creative stimulation I had expected. Tonight was one of the few times that I had felt stretched, uplifted. 'Meeting a fine mind at last,' I sighed – speaking of Lord David Cecil but also intending a shy compliment to the interesting man whose hand was linked with mine so lightly and warmly. At my college gate, he lifted my fingers to his full, red lips and looked at me searchingly. It seemed that years passed before he spoke. I didn't know whether to smile or look grave, remove my hand or leave it where he was holding it, pressed to his heart. He said, finally, 'We have talked of so much but we don't know each other. There could be more if you want it. Say the word, Laura.'

That was typical of Pete, I later discovered. If you leave it to the woman to make the first move, she will be likely to commit herself further than she really wants to and anything that goes wrong afterwards will therefore be entirely her fault. But I was too green to be trapped in this way. I had no idea what 'word' he was waiting for, and so I simply smiled nervously. He sighed, kneading my fingers against his tweed jacket and then smiled forgivingly (what he was forgiving me for I didn't know, I only knew I felt guilty) and asked me if I would dine with him in three days time. We could drive out to The Bear at Woodstock. He had a motor car. Think it over, he said, don't decide now. Perhaps, when I had made up my mind, I would leave a note for him at his college.

I was pitifully agitated. (I have chosen this adjective carefully; in spite of all I have said, I do pity that silly girl sometimes.) I looked for Hilde, to ask her advice, but her room was empty. I went to my own and lay on the bed smoking one cigarette after the other. Joey had no motor car. He couldn't afford to take me out to grand dinners. Would he be hurt? We had always talked about the importance of not being tied to each other. But it wouldn't be *untying* myself from him, surely, just to drive out to Woodstock? If that was all, of course not! It might not be all, though. What had Pete meant by there being 'more'? Would he fall upon me, after dinner, in the back of his car? If he did, and I couldn't stop him (or didn't want to – this novel thought made me laugh aloud, excitedly), what about contraception? A man of his age might expect a girl to carry a diaphragm in her handbag. On the other hand, it seemed a little presumptuous to think on those lines, to flatter myself that a man like Pete might actually want me. And I didn't own a diaphragm, anyway.

The morning was no better. The awful decision stared me in the face the moment I opened my eyes, and consumed all my attention as I sat in the library and tried to read Bishop Berkeley. There was no guide to my problem in *A New Theory of Vision*. The Agony Column in some woman's magazine might have been more appropriate reading, but probably just as unhelpful. The truth was, I wanted to go and I didn't; no one but myself could solve this dilemma. Unless it were *Joey*, I realised suddenly – and, at once, although I wasn't sure what I hoped he would do, forbid me or give me permission, the hideous burden seemed to lift from me.

But when I got to his room, just before four o'clock, Hilde was there, curled up in the corner of the ancient sofa where I always sat, and Joey was kneeling in front of a small, smoky fire, a knife in his hand, about to cut into a fruit cake. As I came in, they were laughing. Their flushed, laughing faces looked up at me and I felt like an intruder. Resentful, too – though I knew this was foolish. After all, I had urged Joey to 'do something' for Hilde . . .

I perched on the arm of the sofa. 'You should be honoured, Hilde,' I said playfully. 'He never offers me cake! Limp toast is all I get. If I'm lucky.'

'My mother sent it,' Joey said. He was slicing the cake very carefully.

Hilde laughed. 'He told me last night that he'd had a parcel. Home-made jam, too. That's how he lured me to his den.'

'Cupboard lover,' Joey said. He prodded the point of the knife into a chunk of cake and offered it to me.

I shook my head. 'I can't stop. I promised to have tea with Rosie. Where were you last night? I went to listen to David Cecil. I didn't know there was a Labour Club meeting.'

Joey looked at Hilde. She said, 'Oh, it wasn't the Labour Club, just a party.' And I thought I heard guilt in her voice, read guilt in his face.

I said to Rosie, 'I really do despise myself sometimes. After all, Joey isn't my *property*, and I was with someone else last night anyway. So it's hateful of me to be jealous. Like some spoilt, horrible brat who can't bear other children to play with its toys. But I can't help feeling just a little bit hurt.'

Rosie said, pouring tea, 'Well, of course, darling. But it's only sex, not important. Try and tell yourself that. You know what Hilde is, it doesn't mean what it would to most girls. I mean, *virgins*. In some ways, I envy her. Sometimes I think it would be sensible if we all got this physical thing over, out of the way and out of our minds, so we could get on with our *work*! Only then I think how much it would upset my mother if she knew. And I'm sure it matters very little to Joey. Medically speaking, men are quite different from women in that way. Wham, Bam, thank you Mam!'

I felt giddy – as if I were standing on the edge of a chasm. I wailed, 'Oh, I didn't mean that. . . .'

She put down the tea pot. 'Then, what did you mean, Laura? I mean, I assumed . . .' She stopped, her eyes fixed on me with an expression of horrified sadness. 'That was why I was being so digustingly *coarse*, I thought it might make it easier for you. I was so sure you must know! I mean, everyone . . .' She bit her lip and blushed. 'I'm so sorry, so *clumsy*. I shouldn't have told you.'

My ears were singing. It seemed I really did have a problem with balance. I said, speaking slowly and carefully, 'I'm glad you did. I'm such an idiot, I never notice these things, I would never have known if you hadn't told me. Though how anyone *really* knows has always escaped me. Unless you actually *see* them, rolling round on the floor with their clothes off!'

Perhaps, if I had got to Joey's room a little bit earlier, I would have caught them! To think I had gone to ask Joey if he would mind if I went out with Pete! I laughed wildly.

Rosie said, 'Well, of course it has to be gossip. But they've been seen around – very much, sort of *together* – and Hilde doesn't go in for platonic relationships as a general rule, does she? Of course Joey could be an exception.'

I laughed again. 'Not if she offered herself, so to speak. He would think it unkind to reject her.'

Rosie was looking anxious and humble. 'Oh, Laura, I can't think it will last, I'm sure Joey loves you. I'm so desperately sorry! And so ashamed! If I hadn't opened my stupid mouth you might never have known.'

This was only too likely. Pure-minded Laura! I said, 'I'm not sure being ignorant is all that desirable. You can look such a fool!'

Rosie sighed. 'Of course, people do jump to conclusions.'

'Lay not that flattering unction to thy soul,' I quoted, and pulled a wry, comic face to try and make Rosie smile. But she was too conscience-stricken. She shook her head, turning away to hide the fact that tears threatened, and said, in a husky voice, 'Can you ever forgive me?'

Her penitence touched me. I rushed to console her. 'Dear Rosie, honestly, it's not *your* fault, *you* haven't hurt me! If I had to hear it from someone, you're quite the best person. Although it's a shock, I'll get over it. And, to tell you the truth, I'm not altogether as sorry as perhaps I should be! I wasn't exactly going off Joey, but there *is* someone else. Rather interesting, actually. Shall I tell you?'

Rosie looked at me doubtfully. I smiled cheerfully. She murmured, 'You are so sweet, Laura.' She put her hand to the tea pot and frowned. 'I'm afraid the tea's cold.'

I wasn't surprised that Rosie knew Pete. Where people were concerned she was naturally inquisitive, harvesting friends and acquaintances and friends of acquaintances like a bright-eyed, busy squirrel. She remembered everyone she had met, or had heard spoken of, and could always be relied upon to produce information; a few nuts from her store.

Pete's father, who was a publisher, was a friend of her father's. The two men often travelled on the same train from London to Brighton together. From her father, Rosie had learned that Pete, who was an only child, had been 'over-indulged' by his mother, but that his years in the army had changed and matured him. Before the war he had scorned the idea of publishing as a career; too safe and too dull. Now he seemed quite prepared, when he had finished at Oxford, to go into his father's firm and work his way up from the bottom. Rosie was sure that in all sorts of ways he was much more suitable for me than Joey, who was just a boy still. 'You need someone mature,' she said, 'someone to lean on. You're a creative personality, and creative people tend to be young in some ways. It's as if they need all their vital energies for their creative development.' She sighed, rather wistfully. 'You know, I've often thought I'd like to marry an artist, a painter or a musician. I'm such a practical person, I could do all the humdrum things for him, make his life easy . . .'

I said, 'Are you suggesting I should marry Pete, Rosie? I've nothing against the idea in principle, it's just that it seems a bit premature. I'm not sure that I want to get involved with anyone, anyway. Certainly not at the moment.'

Rosie was blushing. 'Oh dear,' she said. 'You're still angry with me.'

'Not with you. Perhaps a bit angry in general.'

She gave me a long, thoughtful look. 'I suppose that's really quite *good*. Psychologically speaking, anger can sometimes be a healthy reaction. But – oh, I know it's a lot to ask, but try not to blame Hilde too much. The last thing she'd want is to hurt you. Or at least, the good, true blue part of her wouldn't want to. The thing is, I don't think she's fully in control of herself at the moment. The way she's behaving looks like desperation to me. Taking refuge in promiscuous sex can be a sign of deep in-security. She loved Fritz, you know. I think he did her more damage than we ever realised; broke her in *pieces*! Once or twice lately I've felt she was making a tremendous effort to hold all those pieces together. As if there was a kind of *chaos* inside her.'

I was genuinely surprised that Rosie should think I would want to blame Hilde. And piqued by this show of concern for her – as if Rosie could possibly understand Hilde and care for her more than I did!

I said, 'I'm not blaming anyone. Only myself for being half-witted. So don't worry, Rosie! I won't do anything that might upset Hilde! I shan't say a word to her!'

Nor did I. I said nothing to Hilde, nothing to Joey. Pride and a shuddering embarrassment ruled me. I could not bear either of them to know what I knew. Or what Rosie had told me. If it was the truth or not, I never discovered.

Nor do I care. Apart from the fact that it amuses me to reflect that if Rosie recalls these various conversations between us as clearly as I do, she must be as mortified by her young self as I am by mine, this episode bores me. Especially my part in it. My reactions were so humiliatingly juvenile; the resulting events so predictable.

Rosie interests me more. Setting down that last little scene, I believe I have discovered something about her, a clue to her character. Although she is a manipulator, she has never been mischievous. (I really do believe that her revelation about Joey and Hilde was an innocent blunder.) What makes her play puppet master – give these good parties, bring the 'right' people together – is a frustrated creative urge.

She had a strong minded Jewish father who had loved and valued his sons – not more than his daughter, but differently. He was proud of Rosie, who was a clever and promising pianist, but his boys were his stake in the future and, as Jewish fathers do, he had made his plans for them. He owned a small, influential, art gallery. One son was to go into the business, the other was to become a doctor. When both were killed (within three months of each other), Rosie, who already had a place at the Royal College of Music, decided to study medicine, to comfort her father.

It may seem a little strange that her parents accepted this. Presumably Rosie had made up her mind while they were absorbed in their grief, and she would never have presented her decision as a sacrifice, nor consciously looked back herself once she had made it. Perhaps she was even, in her heart, uncertain about her own talent – better, after all, to be a good doctor than an indifferent pianist, a successful 'practical person' than a failed artist. But since she never had the chance to find out, she has never lost her solemn, adolescent respect for the 'creative' professions and I have sometimes wondered if she would have married William if he had not been an amateur painter. Certainly she has always taken his hobby more seriously than she takes his job – if William is 'working', he is in his studio at the top of their house, not in his office in London. 'Of course once he's established,' she used to say in the early days of their marriage, 'he can give up the rat race.'

William has never become established (nor wants to, in my opinion: he has always seemed to me a most contented rat) but Rosie has kept his brush to his Sunday easel and their house is full of his pictures; pretty landscapes, and slightly sentimental pen-and-ink drawings of his daughters at various stages of growth, all expensively framed and carefully lit. Rosie's pride in them is touching or foolish, depending on how you are feeling, and her friends' affection for her is such that no one, as far as I know, has ever dared to murmur a hurtful opinion.

Not even Amanda. Standing by the fireplace with Andrew, narrowing her eyes against her cigar smoke, she was gazing up at William's latest effort; a water colour of the house seen from the river, a cherry tree in full, romantic bloom in the foreground.

She was saying in her deep, rusty voice, 'Is that a new extension on the top storey?'

'I think so,' Andrew said in the same reserved, thoughtful tone. 'At least, it's what they hope it will look like. Rosie says they are enlarging the studio, but apparently they've run into trouble. They want to build out, over the balcony, but when they started to take off the bitumen, or whatever that tarry substance is called, they found dry rot underneath and they're not sure yet how far it extends. If it's already in the house, in the joists and the floorboards, it could be expensive.'

'So this is what you might call work *not* in progress.' Amanda laughed raucously and jerked her head at the picture. She winked at me in a vulgar, sardonic way. 'Interesting artistic licence.'

'I think it's a very good painting,' I said severely. 'How awful, though, about the dry rot.'

Dry rot, wet rot, rising damp, fungus creeping over the walls of the cellar, death watch bettle ticking away like a time bomb in the rafters. All these people here, eating mushrooms in pastry, red caviar on slivers of toast, little smoked sausages, laughing and talking and showing off to each other, and, though none of them would wish to be thought sycophantic, edging their way into the tight little groups round the more distinguished of our Oxford contemporaries – Rosie always asks a few lions to pep up her parties and there is a Cabinet Minister here today and a famously rude television personality – all these happy innocents believe themselves to be safe at the moment. But no house is safe. Not even Rosie's.

Andrew was watching me. 'Don't worry, sweet. The ceiling won't fall down on us.'

I tried to laugh. 'I wish we didn't live in a property-owning democracy.'

Amanda grinned at me drunkenly. She was wearing a green hopsack shift, unbuttoned almost to the waist in front, exposing plump, sallow flesh and a lot of pendulous, heavy gold jewellery that clanked like loose armour as she swayed slightly towards me.

'Nice Laura, pretty Laura, it's super to see you. I've been monopolising your lovely husband. I hope you don't mind. You always have such lovely husbands, how do you get them? Have you come to break us up?'

'No, but we have to go soon. That is, we have an appointment. We can't stay for the Boat Race.'

I was longing to leave suddenly. Since I no longer get drunk at parties, it offends me to hear voices slurring, see features slip sideways. There were raised, red lumps on Amanda's cheekbones, and her lower lip dribbled slightly.

I said, conversationally, holding my arm out, 'I've been trying to get rid of this stain but without much success, I'm afraid. The wretched Joey spilled his wine over me. He got excited, telling me about his new baby.'

Amanda groaned. 'I thought we were past the stage of child worship. Now all our bloody kids are entering the danger zone, most of us prefer to keep silent. Though perhaps yours are perfect. If they are, for Christ's sake don't tell me.'

'Oh, we have the usual problems arising,' Andrew said easily.

She shuddered and her jewellery jangled. 'I don't want to know.' Her voice was shrill with anger. She turned her back on Andrew and leaned towards me. 'As a woman, I find kiddy-talk plain insulting. You understand, don't you, Laura? You go to a party for *fun*, for a bit of the old hanky panky. But all the men can think of to talk about once you're menopausal and they're no longer dead keen to fuck you, are your ghastly *children*! For Christ's sake, the last thing you want to be reminded of is your extinct biological function. Your shrivelled up *womb*.'

'Oh, come on,' Andrew said. 'I thought we'd been having an intelligent discussion about the law on rented accommodation and its effect on the housing problem in inner cities. You were telling me about the article you were writing on single homeless persons and the importance of the rate support grant.'

'Oh Christ!' Amanda said. 'Oh, dear Christ, was I really? Tell me now, were you interested? No – *don't* bloody tell me. Even if you were, you bloody shouldn't have been. You should have been making a grab at my cunt.'

'It's not that kind of party, dear,' Andrew said. He moved to stand next to me. Together, we shielded Amanda from the rest of the room. People didn't get drunk at Rosie's parties. If they did, she seldom asked them again. I wondered who we were protecting – Amanda, or Rosie? If Rosie saw Amanda in this state she would be distressed. Was she fond enough of her to put her on the list of friends who needed special care; luncheons *à deux*, therapy sessions? Would Amanda respond graciously if she were offered this kind of attention? I doubted it. I giggled, and Andrew nudged me warningly. He glanced over his shoulder and smiling shook his head at one of Rosie's pretty daughters who was approaching us with a bottle. 'Thank you, love, but we're doing fine in this corner.'

'Oh, you *bloody* man,' Amanda said. She pulled a face at her empty glass, then looked at me mournfully. Her large, amber-coloured eyes – a ginger cat's eyes – were streaked with blood in the corners and swimming with moisture. She sniffed, wiping her nose with the back of her hand. 'Do you remember, Laura, what it used to be like? Going to parties, once upon a lovely time, long ago? When we were *nubile* – God above, I don't think I've heard that word for just about five hundred years! Drinking ghastly wine like gnat's piss, and talking about ourselves and our golden, marvellous futures, while all the lovely men peered down our bosoms? Never getting tired, never going home till the morning, unless someone we fancied offered to take us to bed. Now no one wants to, or only old age pensioners down on their luck, women our age don't *exist* for anyone else any longer. If some poor bloke does get stuck with us, all he can think of is to ask if little Johnnie has passed his exams yet, and what do we think about the rate support grant? Bugger the rate support grant, and fuck little Johnnie. Fuck big Johnnie, too – though I should be so lucky! Your lovely husband is just as old as me, Laura, just as battered and flabby, but it hasn't crossed his mind that *his* party is over! You see his eyes wander, undressing all the young, juicy girls, ripping their pants off.' She snorted with contempt. 'Rate support grant on his lips, and rape on his mind.'

'I don't think I'm flabby,' Andrew said. 'I take proper exercise.'

She started to weep noisily and he put his arms round her, stifling her sobs in his jacket. 'You don't feel all that flabby, either.'

She pushed him away, a bit roughly. 'It's all right, I'm all right now. Nasty scene over. Too long at the fair, that's my trouble. I better get home.'

Andrew offered his handkerchief and she trumpeted into it. 'Bloody toothache,' she said, 'that's another thing. Sloshing down brandy and aspirin all night. Scared stiff of the dentist.'

She smiled shakily. 'That's my excuse, anyway. Sorry, Laura. What an exhibition! I never thought much of the Women's Libbers. Moaning middle class bitches, their own worst enemies for the most part, rather like that woman in the novel you wrote, and here I am behaving just like one. Full of female machismo but whining because I'm no longer a lovely sex object.'

'Roaring, not whining,' I said. 'Did you drive here?'

'I don't have a car. Friend of the Earth, and all that. And my bike had a flat tyre.'

I looked at Andrew. He nodded. I tried to remember where Amanda lived. A large house on a common, full of children and bouncy, flea-ridden dogs.

'Clapham,' I said – for Andrew's benefit. 'It's more or less on our way, Amanda. We can give you a lift if you like.'

'Dear Laura, always the Good Samaritan, little friend of mankind!' She looked at me, blinking. 'Sorry,' she said, 'that was *nasty*!' She heaved a deep sigh and, as a further apology, plucked at my arm and tried to focus her eyes on my sleeve. 'Pity about your lovely dress, dearie. Bloody Joey! You'll never get it out. Red wine is the *devil*.'

PART THREE

The Prison

At one end of Fleet Street, in the City of London, there is what looks like a fairy tale castle. The pale, elegantly frivolous towers of the Law Courts suggest dreaming princesses, confined by some tender enchantment, waiting for a prince's kiss. Although for ordinary mortals rescue comes more expensive (when we sprung Jeremy after he had been arrested and remanded in custody from the magistrate's court, it cost a hundred pounds to get bail from a Judge in Chambers) the atmosphere inside this lovely, preposterous building remains that of a fantasy in which all who enter are condemned to perpetual motion. The intricate medieval architecture may explain to some extent why no one appears to know where to go, what to do, but the lawyers and ushers scuttling up and down the warren of halls and turrets and twisting stairways seem to be in the grip of a more mysterious agitation – as if they had been transformed, by some arcane spell, into characters in *Alice in Wonderland*. 'Like trying to catch the White Rabbit,' Andrew said as we chased a hurrying, black-gowned official to try and discover where 'our' Judge was sitting. And when we caught up with this usher and saw that his mouth was deformed by two long, yellow, grass-nibbling front teeth, we were overcome with unseemly, nervous hilarity.

Perhaps there is always an element of the absurd in moments of crisis. You are never prepared; always caught unaware. As soon as Jeremy had telephoned from the prison we had acted swiftly and rationally, rung our lawyer, taken advice, made arrangements, reassured each other that what had happened was a mistake, a ludicrous miscarriage of justice, but we had passed, without knowing it, through a barrier. Beyond it, on the other side of the looking glass, the rules of the game were not ones we knew; civilised order, as we understood it, had vanished.

We were not aware of this yet, at this point of the morning. The system worked in our favour as we had expected it to. The police did not oppose our application for bail and the Judge was polite to us – no doubt impressed by our educated voices, our good clothes and calm, responsible air. We were a little discomforted to find that we had to proceed to a police station to get an official form of release to present at the prison, but this was just a formality, our lawyer said comfortingly. He shook hands and left us. Andrew glanced at his watch. He had a luncheon appointment. We would take a taxi to Bow Street, he had time to do that, but I wouldn't mind, would I, going by myself to the prison? Jeremy, he thought, might prefer it. Easier for him, after this humiliating experience, to be alone with one parent to start with. 'Take him somewhere for a good meal,' Andrew said. 'Let him unwind. We can have a proper discussion this evening.'

The sun was shining outside the Law Courts. The cold spring air sparkled. We looked up at the newly cleaned stone of the pretty towers and smiled at each other. Andrew held my hand in the taxi; we walked hand in hand into the police station. The reception area was painted a dingy green. There was an elderly woman sitting on a bench by the wall and a young policeman behind the counter.

He glanced at the Order indifferently. His voice had a nasal twang – a London cockney with a cold. He couldn't deal with this, we had to sign 'the book' and he had no authority. The duty officer would be back from lunch at about two o'clock.

Andrew said, in a mild, surprised tone, 'It isn't midday yet. A long lunch hour, surely?'

'Might be a bit earlier. You can wait if you like.'

'I don't understand,' Andrew said. 'We were told this was only a simple formality.'

'That's right.' The young, plump face was expressionless.

'The officer will see to it when he comes.'

'You mean there is no one else who can help us?'

The policeman shrugged his shoulders in answer. Then, looking at Andrew, expanded grudgingly. 'The book's locked up. The bail register.'

'And the duty officer is the only one with a key?'

'I can't tell you about that. I'm on the desk, sir.'

I said, 'But this is *ridiculous!*'

Andrew frowned. He took my hand again and stroked my palm with his finger.

The policeman said, hopefully, 'You could go away and come back.'

'We will wait,' Andrew said.

We sat on the bench beside the old woman who was rolling a cigarette. She was wearing an ancient fur coat and pink carpet slippers on her stockingless feet. Andrew produced his lighter (although he has never smoked, he always carries a lighter) and lit her cigarette for her. She coughed and said, wheezing, 'Playin' cards down the basement. That's what they're all doin'. I bin down to look. They don't care, do they?'

The young policeman laughed. Stiff with us, he was at ease with her. 'Come on, Ma! You'll get your old man out soon enough, what's the hurry? Bashed you up, didn't he?'

She giggled and winked at me. Merriment cracked her face finely, like an old, china plate. 'Silly old fool. Though it's not right to lock 'im up really. It's his terrible nerves, he can't help it, he's under the doctor.'

Andrew was staring at his hands, clenching and unclenching them, examining his nails. A muscle twitched in his cheek. He was thinking of his luncheon appointment; how to get out of it. *Should* he get out of it? He had taken the morning off to go to the Law Courts, but he had work to do. Perhaps, in this situation, his work was not so important. Wives and children came first when their needs were urgent. It was a matter of getting priorities right. And this old woman was waiting quite cheerfully. She had nothing else to do, probably. Living on social security, a bit of free warmth in the police station might be quite welcome. That wasn't the point, though. He had no right to claim privileges, expect people to jump to attention, just because he was more socially fortunate . . .

This is, of course, what I *thought* he was thinking.

I whispered, 'Darling, go if you want to. I can handle this now. It's only boring, not difficult.'

The old woman stubbed out the butt of her thin, brown cigarette with her small, slippered foot. She had very white and delicate ankles. She said, in a hoarse, plaintive voice, 'It's the time gets you down. The hours you spend waiting.'

Andrew looked at her. His face, which had been pale up to now, suddenly darkened. He clapped his hands on his knees, jumped up energetically, marched to the counter, thumped with both fists and shouted. Words tumbled out so fast I could only catch a few phrases. *Insulting contempt for the public . . . casual and careless behaviour . . . petty bureacracy . . . the sort of thing you might expect in a police state . . .*

I was astonished by this performance. My restrained and well-mannered husband with his deep respect for rules and authority, dressed (as if for a funeral) in his best city suit and dark overcoat, was swollen and scarlet with rage and yelling as if some vulgar demon possessed him. 'A disgrace to a free country,' he thundered, and then, realising perhaps that this was not the most felicitous phrase in the circumstances, reined in his anger and went on, with more dignity, if somewhat pompously, 'I accept that the police force is understaffed and overworked and that in a capital city there are bound to be more pressing priorities, but I cannot believe there is no one in this building at this particular moment to deal with this matter, produce the correct form, piece of paper, or whatever is needed to get my son out of prison. I intend to go downstairs, to the basement, and if I discover that there are in fact police officers there, playing cards, as this lady has just suggested, I shall not only report it to the proper authorities but see that it is brought to the attention of the public prints. And if I find that you yourself have been derelict in your duty, it will be my personal pleasure to have your hair and hide.' He looked at his watch. 'I will give you three minutes.'

The policeman turned his back and lifted a telephone.

Andrew came back to the bench. He sat down, closed his eyes, and said, in an undertone, 'Oh God. Laura.'

The old lady cackled. 'You'll be locked up yourself, sonny boy, if you ain't careful.'

I felt I could burst into tears. Or hysterical laughter. Either reaction seemed perfectly natural. I said, touching Andrew's arm, 'Was that deliberate?' and was surprised to hear myself sounding so light and dispassionate.

Andrew opened his eyes. 'I don't know.'

The policeman put down the telephone. He said, in a toneless voice, 'The officer is coming now, sir.'

Andrew blushed painfully. He was rubbing his hand over his chin as if feeling for bristles. He muttered, 'I couldn't stand it. Thinking about Jeremy, waiting for us to get him out, trusting us. Something exploded.' He looked at me, awed and ashamed. 'I could have killed someone.'

I am afraid the house will fall down. Andrew is frightened of maggots and crawling things and of being shut in. He cannot bear to sleep with the curtains drawn and the window closed. At night, we always leave our bedroom door slightly open. Jeremy in prison was his nightmare come true.

Worse, even. He has always been afraid that things will go wrong for Jeremy. It is not that he loves him more than the others (at least I don't think so) but it is a different kind of love, more acutely aware, more anxious, more suffering. When Jeremy ran away from his school it was Andrew who opened the door of our London flat when the bell rang at midnight (this was before Henry and Isobel were born, before we moved to the country) and found him standing there, a thin boy of thirteen, shivering, weeping; Andrew who stayed awake all that night, sitting beside his bed, even though the child was fast asleep with exhaustion; Andrew who promised him the next day that he would not be sent back to his school, that he could live with us if he wanted, that we would look after him always.

Andrew feels he had failed him and it fills him with anguish.

He doesn't speak of his pain, he would be ashamed to, but I know when he is thinking of Jeremy and finding his thoughts hard to bear, because he grinds his back teeth together.

He was grinding his teeth as we drove away from Rosie's house, after the party. Amanda was sprawled in the back of the car, mouth slightly open, snoring in little puffs like a labouring steam engine. She looked like a large, weary schoolgirl who had fallen asleep after a fierce game of hockey.

I whispered, 'Andy, stop grinding your *teeth*.'

He shook his head fretfully, stretching his jaw. 'I didn't know I was. Sorry.'

'It won't help Jeremy if you lose your gold fillings.'

'I can't help it. I *said* I was sorry. Is Amanda asleep?'

'Yes. I know it's a bit of a nuisance but we couldn't have left her. We won't be late, will we?'

He gave a loud, aggrieved sigh and accelerated through a red light. A truck, pulling out of a side street, almost hit us.

I said, 'There's no need to drive like a lunatic.'

'I thought you didn't want to be late at the prison!'

I laughed. He glanced at me, forcing a smile. I saw tears in his eyes.

I said, speaking quickly to stop myself crying too, 'Do you remember that old woman at Bow Street?'

'The nice old girl with pink slippers?'

'Yes. She was sweet, you know, when we went to the prison. We had to wait ages, of course, and we sat in the hut outside and drank cups of tea, and she insisted on paying for mine because I had paid for the taxi. She rolled me a cigarette and I took it, to be polite, and it made me feel faint. Or perhaps it was the strain catching up. Anyway, she made me put my head down and when I felt better, she said, trying to comfort me, that it was always worse the first time. And, you know, I had to fight like mad not to *laugh*. I mean, it was funny – at least, it seemed funny then – but she was so obviously, well, a regular *customer*, and I thought, if I laughed, it would seem dreadfully patronising. As if I was saying that the idea there could be a second occasion like this, for someone like *me*, was so profoundly ridiculous . . .'

My voice dried. I swallowed and said, 'I wonder what happened to her.'

'Perhaps we'll find out,' Andrew said. 'If you're right about her being a regular customer, her old man may be inside, we may run across her. I suppose that would be a bit of a coincidence, really, but I daresay we shall make a few new acquaintances. In fact a whole area of social experience will open up for us.' He smiled at me suddenly. 'It could be rewarding. Think how dull life becomes for most middle-aged people.'

'May you live in interesting times,' I said. 'A famous old curse.'

Amanda groaned and muttered in the back of the car, flinging her arms about. Andrew said, 'Amanda?' and she came fully awake, yawning hugely. 'Nearly there,' she said. 'Christ! You almost went past the turning. Left by that pub. First house by the common.'

The unfenced front garden of Amanda's large, Edwardian house was littered with bicycles. A rubber paddling pool lay airless and flat on the grey, trampled grass. A small black boy was swinging by his knees on a metal climbing frame. When he saw us he dropped down, performed a neat somersault, and ran to the car. Amanda got out and he flung himself at her, hiding his face in her stomach.

Amanda said, 'Ben, say hallo to the people.'

Clutching the folds of her dress, he peered at us shyly.

She patted his woolly head. 'My new one,' she said. 'He's not very sociable yet.'

'Hallo, Ben,' Andrew said. 'How many does that make, Amanda? Or is it an insult to ask you?'

'Oh. Well. Six. My own ghastly pair and my four little delinquents.' She pulled a wry face. 'Did I make such a frightful ass of myself? The thing is, my kids aren't exactly a conversational asset among the lumpen bourgeoisie. I can see them all wagging their wise heads and questioning my motives. Poor old Amanda's little bit of sublimated sex, aren't you, my Benjie?' She picked him up and he wound his skinny legs round her, settling comfortably on her broad hip. 'D'you want to come in? It'll be bloody chaos, I warn you, but I could give you a drink. Or some sobering coffee.'

Andrew looked at me. I said, 'We can't, I'm afraid. We've promised to visit this – this old aunt of Andy's. And we're a bit late already . . .'

'Another time, then. Bless you both.' She waved goodbye and strode sturdily up the muddy path, the boy bobbing up and down on her shoulder.

Andrew said, as he turned the car, 'You didn't have to lie. We could really have told her.'

'Did you want to?'

'Mmm. Perhaps.'

'Why didn't you, then?'

'It was your decision, I thought. Your old friend. If she is. I mean, you don't really like her.'

'Do you?'

'Very much. I think she's amusing and plucky and clever. And she sticks to her guns.' He was quiet for a minute, frowning and chewing his lower lip; then went on in a low, angry voice, 'I know you don't think much of her writing, all that marketing woe, as you call it, but there aren't many like her. Not from our generation. I was thinking about this at the party – not that there's anything new in it, really. It was just that looking round at all those nice people, all so well fed and comfortable, it suddenly struck me how obsessed we've all become with our own private lives. Nothing matters except ourselves and our families. As if we'd retreated into our own tiny castles and pulled up the drawbridges. Though that's really too attractive a picture. Defending our own cabbage patches against starving peasants is closer to the truth of it. We still affect an interest in what's going on, read newspapers, vote at elections, but we don't take part any longer. If we argue politics it's only a social amusement, after-dinner talk, a branch of the entertainment industry. Basically, we've opted out. Oh, we may feel the odd stab of guilt, even pain perhaps, when there's some enormous disaster, famine or flood, but we don't really *care*.'

'And Amanda does? I suppose it is brave of her to take in those children. Are they really delinquents, do you think, or was she just boasting?'

'I don't know. I wasn't thinking of them – after all, she was making a point of not talking about the kids, wasn't she? No, what I mean is, she hasn't retreated, she's still charging into the battle. I know that crusading journalism is what she lives on, but it's also what she lives *by*. She means every word that she writes, every cause she takes up. It amazes and hurts her that other people don't feel as strongly as she does. That's why she got drunk.'

'Andy! What absolute *drivel*. She was drunk before she came to the party. She said so, remember? She'd had a bad toothache.'

'Oh, all right. Maybe. It doesn't alter my point which is that she hasn't shut herself off. She still feels – well – one's stuck with old-fashioned expressions – a duty, if you like, to society. The fact that this sounds stuffy and pious is a clue to what's wrong with us, isn't it? And what she was complaining of, the way people of our age and kind carry on about children, their achievements, exam results and so on, is another sign. Getting on, coming top, winning – that's all we've taught them to care about, isn't it? Not in so many words, perhaps, but it's what they see when they look at us. It's not much of an example to follow.'

'This is nothing to do with Amanda. You were thinking of Jeremy. Finding some new way to blame yourself!'

'Not altogether. Though of course Jeremy is mixed up with it. Look, let me explain. All I really care about at this moment is *him*, the thought of him locked up for six months tears my guts out, but for God's sake, people have been rotting in prison for years, and they haven't mattered a damn to me. Even though I may have sent the odd cheque to Amnesty. I find this very shameful. As if my feelings were too blunt to operate properly – the way old people's finger tips get calloused with age. I'm impressed by Amanda because that hasn't happened to her. She's not blunted.'

'Nor are you. There's nothing shameful in caring more about

people you know and can help, than about political dissidents in labour camps, or starving millions in Asia. That's an old trap.'

Andrew said, coldly, 'I am aware of that argument, thank you. It wasn't one I was putting forward. I was simply using my own experience to make a more general statement. Perhaps it was a mistake to go to the party. I found myself getting resentful because everyone except Amanda seemed so bloody complacent. Though I still think what I said was quite valid. I mean, that we're not aware of our apathy, our lack of imaginative sympathy and so on, until something strikes close to home. If you didn't understand that, I'm sorry.'

'Oh, I *understood*. I understand how Amanda affected you. She was maudlin drunk and unhappy and that appealed to your quixotic instincts, and so you've convinced yourself that she's more noble than the rest of us, a gallant idealist, carrying the sins of the world on her shoulders. And then, because Jeremy hurts you, you've persuaded yourself that you shouldn't really be worrying so much about him, it's horribly selfish when there are so many other poor prisoners, so many suffering people. If you could spread the load that way, and be sorry for *everyone*, it would be a whole lot more bearable.'

I was unwilling to identify the rage that possessed me. I turned my head away and glared out of the window.

Andrew said, 'Darling, you do like to put me down, don't you? Don't let's quarrel, just because I was being silly and pompous. Or because I stuck up for Amanda. Did that upset you?'

'No, of course not. How ridiculous.'

Andrew laughed. 'Pete never liked her, did he? I think you're still stuck with some of his prejudices. Sometimes that irks me.'

Softened by this admission, I found myself smiling. 'It was only because she didn't grovel with admiration for him. She actually dared to say, at our wedding reception, that I was mad to get married straight out of college. So he punished her for not seeing how amazingly lucky I was to be marrying *him*, by saying she had a second class mind.'

*   *   *

Like Richard, the husband in my Women's Lib novel, Pete graded people in a peculiar way. They had first, second, or third class minds. A second class mind was his nastiest insult. Third class minds usually had something else going for them – an untutored, *natural* intelligence – but to be second class simply meant mediocrity.

Pete's system had nothing to do with academic results. He had a second class degree himself, as I did. Amanda got a first. So did Joey. And Fritz – ambitious Fritz – got a third.

Hilde did not take her degree. The day we all trooped into the examination halls wearing our silly uniforms, black stockings, black hats and gowns, and white blouses, she was in hospital. In what we called then an 'asylum'.

She had not returned to Oxford for the last summer term. Miss Loomis had written to me in the Easter vacation to say she had suffered a 'nervous breakdown.' It was not very serious and I was not to worry about her and upset my own work to no purpose. There was no need to visit her. What Hilde needed was several months rest and quiet. When I telephoned, Miss Loomis was even firmer. Hilde didn't want to see anyone. She found it an effort to talk. The kindest thing was to leave her alone to recover. I could write if I liked but I must not be hurt if she didn't answer.

It wasn't too hard to accept this. I was busy, I had exams to take, and, when I wasn't working, Pete absorbed all my attention. We were lovers by this time and if sex hadn't turned out to be quite the earth-shattering experience I had expected, I found it an agreeable way of relaxing. My life altogether seemed to be forming into a fulfilling and positive pattern that, for the moment, excluded Hilde.

I cannot remember what I really thought could be wrong with her. I think I envisaged a romantic decline, a delicate Victorian weakness of body and spirit. Hilde lying on a sofa with a rug over her knees, reading poetry. I sent her postcards with loving messages, and, towards the end of the term, an invitation to my wedding. I hoped she would come but I wasn't surprised when she didn't reply.

Pete and I were married in Oxford in the first week of the

summer vacation. To my parents' relief and Pete's mother's fury (although she didn't think I was good enough for Pete, she would have liked a full blown, conventional ceremony as a background for her martyred displeasure) we made all the arrangements ourselves. We gave a party (the party at which Amanda made that unfortunate remark), went to France for our honeymoon, and came back to a flat in Chelsea that belonged to one of Pete's aunts who had moved out to stay with a friend in the country until we found somewhere to live. We found a small Georgian house in a Surrey village for four thousand pounds and Pete's father bought it for us as a wedding present. Since the owners were going abroad we were able to move in very quickly, buying their carpets and curtains and furniture out of a legacy another of Pete's aunts had bequeathed him. Both house and contents were excellent bargains, Pete said, though five thousand pounds, which was what had been spent by the time contracts were exchanged, seemed an immense sum to me.

I think I was happy. What I am more certain of is that I was astonished by my own luck. Perhaps I didn't love Pete in the way I had believed I loved Joey, but I was in love with the wonderful ease of the life he was giving me, with my pretty house and garden, my own bank account with a 'float' of five hundred pounds so that I should feel independent, and my exciting, new position as a young married woman. I was grateful to Pete for these things and if I knew, in some part of my mind, that there would be a bill presented for them eventually, I didn't doubt that I would be able to pay it. I meant to be a good wife to him, the kind of wife I imagined he wanted, cooking the meals that he liked, looking after his clothes, giving dinner parties for the eminent authors that he would wish to entertain once he had served his apprenticeship in his father's publishing firm. In retrospect, of course, this attitude seems shockingly subservient; absorbed in cosy dreams of living my husband's life, I was abdicating responsibility for my own. But in the early fifties marriage was not yet thought to be a stifling martyrdom for a woman; I saw my role as creative – and not just where Pete was concerned. None of my friends were married; none, except

Rosie, were as comfortably fixed. I saw my house, proudly, as a warm sanctuary for them; a safe house where all would be welcome, a refuge from dull jobs, from illness, misfortune.

I longed to begin to play Lady Bountiful. I rang Miss Loomis to ask if Hilde was well enough now to come and stay for a while, but there was no answer. I telephoned Rosie and she said she thought that Hilde had come out of hospital and Miss Loomis had taken her away for a holiday. 'I think it's rather mysterious,' Rosie said. 'Did you know that my parents haven't once been allowed to see her? Miss Loomis told them that the doctor was against visitors. Really it is a teeny bit strange, don't you think, since we've always been so concerned for her? In fact, my mother said rather a *naughty* thing!' Rosie giggled. '*I wonder if the poor girl's neurosis has been wheeled out in a pram!*'

I wrote to Miss Loomis. I said that I had tried not to be hurt by Hilde's silence, my unanswered letters, and of course I didn't want to intrude if, for some reason, Hilde had decided to 'cast me out of her life', but I longed to know if I could help her. Although I had my household to run and would be very busy once my baby was born, just now I had time on my hands. And, in case Rosie's mother was right about Hilde's trouble, I added a delicately obscure postscript. 'Being a married woman widens one's sympathies, as I'm sure you will understand.'

Miss Loomis wrote back three weeks later. She had been glad to hear I was happily married but she hoped that I wouldn't waste my good education. Indeed, since I was pregnant and therefore unlikely to be looking for a job at the moment, this might be the time to think seriously about writing. A literary career was one that could easily be combined with running a house and being a mother. It was important to discipline oneself, establish regular habits of work. She believed I had perseverance and talent and hoped for 'great things' from me. 'And remember, dear Laura, that to write fiction is not necessarily to be out of the battle. The pen can be mightier than the sword. Look how Dickens exposed social evils!'

The tone of this letter was pure Miss Loomis; her sharp, angular handwriting firm and black on the page. The next paragraph seemed to be written not only with a different pen, but by someone else altogether; the strokes pale and spidery, the unformed words sprawling distractedly. Hilde had had a relapse and was in a North London Hospital. 'Please visit her,' Miss Loomis wrote, in this unfamiliar, pitiful scribble. 'And forgive her if she seems not to trust you. It is a cruel illness and you will see why I tried to spare you. I can only pray that your love will comfort and help her.'

And remembering the only other time that Miss Loomis, that stout tower of strength, had crumbled in front of me, I knew that something was terribly wrong.

I didn't show this letter to Pete, nor tell him I was visiting Hilde. He was taking my pregnancy solemnly; to be a prospective father was a weighty responsibility, he often said, and he was not a man to make light of his burdens, although, as I soon discovered, his concern had its limits. It was all right for me to do housework, carry shopping and coal and do all the gardening. These activities were a wife's proper functions, and since he was not at home to observe me performing them, he was content to ignore the fact that feeding the old solid fuel boiler, and digging the clay soil of the vegetable patch, might be heavy tasks for me. But if I did anything outside these necessary duties, went to London to have lunch with a friend, see a film, or even went for a long walk alone, he was disapproving. It was wrong of me to 'wear myself out'; I might catch a cold in the train or the cinema – or German measles, or polio! Could I not see that I owed it to him and the baby to keep myself healthy? When I tried to make him laugh by asking if he wanted to keep me in purdah – should I, perhaps, wear a *veil*? – he grew pompous and sulky. I was younger than he was; too young, he was beginning to think, for marriage and motherhood. He didn't blame me for that, of course, but it did mean he had to take his job of looking after me extra seriously. The first time he said this I was flattered; when he repeated it, as he did whenever he thought I was indulging myself by doing something that was not directly related to the house or his comfort, I began to be irritated. I pointed out that I had been looking after myself quite successfully since I was eleven years old. My father had been at sea for most of the war and except for brief periods I had only lived with my mother during school and university holidays. 'That's part of the trouble,' he sighed. 'You didn't have proper parental guidance during your formative years and so I have to be father and mother to you, as well as a husband.'

His sad, wry smile implied that I had forced these extra roles on him unfairly. I knew this was affected nonsense, but felt, all the same, uneasy and guilty. It seemed that the only way to avoid this kind of discomfort was to give him no cause to reproach me and I was relieved to find that for such a sensitive man he was curiously easy to deceive. If I was out when he rang in the afternoon he always believed me when I said I had been resting and had turned off the bell on the telephone in the bedroom. And it was simple to invent acceptable reasons for going to London. Although we were better equipped than most post war young couples, we needed odd items of furniture, linen and crockery, clothes for the baby. If I hurried, ran instead of walked from one shop to another, I could fit in time for a film. Collapsing (sometimes with real exhaustion) in the warm comfort of the cinema, it didn't occur to me that my behaviour was cowardly. I was too much in awe of Pete still, too nervous of 'hurting' him, to question his anxiety for me, or to see my deception as anything more than a temporary expedient. Once the baby was born, Pete would stop worrying and we would have a more balanced and adult relationship.

The day I was to visit Hilde, I told Pete I was due for a pre-natal check. The hours I would be notionally waiting in the clinic gave me plenty of time for a journey to London and back. 'It's cold and misty,' Pete said as he kissed me goodbye in the morning. 'If it gets worse, wear a scarf over your mouth. And try to get home before dark.'

The mist was thickening as I took the main line train to London, and by the time I came out of the Underground near Hilde's hospital, the air was dense with choking, mustardy fog; the kind of London pea-souper we no longer see. The mood I was in, both nervous and exultant, made me regard this hideous pollution as mysterious and magical. Traffic crawled by, horns muffled and melancholy, romantic as the sirens of ships on the river; street lamps bloomed softly, fuzzy yellow flowers, casting no light; the trees in the grounds of the hospital, lifting black branches above me, were tangled and motionless like trees in an enchanted wood. I trod on their wet, fallen leaves with a sense of adventure and a rising excitement, convinced, suddenly, that Hilde knew I was coming, was waiting and longing to see me.

Inside the building, the fog was still present; an acrid taste in the air. I went to the desk, asked for Hilde, and a nurse took me up in a lift and along a short passage. We came to a door at the end and she unhooked a bundle of keys from her waist. She smiled at me as she turned the key in the lock. 'Don't worry, it's just a precaution. Some of our guests are a little anxious to leave us.'

Beyond the door, a long, narrow corridor with doors either side. She rapped briskly on one, pushed it open and said, 'Hilde. Wake up, dear, you have a visitor.'

Her voice was loud and bright as if she were speaking to a deaf person. The mound of blankets on the bed did not stir. The nurse winked at me. 'I expect she'll be lively enough once I've gone. Ring the bell by the bed if you need anything. Someone will be along very quickly. If I were you, I should leave the door a bit open.'

She bustled away, starched apron and polished shoes squeaking. I closed the door firmly. Approaching the bed, I said, 'Hilde?' – and, slowly, like a child playing Peek-a-boo, she pulled a corner of the blanket away from her face. One dark eye regarded me warily. I said, 'Darling . . .'

She sat up. She was wearing a cotton shirt with a hospital monogram embroidered on the front. Her face was rosy – it was hot in the room – and, in an odd way, both thinner and heavier. Her bones, her strong nose and the arch of her brows, seemed more prominent.

I said, 'I've brought you some flowers. And some chocolates.'

I put the damp bunch of violets on the bedside table, the chocolate box on the bed. She looked at it and shook her head.

'I'm not allowed to eat anything. Only what the nurse brings me. Didn't they tell you?'

I was delighted to hear her speak. I laughed and said, 'No, they didn't say anything. Are you on some sort of diet?' Too shy to kiss her, I sat on the bed, smiling. 'I should have come before. I'm so sorry I didn't. But Miss Loomis said you wanted to be left alone, and I was so busy.'

'You married that frightful man, didn't you?'

'Pete's not frightful. Honestly, Hilde! I'm terribly happy. And I'm having a baby.' I moved closer to her. 'You can feel him already. He's started to jump about. Like a frog. Or a footballer.'

Tentatively, she stretched out her hand. I took it and pressed it against my stomach.

She shook her head. 'It's not moving.'

'Wait a minute. Be patient. He's more active in the bath, he likes hot water. But it's quite warm in here.'

The baby kicked into her hand, a small foot or fist, a hard bump, like an apple. She smiled slowly and broadly and I saw that one of her front teeth was broken and jagged. She said, 'How amazing! Why didn't you tell me?'

'I did write. Lots of letters.'

'Did you? I don't remember. They've been giving me electric shocks and it makes me forget things. Or perhaps they just didn't want me to have them. I'm under guard here, you see, and they have to be careful. They censor my letters and see that no one brings in food in case its poisoned. That's why I was surprised they allowed you to bring in the chocolates.'

She sounded perfectly sane. I said, 'If you like, I'll open the box and eat one so you can see that they're safe. Who is trying to poison you?'

'Rosie's parents, of course. It was lucky I found out in time. That's why they paid for me to come over to England. They mean to destroy me.' She frowned. 'I don't quite know why. I think it must be something to do with the money.'

'What money?'

'I don't know exactly. It may be the reparations that the Germans are going to pay because they killed all my family. If I died, they think they would get it because they've done so much for me. Rosie's mother tried to get in to see me, to make me sign all my rights away. It was lucky that one of the doctors saw the danger and stopped her.'

'That can't be true, Hilde.'

She looked at my slyly. 'Oh, I know it doesn't *sound* true. That's why I don't talk much about it. It gives me a headache when people say I am making it up. Hurts my head – oh, so *badly.*'

She put her hand to her forehead. 'I can't think when my head hurts. So many different voices start talking.'

'Would it help if I said I believed you?'

'It might. I don't know. If I try and tell myself it's not true, the bad voice gets angry.'

This seemed interesting. 'Does the good voice say that Rosie and her parents are fond of you and don't mean to harm you?'

She nodded. 'Only it isn't as strong as the bad voice. I hate it when they start quarrelling. I have to hold my head so they won't break it open. It feels – I can't really explain it – so fragile. Like a parcel of broken glass. Sometimes I tie my handkerchief round to hold it together.'

I touched her head gently. 'It seems tough enough. Skulls aren't made of paper.'

She said, like a fearful child, 'Don't tell on me, will you? They don't understand, they're so stupid. They'd make me have some more treatment.'

'Of course I won't tell.' I didn't want her to see the tears in my eyes. I put my arms round her, hid her face on my shoulder, stroked her strong, wiry hair.

She was stiff at first. Then she was hugging me tightly. She whispered, 'Oh, that's nice, Laura, don't let me go. We're not hurting the baby, are we? I wish I could have one, tucked up inside me. Someone that belonged to me.'

'You will, one day. You can share mine, in the meantime. Perhaps, by the time it's born, you'll be better. You can come and help me look after it.'

She moved out of my arms. Her black eyes were shining. 'I'd like that. Oh, I *would* like that, dear Laura. Even if you change your mind later, thank you for asking me!'

'Why should I change my mind?'

'Someone will make you. Miss Loomis said I could stay with her, but they took me away and sent me here. I don't know if they'll let me out. Will you ask them?'

I nodded and she caught my wrist, twisting it painfully. Her eyes had gone dull; dark grapes with no bloom. 'Sleep now,' she said. 'I get so tired, talking.' She lay back, looking exhausted. I held her hand for a while, until her breathing grew regular.

But she wasn't sleeping. As I got off the bed, she sat up and threw the box of chocolates at me. It struck me on the side of my face. She said, her voice strong and angry, 'Bring me *cigarettes* next time, you old sod, not chocolates. And matches. They make a fuss about matches, but you can sneak them in, can't you?'

'I'm afraid you can't see the doctor, dear,' the nurse said. 'Not without an appointment. Besides, he's not in his room at the moment.'

'I don't mind waiting.'

She pulled a sour face. 'I can't stop you, can I? But you won't get anywhere. Doctor's very busy, he has a lot of patients to see to.'

'I'll chance it,' I said.

I waited for an hour outside the doctor's empty office. When he came along the passage, white coat flying, and slammed into his room, I jumped up before he could close the door on me. He was short and plump with a tired, pale, puffy face and lank, thinning hair. While I stumbled out my first questions he drummed pudgy fingers on the desk. A busy man. Too busy to listen.

Eventually he said, 'Are you a relation?'

'No. But . . .'

'Then I can't tell you anything.'

'She hasn't got any relations. All her family died in the concentration camps. You ought to know that – it's in her notes, isn't it? If it isn't, it should be. I'm her best friend. There's no one to care about her, except me and Miss Loomis.'

'Oh, yes. The old lady. Your friend is too much for her, she couldn't cope any longer, you know that, don't you?'

'I didn't know. Miss Loomis only told me that Hilde was ill.' I found I was shaking with anger. 'That's why I've been sitting outside your office, waiting to catch you. I have to know what is wrong with her.'

'I suppose there's no harm.' He picked at his nostrils which were black with the fog, watching me. 'She's schizophrenic at the moment, exhibiting some paranoid symptoms. She may recover from this episode or she may not. Either way the prognosis is poor.'

'She didn't seem so terribly ill to me. She's scared that someone we both know is trying to poison her. Otherwise we had a sensible talk.'

'She covers up well. She's an intelligent girl, it's a pity.'

I pleaded with him. 'She'll get better, won't she?'

He didn't answer. He took out a handkerchief and cleaned his nose carefully.

I said, 'What's going to happen? You must have some idea. Can't you tell me? I do want to help her.'

He looked at his blackened handkerchief and put it back in his pocket. He smiled, a bit helplessly, and I saw he was younger than I had thought. He said, 'Well, we'll keep her here as long as we can, as long as she seems to be improving, that is. This is an acute unit, you see, and there's a lot of pressure to discharge patients as soon as they're stabilised. In her case there seem to be only two options. A long stay hospital, or, if she's well enough, and we can find a place for her, a suitable hostel. Since she's young and alone in the world we might be lucky enough to get a priority placement.'

'She's not alone in the world. She's got me! I could look after her!' I started to cry and he poured a glass of water from a jug on his desk and got up to give it to me. He stood by my chair as I drank, then put the glass down. He said, awkwardly kind, 'Look, I can see you're a jolly nice girl, very sympathetic and all that, but you're young, starting your life, you don't want to lumber it up. You've no idea what you'd be taking on. I don't suppose you'll take my advice but I'll give it to you all the same. Go home and try and forget all about her.'

I stared at him. 'How can you be so wicked! So *callous*! You're her doctor, she's your patient, you should be glad she has someone to turn to, someone who loves her and is anxious to help her.'

He went to sit behind his desk. His tired face expressed nothing. He said, 'I'm not sure how you think you can help her. If you had any idea, for example, of offering her a home, you should put it out of your head. This type of patient can be very hostile, sometimes aggressive. There are often bewildering personality changes. And to raise her hopes by making promises you can't carry out would be cruel. She has enough to suffer without that. If you must keep in touch, stay at a distance. Letters, the occasional visit. Any more, and you'll be out of your depth. I'm saying this for your sake, not hers. Get too close and she'll drown you.'

'But you don't understand,' I said. 'Hilde's my *friend*.'

'She's my friend,' I repeated sullenly, several hours later. My train had been held up in the fog and Pete had got home before me. He had taken the afternoon off and driven to the ante-natal clinic to pick me up so that I wouldn't have to hang about waiting for buses in this dreadful weather, and so he was doubly angry: I had not only deceived him but made him look foolish when he got to the clinic and insisted that I must be there, that he knew, for a fact, that I had an appointment . . .

'Perhaps looking a fool doesn't matter,' he conceded magnanimously. 'At least I didn't look like a cuckold. They could hardly have thought that a woman in the fifth month of pregnancy was using the clinic as an alibi for an afternoon with her lover. No – what really hurts, screws me up, is that you should have felt you had to lie to me for such a paltry reason. As if I were some kind of tyrant, a jailor you had to escape from.'

I said, goaded, 'It's a bit like that, isn't it? I mean, you're always making objections. I'm not allowed to go anywhere or do anything you don't approve of. I know you worry about me, and for my own good, as they say, but I do sometimes feel like a sort of cossetted *prisoner*.' To take the sting out of this, I laughed and added, 'What the Victorians would have called a bird in a gilded cage!'

Pete's fleshy, handsome face sagged mournfully. He looked like a depressed Roman Emperor. He said in a deep, throbbing voice, 'I hope you don't mean that. I pray you don't mean it. If you really do, then I must tell you, Laura, that I see very little hope for our marriage.'

I was already distressed by my visit to Hilde, tired from the long, foggy journey, and this threat weakened me further. I had no strength to fight and I was in the wrong anyway. There was only one card I could play. 'My back aches,' I said tearfully.

'No wonder,' he said. But he fussed over me then, made me lie on the sofa, tucked cushions beneath me, fetched a glass of warm milk flavoured with honey and brandy. Having settled me comfortably, done his husbandly duty, he felt free to attack me. 'You see why I have to look after you? You're incapable of looking after yourself. The idea of dragging all that way in your condition and in this appalling fog was really quite irresponsible. If you felt you had to see Hilde I would have driven you to the hospital at the weekend, though I must admit I wouldn't have been too keen on the notion. Emotional strain is something you ought to avoid when you're pregnant. It's not just *your* baby you have to take care of, you know! He's mine, too!'

His eyes grew moist and he brushed them with the back of his hand in a theatrical gesture before kneeling beside the sofa, taking my hands and regarding me intently and sadly. 'What hurts me most deeply is that you never think of my feelings. You always say *my* baby. Never *our* baby!'

'Pete, you know that's not true!'

'Oh yes it is,' he said angrily. 'Having a child should be a great, shared experience. A knot to bind us together. But you want to deny me my rights as a father. I can see that once he is born, you will shut me out, diminish me. I won't be your lover, just a useful provider for you and *your* baby.' He lunged at me, arms about me, burying his face in my lap and groaning. 'Don't do that, my angel, swear you won't do that!'

He wept. Although I stroked his hair and tried to feel tender towards him, his anguish seemed embarrassingly false, a kind of strategy. All this moaning and groaning and pretended concern for me was nothing but jealousy. He was jealous of all my friends; he was jealous of Hilde . . .

I think now that this was unfair. If Pete was jealous, it was only in a general way; he wanted to come first with me and resented anyone or anything that distracted my attention for a moment. But he had an urgent need to dramatise. He had been a spoiled, petted boy, he had had what we called then a 'good' war, and he was terrified that nothing more was going to happen, that he would wake up one morning and find that his life had become commonplace. And, of course, the bourgeois comfort in which we were living that I found so new and delightful, an amazing achievement, was commonplace to him. He had never been without a warm house, a car, and money in the bank. He often spoke of the stifling boredom of suburban existence, and was genuinely astonished by my contentment. 'I thought I had married a sharp little alley cat,' he said ruefully. 'Not a cosy little puss, happy to sit by the fire.'

I did not see that this was a complaint, that he really thought he had done something rather dashing in marrying me, a bright 'working class' girl, rather than the moneyed miss his mother would have preferred. Nor that he was disappointed when he invented small hurts and grievances and I did not rise to the bait. A few passionate rows and reconciliations would have made his life more interesting, but pregnancy had made me too placid to quarrel. I understood, because he told me, that he was afraid of dwindling into a husband and father, but not how deep his fear went, or how contradictory his emotions were. When he quoted, 'The enemy of promise is the pram in the hall,' I thought he was being affected. After all, he didn't work at home. And he also said, repeatedly, that he 'longed for' a son . . .

In fact, Jeremy's arrival gave Pete a fine chance for drama. He suffered terribly while I was in labour. I came round from the anaesthetic at five in the morning to find him sitting by my bed, white-faced and grim, waiting to tell me how terrible his sufferings had been. 'I walked round in the pouring rain all night,' he said, and there was such triumphant anguish in his voice that I refrained from pointing out that even in my dozy state I could see his clothes and hair and shoes were dry. 'Poor Pete,' I murmured tactfully, and he held my hands against his chest and sighed. 'Oh my love, my little love, I could never go through this again, don't make me, will you? I was so afraid that you would die . . .'

He suffered all the time I was in hospital, arriving every evening pale and exhausted with the forebodings that had plagued him through the day, bringing me tales he had heard from other fathers of post-natal depressions, post-partem haemorrhages, along with his offerings of flowers. And once I was safely home, too obviously fit to be a suitable subject for Pete's obsessional anxieties, he worried about Jeremy instead. He weighed him night and morning, saw developing pneumonia in every sneeze and snuffle, and questioned visitors about their health before he took them to the nursery; frisking them, like suspected terrorists, for germs.

It was just another act, I thought. The role of protective and adoring father was new and interesting to him; he would get bored with it eventually and we would be able to resume a normal social life. And, indeed, he was aware of other obligations. When the hospital welfare department telephoned to say that Hilde was being discharged and to ask if we could take her in (making no mention, naturally, of the doctor's advice to me) Pete agreed at once. Miss Loomis was old and ill, Hilde had nowhere else to go, it would be monstrous behaviour on our part to turn her away! But soon after she arrived, he grew nervous. She was a little quiet and slow with all the medication she was taking, and Pete began to see an awful menace to his baby son behind her sweet, drugged smile. Late at night, whispering to me in our bedroom, he indulged in histrionic fears. He thought he had noticed Hilde looking at me oddly while I was nursing Jeremy. Perhaps, without her being conscious of it, she was jealous of the place Jeremy had taken in my life and my affections. Or resentful, because she did not have a baby, too! Of course he didn't think Hilde was *dangerous*, she would never dream of harming the child *in her right mind*, but was she in her right mind *altogether*? Suppose, for example, she should walk in her sleep?

Although I protested this was nonsense, that when we were alone Hilde was her old self, quite recovered, and it was only when Pete came home in the evenings that she became so withdrawn and shy, his fear infected me. Not fear for Jeremy – since Hilde loved me, I was sure she must love my baby, too – but fear for Hilde. I was terrified that now Pete had decided to see her as a threat he might, by some careless word or look, make her aware of it, humiliate and hurt her, destroy her fragile self-confidence. Because she was not her 'old self', of course . . .

Physically, she looked marvellous. Her broken front tooth had been capped and her lovely face was rounded again, smooth and blooming. While we were busy together, shopping and cooking, playing with Jeremy, weeding the vegetable patch or cleaning out the rabbits I was keeping in a shed at the end of the garden, she seemed content, almost happy. She could still be coaxed into laughter; when I explained that I was breeding the rabbits in case war broke out again and meat was rationed, her eyes danced in the old way, joyfully teasing me. But though she was usually ready to do whatever I asked, she never initiated any activity, and even with me she could be very silent, sitting in a chair for an hour at a time, staring at nothing, rigid, unmoving. If people came to the house she would make social efforts, smiling quickly and over-brightly whenever they spoke to her, pathetically anxious to please, appear normal. And when I asked Rosie to visit us, hoping to break down the barrier Hilde's illness had erected between them, her tension was pitiful.

Rosie seemed not to notice any change in her. Or pretended not to notice, perhaps. She kissed Hilde fondly and chattered away – about Oxford, about William whom she was shortly going to marry, and about her parents who would be 'so happy' if Hilde would go to stay with them; they would love to see her again and the sea air would be good for her. Hilde didn't answer; she simply sat smiling, that painful, fixed smile that concealed her inner confusion and terror, until I could bear it no longer. I said, 'Oh, Rosie, not *yet*. It sounds terribly selfish, I know, but I need Hilde so badly! It's so boring, being alone with a baby! Jeremy's a pet, an absolute darling, but he has no *conversation!*' And was rewarded by the look of grateful love Hilde gave me.

I was proud to protect her. From Rosie; from Pete. His fears that Hilde might harm the baby seemed grotesque to me, products of a wilfully neurotic imagination, but for her sake I couldn't altogether ignore them. I moved Jeremy into our bedroom at night and when he cried and Pete woke and grumbled, carried the crib back to the nursery and sat on guard by it. Though Pete must have known why I was doing this, he didn't say so, preferring (for his own comfort, presumably) to accept that as I was breast feeding, there was no point in disturbing him when the child was restless or hungry.

During these night watches I started my first novel, a colour-ful, Gothic thriller about a twelve-year-old girl left by her parents in the care of a half mad, vicious old woman, gleefully recreating my time with Aunt Milly and bringing it to a more dramatic and far reaching conclusion than it had in real life. (For those who have not read *The Only Way Out*, which has long been out of print and is unlikely to be resurrected, the girl murders her jailer with an overdose of sleeping pills and grows, since this first crime remains undetected, into a steady, routine poisoner, ruthlessly disposing of everyone who annoys her, seems to threaten her in any way, or utters the smallest of criticisms.) The *New York Times* called it a 'chilling book', and it chills me now when I think of it; when I remember the horrible ease with which I was able to identify with my psychopathic young heroine. I understood her so well, it was almost as if I had been possessed by her. Or – more exactly and frighteningly – as if she were part of me; a vengeful phantom lurking in some dark, unvisited attic of my mind. Perhaps lurks there still. Though I do not think I could murder anyone, the idea of death as a convenient way out of a tiresome situation has often occurred to me. Indeed, there was a time when I used to kill Pete fairly regularly – a road accident, a heart attack, a new strain of influenza resistant to antibiotics . . .

But these are afterthoughts. I remember that I was relieved that Miss Loomis died before the novel was published, knowing that she would be dismayed by its lack of social and moral concern, but at the time I was writing it, I didn't think of publication, nor worry because the story was crudely sensational. I was simply and innocently amusing myself; scribbling naively away. I was never tired, partly because I was able to cat-nap in the daytime, but chiefly because I was happy. I remember this happiness – it comes back to me as a warm wave of loving energy that carried me along with it, buoyant and hopeful and strong. I had no night terrors then. The house that I lived in had stood for a hundred years and was good (our local builder assured us) for another century. I was happy in this solid, safe house, and happy that the two people I loved best in the world, my baby, and my friend, Hilde, were safe with me under its roof. I was pleased and proud to look after them. I didn't doubt my ability to keep them both safe, for ever.

I was crying in the car on the way to the prison. Andrew gave me his handkerchief. He said, 'Dry your eyes, silly. If you cry you'll make your face puffy and upset poor old Jeremy.'

I swallowed my tears and blew my nose. I said, 'I can't believe this has happened.'

We had been so sure it would be all right. If Andrew had doubts, he kept them to himself. And Jeremy, I think, had lived for the moment. Rescued from prison by his mama and stepfather, bailed into our loving custody, he put himself into our hands, passively, sweetly; going uncomplainingly to the barber to have his long, beautiful hair cut to an acceptable length, his beard trimmed (to persuade him to shave it off altogether would be too authoritarian, Andrew decided), allowing us to buy him a respectable jacket and trousers, and to coach him in the role of innocent victim he would have to play when he next appeared in the magistrate's court.

It was not a false role – or so we believed. Or I believed, anyway, and I think Andrew tried to. It was too simple a story not to be true, he said, several times. If Jeremy had wanted to lie, he would surely have cooked up something more original and circumstantial than this hoary tale of a sad, waif-like girl with a mass of untidy luggage whom he had met on the boat from Tangier to Gibraltar and helped on the plane to Heathrow. He would have known – or invented – her *name*, for Christ's sake! 'I can't see what difference that would have made,' Jeremy said. 'I mean, she was just a thin girl with too much to carry and I just bought her a drink on the plane and toted her heaviest bag. If she'd told me her name, I would have remembered, but she didn't tell me and I didn't ask. I'm rather glad now, to be honest. I mean, I wouldn't have told the police, anyway, but it's a relief to know that I can't.'

This candour is typical of Jeremy. As is the fact that when he was stopped at the customs and told to open her canvas hold-all, he allowed them to think it belonged to him, even though he had seen the girl scuttle ahead with a frightened glance backwards over her shoulder. 'I supposed I guessed there was something up then, but I didn't think it would matter. That is, I assumed there would be a girl's things in the bag. But as it turned out, there was only this ghastly muddle of unisex jeans and old shirts that could have been mine at a pinch – I mean, she was almost my height – and a lot of squashed paperbacks and this piddling little parcel of hash right at the bottom.'

'But you didn't say the bag wasn't yours, even then,' Andrew objected. 'Not until you were at the police station and they got a bit rough with you.'

'Not a *bit* rough. They bashed me up,' Jeremy said. Then he blushed. 'I just wanted her to have a chance to get right away. I know it sounds crazy now – it seemed *bloody* crazy the moment they started to thump me! But, honestly, Andrew, she was so *pitiful*! She'd been living in Tangier with this Lebanese who'd just walked out one morning and dumped her. He'd left the money for her plane ticket home, nothing more. She said she hadn't eaten for days. And she was desperate to get home to her mother and father.'

Jeremy is quixotic by nature. As a little boy he was always eager to take the blame – for other boys at school, for his sister,

Claudia. He has always suffered, perhaps, from the sense of responsibility some children feel when their parents split up. But he felt this responsibility, this troubled and bewildered guilt, before Pete and I separated. I came out of our bedroom one night, flinging out in the middle of a loud, stupid row, to find my baby son quivering opposite the door in soaking pyjamas, tiny face screwed up and stricken. 'I done wee in my bed,' he whispered as I picked him up and carried him to the nursery. 'Is that why Daddy is shouting?'

He still has this delicate conscience. Inside his grown, young man's body there is an apprehensive little boy watching and listening for angry faces, raised voices, terrified that he is at fault and yet longing to be found out and punished. Perhaps that is why he did not seem to resent what so incensed us – the beating he got at the police station. And why he seemed so tranquil those three weeks before the court hearing, amusing Henry and Isobel like a kind, older brother, playing Scrabble with Andrew and me in the evenings. (We thought we were keeping him occupied but I realise now that he was indulging us, keeping our spirits up.) Although he may have hoped he would be acquitted, he was ready for martyrdom, for his guilt to be exorcised.

I cannot think, all the same, that he imagined he might be locked up. Certainly we did not think it could happen. Even if he were convicted, a fine or a few months probation was the most likely outcome. Our solicitor warned us that he could be sent to prison, but since he was a first offender, there should be social and psychiatric reports before a sentence of this kind was passed. And reports, we were sure, could only be to Jeremy's advantage. Though we realised that a bench of magistrates might not take the same kindly view of our sweet son as we did, he was obviously a decent young man, of 'good character'. The fact that he had left university without taking a degree and had not yet decided on a career should not, in these days, count too much against him. He wasn't lazy, not a layabout, but a wise child of his generation. There were plenty of boys like him, growing up in the tolerant sixties and early seventies, rejecting their parents' boring devotion to the work ethic, taking casual jobs to finance their travelling, sensibly seeing a bit of the world before settling down.

So we comforted ourselves, speaking of our hirsute (though now trimly bearded) twenty-four-year-old as a 'child', a 'boy', as if by using these tenderly inappropriate words we could restore his innocence and make it visible. If he knew better (and sometimes it seemed that he looked at us pityingly) he did not attempt to resist this conspiracy to reduce him to an artificial childhood. Indeed, most of the time he seemed grateful for it, listening with a strained look of hope as we exerted ourselves to comfort and cheer him, assuring him that his offence was only a technical one. As long as he had not known, or suspected, that there were drugs in the bag, he was only a 'carrier'. All he had to do was stick to his story courageously and all would be well.

He had always been a brave boy, we recalled lovingly, reminding each other of instances, turning the clock back. There was the time just after I had met Andrew, before we were married, when we had taken him and Claudia to the sea for the day. Claudia had a kite that Pete and his wife had given her for her eighth birthday. It was too big for her to manage alone, which enraged her. She refused Andrew's help and flew into a passionate temper, hurling the kite to the ground, stamping her feet on it, screaming with frustration. While Andrew and I were trying to calm her, Jeremy slipped away, making himself scarce as he usually did when his sister made public scenes, and went to the far end of the beach where the shingle was cluttered with rubbish swept in by the tide. Jumping off a jetty, he landed on a rusty iron spar and cut his foot badly; a long, ugly gash in his instep. At the local hospital, a plump and kindly Matron gave him a tetanus shot and stitched the wound. He was terrified, tense and trembling, but after one desperate, beseeching look, imploring us to save him from this fearsome torture, he endured the needle in a flushed, unflinching silence that plucked our heart strings. 'A valiant child,' Andrew whispered to me afterwards, and the sharp-eared little boy looked modestly downward, with a proud and crooked smile.

In the court, when he was sentenced to six months in prison and he turned round briefly, searching for us in the public gallery, that scared child's beseeching look was on his face again. Beside me, Andrew caught his breath and I knew that he remembered. Then Jeremy smiled, his crooked smile, and vanished down the steps inside the dock. Andrew said, 'Bloody magistrates,' and struck his clenched fists together. William, who had come with us, to support us, touched his arm. Andrew stood up, shaking off his old friend's warning hand. 'A blatant miscarriage of justice,' he said, in a commanding, furious voice, and the Chairman of the Bench, a bald and prim-faced man in spectacles, looked up and frowned.

Outside the public gallery, in the court's small, crowded entrance hall that smelled of wet clothes and sweat, we waited for the young barrister our solicitor had chosen to defend our son. 'Too bloody young,' Andrew growled. 'He's supposed to know about the drug scene. That's what we were told. We should have insisted on briefing someone who wasn't still wet behind the ears. Brought up some heavy gun.'

'I don't suppose it would have made much difference,' William said. 'In fact, it could have been bad tactics. Steam hammer to crack a nut – make it seem a bit too *serious*, you know? As if there might be more behind the charge than just an ounce or two of cannabis.'

'Half a pound,' Andrew said. 'More than Jeremy told us. Though since it wasn't his, he'd hardly know, would he? I don't suppose they let him weigh it. They knocked him about, Will. That should have been brought out in court, in my opinion. What the flaming hell do we do now?'

He glared round the noisy, smelly hall as if he expected someone – a policeman, an usher, one of the other defendants – to spring to attention at once and answer him. A tall, imposing, angry man, unaccustomed to this kind of defeat, to his son being beaten up in police stations, sent to prison. The young barrister, pushing his way through the crowd, looked at Andrew's face and reddened slightly.

He said, 'I'm sorry, we had dreadful luck. It could have gone the other way so easily. But we struck a dim-witted Bench, a bloody-minded, bossy Clerk . . .'

'They paid no attention at all,' Andrew said. He regarded the young man accusingly. 'Not to you, nor to Jeremy. That court was conducted like a Mad Hatter's Tea Party. Off with the boy's head as soon as he appeared. Those magistrates whispered to each other while he was in the witness box, for Christ's sake! They didn't listen to a word he said.'

'Oh, they listened all right,' the barrister said. 'It was just that they didn't believe him. It might have been different if we could have produced the girl.'

'Jeremy wouldn't have allowed her to give evidence and incriminate herself,' Andrew said. He added, absurdly, 'The boy's a gentleman!'

The barrister stood with downcast eyes. They had smooth, white lids and long, dark lashes. I thought his mouth twitched, secretly.

William said, 'Of course, he can appeal.'

The young man raised his eyes. 'He doesn't want to. I've been to see him and he's quite firm about it. He says he'd rather get it over with, finish with it now. And, well, he may be wise to.'

'But he's innocent!' I smiled at him coaxingly. 'You think so, don't you?'

His mouth twitched again. A nervous tic. He wasn't so young – around thirty. He didn't answer my question, only said, 'If he appealed, it could still go against him in a higher court. And he could get a longer sentence there.'

'I can't believe that,' Andrew said. 'And at least it would be a proper trial, not this bloody awful *farce*. A proper Judge and jury, instead of a Bench of jumped up, half trained nobodies, puffed up with their own importance, toadying to the police. And, for God's sake, what about these reports? I understood there had to be reports before he could be sent to prison. His background, education, all that sort of thing. He's not a criminal!'

The barrister said, delicately, 'It is a criminal charge, sir. Though you're right, of course there should have been reports. But that is only a Home Office directive, it doesn't have the force of law, and some courts, like this one, I'm afraid, don't pay too much attention.'

He glanced at me hopefully. Perhaps I didn't exude the same

air of outraged privilege as Andrew. But I was on Andrew's side. I said, 'It was your job to remind them, don't you think?'

William said, 'If the Bench ignored a Home Office directive, there must be, to put it at its lowest, some kind of argument! Some grounds for an appeal!' He spoke diffidently, his face crumpled into anxious lines, thin shoulders hunched beneath his overcoat.

'Only if he wants to make use of them.' The barrister turned to Andrew and said, with apologetic dignity, 'It's your son who is my client, sir, not you, and so it's his instructions that I have to take. And he does seem to have made up his mind, though I have told him to let me know if he decides to change it. I'll be able to see him in prison. I'll try and find out where they are taking him. Would you like to see him before he goes? I'm afraid that only one of you will be allowed down to the cells.'

Andrew looked at me. I nodded, and he said, 'My wife had better go. His mother. I think that I might punch someone on the nose.'

Below ground, the tiled walls ran with water. The smell of unwashed clothes and bodies was overlaid by an old-fashioned disinfectant, like carbolic. A policeman with a black mole on one weathered cheek smiled when I asked for Jeremy and said, in a soft, regional accent, 'You can have five minutes, dear.'

The cells were the size of small lavatories, and there seemed to be two men in each. Besides his cubicle companion, a muscular, wild-looking man with heavy, bare, freckled arms, Jeremy looked frail as a leaf; a mild, civilised scholar caged up with a gorilla. He was wearing the glasses that he doesn't need but sometimes puts on to hide behind, and reading Henry Troyat's *Life of Tolstoy* in the Penguin edition. At least, he was holding the open book in front of him and pretending to read it. I said, 'Darling,' and he gave a convincing start of surprise, closed the book, and took off his glasses.

Embarrassed by the bars between us, I gabbled breathlessly. 'Only one of us could come. Andrew sends his love.' I remembered my visit to Hilde, in hospital. In some circumstances, love could be an inadequate offering. 'Is there anything

145

I can get you? Do you want cigarettes? There's a machine upstairs.'

'I've decided to give up smoking,' Jeremy said. 'It looks like a good opportunity.' He smiled over-carefully, crinkling his eyes up. 'It was nice of you all to come to the court. Especially William. I mean, that was *friendly*.'

'Yes.'

'Perhaps he'll take you out to lunch. Cheer you up.'

'Lunch is hardly the uppermost thought in my mind at the moment.'

'Oh, come *on*, Mum! Don't be silly. It would do you good, really!'

I said, 'Look – I've only got a few minutes. Do you know where you're going?'

'The Scrubs, I think. Wormwood Scrubs. That's what my friend says.' Behind Jeremy, the gorilla was scratching his arm pit and yawning. He was wearing thin jeans and a shrunken-up Tee shirt. Jeremy said, 'Jake, this is my mother.'

'Pleased to meet you,' the gorilla said. He pulled the Tee shirt down over his hairy belly and nodded. He had a pleasant, broad face and clear, attractive, grey eyes. Apart from the ominous scratching, he seemed perfectly clean. He didn't look like a criminal. But neither did Jeremy. 'Are you sure it will be the Scrubs?' I asked. Jake shrugged his huge shoulders. 'Oh, they keep you guessing. That's part of the game.' He grinned at me sociably and then settled down on the narrow bench at the back of the cubicle, folding his arms and closing his eyes, indicating by this tactful withdrawal that Jeremy and I could consider ourselves alone.

I said, 'Well, at least you've got company. Listen, darling, I know you don't want to appeal, I'm not going to try to persuade you, but I must tell you that Andrew thinks – we *both* think – that the barrister made rather a mess of things.'

'He did his best. I mean, there wasn't much he could do. Magistrates always believe the police, don't they? And if the police don't get convictions, they don't get promotion. That's the way it goes, isn't it?'

I was appalled by this cynicism, by his air of weary acceptance. I said, 'If that's what you think, then you *ought* to appeal!'

'I'd rather not.'

'Why? I mean, darling, I'll have to tell Andrew.'

'It's really not worth it. I couldn't bear to go through it all again. The worst is over, all I have to do now is just stick it out. It can't be much worse than school, and it should only be about four months, with remission.' He looked at me with a sudden, dry grin, amused, and faintly reproachful. 'You know, if you hadn't gone dashing round, getting me out on bail, I'd have served three weeks of my sentence already!'

'Well, we'll know next time not to bother!'

He blinked. 'Sorry. I didn't mean . . .'

'Yes, you *did*!' I was shocked to hear myself sounding petulant. We shouldn't be spending this precious time sparring! It struck me that if I had been writing a scene of this kind in a novel, the dialogue would have been a good deal more poignant. Spurred on by this thought, I said, 'Darling, this is awful for you. Four months must seem like an eternity stretching ahead. But it will pass, believe me, and – who knows? – you may even find it a useful experience. A chance to reflect, reconsider! Just don't be *resentful*. You've every right to be, but it's a terrible waste of one's spirit. Even if what has happened is wrong and unfair, if you can accept it, take it *into* your life instead of rejecting it, then you will have achieved something, won't you? A kind of moral victory!'

He was looking beyond me. He said, 'I think it's time you went, Mum.'

I turned to the policeman. He had been watching us. Now he nodded and held up two fingers. *Two minutes left!* I felt cold and sick, my head buzzing. There was something else I ought to say, surely? Some comfort for my poor child. I said, 'Remember we love you. We'll be thinking of you all the time. Every day. Andrew and me and the children . . .'

'You're not going to tell *Henry* and *Isobel*?'

'No. No, of course not. I only . . .'

He said, urgently, 'Promise me! *Please!*' He smiled, a creased, worried smile. 'You know how you get carried away! Anything that might make a good story! I don't expect it would upset

Isobel much, she's tough like you are, takes things in her stride. But Henry is different. He'd be horribly frightened. Thinking of dungeons and torture.'

'Do you really think I would frighten Henry? That's a bit unkind, isn't it?'

'I suppose so. I'm sorry. I know you wouldn't mean to frighten him. It's just, I remember, you used to frighten me sometimes. Telling me things I was too young to cope with. They were beyond my experience. Like when you left Daddy.'

'Are you blaming me, Jeremy?'

He shook his head. There was an exhausted look on his face, the kind of exhaustion you see on the faces of invalids when their visitors are staying too long. He said, softly, wearily, 'No, I'm not blaming you. Really Mum!' And put his hand through the bars, to touch mine.

But of course he was blaming me! This is the new generation game. Cursing the parents! You drop out, smuggle hash, throw the dice so that it always lands you at the head of the snake, never at the foot of the ladder, every move courting failure, but it isn't your fault, it's the fault of your mother and father who never explained the rules properly; only said, truth is relative, nothing is certain, instead of this is right, this is wrong. Fair enough in a way – why should we pass on these absolute rules when we no longer believe them? The trouble is, although we no longer believe, we were programmed by people who did, and so when it comes to the crunch we are shocked and surprised to find that our children cannot hear, as we do, the clear and confident voices of our parents and teachers. (There are times when I still listen to the voice of Miss Loomis.) When our children disappoint us, fall into traps that we knew were there but forgot to warn them about, we go red and gobble.

Andrew said, 'Silly young fool. When the magistrates asked him what sort of job he was looking for, why on earth did he say he had nothing in mind at the moment? It sounded so arrogant. Couldn't he see that was just the sort of thing that was likely to turn them against him?'

148

'How should he know?' I said. 'We didn't tell him.'

We have always been gentle with Jeremy. Nervous of hurting him. He is so gentle, so painfully, anxiously sensitive. This is the character we have given him. I thought – now he is using it as a weapon against me! I said, 'Andrew, tell me something. Honestly. Do I frighten the children?'

'I don't think so. What an odd question.'

I was ashamed to tell Andrew why I had asked it.

When I left Pete, he carried the suitcases to the taxi, and put Claudia, sound asleep in her carry-cot, on the back seat. Then he lifted Jeremy, and held him tight, kissing him, weeping. 'Mummy is taking you away, she wants to leave me, divorce me. But you love Daddy, don't you?'

Jeremy was four years old. He held out his arms to me. I took him from Pete and said, over the little boy's shoulder, 'You know that was *wicked*.' And, as the taxi drove off, 'It's all right, Jeremy darling, naughty Daddy was just cross with Mummy. He was trying to hurt me, not you, so don't cry. You've got to be a big boy and help Mummy look after Claudia.'

He wriggled round, kneeling on the seat and looking out of the back window. He was wearing a woollen coat with a round velvet collar and white socks and red shoes. He said, 'Oh, poor Daddy!' in a plaintively whining tone that made me jealous and angry.

I jerked him round, pulling at his legs so that his white socks and red shoes stuck out in front of him. 'Don't speak in that silly voice, don't be stupid, he's glad to be rid of us. He's only pretending to be sorry we're going, so we will be sorry for *him*. He likes to have it both ways, your dear father!'

He looked at me in sad, scared confusion, screwing up his face, trying to make sense of this, wondering how to placate me. 'Why can't we take the rabbits? Who's going to feed them? Where are we going?'

'You'll see when we get there.' I was punishing him for not understanding. He looked at me dumbly and I wanted to hit him, smash my fist into that dumb, vacant face. I said, 'Of course, if you'd rather stay behind with your father and Sophie than come with Mummy and Claudia, I'll ask the driver to stop the taxi and you can walk back. Make up your mind and see if I care!'

He started to cry. I pulled him on my lap and kissed him. I said, 'I'm a pig.' I snorted comically. 'Horrid Pig-Mummy.'

His tears dried. He snuggled close and asked again where we were going. This time I told him. 'To Hilde's flat. You like Hilde, don't you?' and he said, 'Not as much as Daddy. Why can't we stay with him?'

Honest, irritating, foolish child. A born victim. I said, stiffly, 'He doesn't want us. He wants Sophie to live with him.'

'Why can't we live with them too? With Daddy *and* Sophie?' He smiled up at me. 'I like Sophie.'

'Just because.'

'Because what?'

'Because you can't have two wives, not in England. It's against the law.'

'Would they send us to prison?'

'Perhaps. That's why we're running away.'

His eyes were round and wild with fright. 'What if they catch us?'

'They won't, if you're good.'

He shivered against me. 'Oh, I will be good, Mummy.'

This is a sickening episode. Setting it down I am sickened and sorry, as I was at the time as soon as I'd spoken, and was to be on other occasions when I tormented Jeremy to ease my own misery. But I was in such bitter turmoil. I couldn't believe what I was doing, running off with my son and my baby daughter, leaving my husband, my safe house, my rabbits. (Suppose Pete forgot to feed them? Or let them out of their hutches? Free, in the wild, they would be attacked by wild rabbits, catch myxomatosis!) I was twenty-six, sore and humiliated because Pete preferred another woman to me, and afraid of the future. I had been victimised, and so I victimised my four-year-old boy. (Not very often; indeed, when I look back with a charitable eye and consider my circumstances, really quite *seldom* – but even once is enough to remember with shame.)

* * *

As in all wars, there has to be a build up of tension before the first shot is fired. And Pete and I had disappointed each other. He had hoped for a rich, emotional life, an invogorating, operatic existence, full of colour, loud cries and a constant renewal of passion. But his stagey behaviour, his need to turn every small, daily event into drama, embarrassed me. I couldn't respond to him as he expected (and as I felt that I ought to) and so I felt helpless and cheated. And, after Claudia's birth, I couldn't bear him to touch me. In bed, I shrank from him as if from an enemy.

This embarrassed me, too. Both my inability to be a good wife in what I still thought of as 'that way', and what seemed to be the cause of it. The truth was, I had discovered with Claudia what I had been too young and apprehensive to discover with Jeremy, a startling, physical pleasure. Bathing and cuddling and feeding her fulfilled and exhausted me sexually; her warm, greedy lips on my nipple made me throb and grow moist. I couldn't explain this to Pete, I was far too ashamed. I must be perverse, I thought, to get this 'wicked' joy from my 'innocent' baby. When I had to wean her at six months because Pete had arranged for us to go to Morocco, I missed my small daughter as one might miss a new, ardent lover. My breasts ached with missing her and I was sullen and cold with Pete for coming between us in this cruel way. On that trip to North Africa, our marriage was as dry as the desert. We slaked our thirst quarrelling.

We fought over my novel. Or, rather, that was the ground we chose to fight on, the flat plain on which we drew up our battle lines. But the grenades we lobbed at each other came from a long way behind; from rougher country, deep cover.

It was not true, as Pete said, that I had deliberately deceived him to make him look foolish. While I was writing my little book, I had kept it from Pete because I was afraid he would laugh at me – or, worse still, 'encourage' me, insist on seeing what I had written and crush me with good advice. (I had some reason for fear. Although I am told that he is now an excellent editor, helpful and sensitive, he was then only a tyro, boasting about the 'creative' work he was doing on the novels his father had given him to 'lick into shape', and I had trembled for the poor authors, suffering his rough tongue.) And later on, when my story was finished, I was nervous of showing him my five childish exercise books, full of crossings out and scrawled notes in the margins. Pete had often said how difficult and tiresome it was to decipher handwritten material. He had brought an old Remington home from the office so that I could type the letters of complaint he insisted I write to inefficient workmen – to the plumber who had not come immediately to mend a leaking pipe, to the Gas Company who had been slow in repairing a fault in the heating system. Typing out a fair copy on this ancient machine, admiring the slowly growing, neat manuscript, I decided to wait until it was accepted before presenting Pete with my triumph. I wanted to have a solid achievement to show him, to prove I was somebody in my own right before I told him what I was doing – and, since the novel was returned seven times in the next eighteen months, it seemed my caution was justified. Pete wouldn't have laughed at my failure as he might have done earlier, at my presumption; he would have been kind, tried to cheer me up with little treats, theatres and dinners, humbling me with tact and solicitude, and my self-confidence was low enough without that. But when it was accepted by the eighth publisher, I still didn't tell him. Suppose he should interfere, take a dislike to the typeface, the blurb on the jacket? He might even write indignant letters on my behalf (the kind of letters he made me write to tardy tradespeople) to my publishing firm, which was smaller than his, less old and distinguished. I had to protect my nice, elderly editor, as well as my book . . .

I told myself that all these inhibitions were not only natural, but proper. It wasn't just that I was afraid of Pete's criticism. I was also anxious that he should not be embarrassed by my amateur efforts. I was deceiving him, in fact, for his own comfort and good! I came to believe this so strongly that when I finally presented him with a copy of *The Only Way Out* (a week before publication, on the plane to Marrakesh) I was astonished and hurt when he accused me of spitefulness. How could I have done such a thing behind his back, made him look such a fool? For God's sake, he was a publisher, wasn't he? Oh, he could understand that I might not have wanted him to read it in manuscript, but once it had been accepted, the obvious thing, if I had any care for his feelings, any respect for his professional judgement, would have been to ask his advice. What on earth would his father think if he saw the book reviewed, for example? What would he think of Pete, *as a husband*, when he realised that his wife despised his opinions so much that she had not even told him she was writing a novel? But the worst thing, the cruellest thing, was that I had chosen to deny him the happiness he should have had in my success. In a sense, it was as cruel as denying him his rights as a father! 'You have done that with Claudia, made me feel an intruder, kept her to yourself, for your own pleasure,' he declared emotionally – and with more truth than he knew! Then, more practically, and in a cold, sneering voice, he invited me to look at the result of my ridiculous secrecy. The illustrated jacket was, frankly, appalling. Of course, the book might not merit a better one, he couldn't tell that until he had read it, and he wasn't sure, at the moment, that he *wanted* to read it. And why on earth had I dedicated it to Miss Loomis? She was dead, wasn't she? Oh, he knew that I felt I owed a good deal to her, but to dedicate a book to a corpse seemed a kind of sentimental necrolatry . . .

All this, in lowered tones, on the plane, switching from a furious glare to an open and charming smile whenever the pretty stewardess brought us a drink, or simply passed by on her way through the cabin. Ordinarily, this Jekyll and Hyde act might have amused me, but my breasts were sore and I was grieving for Claudia. Jeremy was fond of my parents, who had moved into the house to look after them, but the baby was too young to understand that I had not left her for ever. I thought of her lying in her cot crying for me, waving her fat little fists, and then screaming in panic as strange faces bent over her, and had to concentrate hard on not crying myself. Pete would see tears as an admission of guilt, and although I did feel, as he ranted self-righteously on, quite remorseful and guilty because I could see that he really did believe I had cheated him, I refused to admit it. A stubborn, slow burn of anger was building within me. It was so unfair of Pete to attack me like this in public! He knew I was too inhibited to answer him back. Well, he needn't think he could bully me into submission so easily! As soon as we were alone, I would put my case, insist on a right of reply. Forming aggrieved responses in my mind stiffened and cheered me. I had been dreading this trip, I realised suddenly, and not just because I was miserable at leaving my baby but because I had been bored by the prospect of ten days alone with Pete. At least we had something to talk about now. We would not bore each other!

Years later, when I was planning my Women's Lib novel, I went to Morocco a second time and took Hilde with me. She had been ill again and was just out of hospital. We flew to Gibraltar, took the boat to Tangier, hired a car and drove across the Atlas Mountains to Tinerhir and Zagora, taking almost the same route as Elizabeth and Richard, the middle-aged couple I was writing about in my story. Both these Moroccan visits were a long time ago and my memories of the first one with Pete are often confused, not only with the journey that Hilde and I made together, but with my own fiction. I hear Pete speaking Richard's lines, see him wear Richard's clothes. And sometimes, half asleep, drifting, it seems that it was Pete and not Hilde with whom I drove over the mountains and through the Sahara.

A satisfying conceit for a writer, and in my book I made use of it, equating the harsh red dust, the empty, stone sky, with the dead marriage. (Which is not to say, as Andrew does sometimes, that writers are liars. If we are compulsive rearrangers, obsessional shapers of patterns, it is only to make the truth clearer.) But in fact, Pete and I never went to the desert. We were not entirely on holiday. Pete had been sent by his father to sign up an author, a woman anthropologist who had been living with a Berber tribe for two years and had turned in an interesting first chapter and a promising synopsis. While we waited for her in Marrakesh, in a luxury hotel with a swimming pool surrounded by palm trees, we passed the time quarrelling.

Our dialogue was confined, on the surface anyway, to Pete's complaint on the plane. I had not 'trusted' him enough to show him my novel, which meant I despised him; he was 'nothing and nobody' to me, just a comfortable house, a fat monthly cheque, a provider for me and my children. All this, I began to see, was true enough. I only denied it to keep the argument lively, and to avoid sexual contact. Once, when I was sleeping, Pete tried to rape me. I woke to find him on top of me, hot and sticky, clumsily thrusting. I fought him off, scratching and biting. He fought back, pinning me down to the bed, saying, 'You see, it's true what I say, I disgust you, don't I?' and laughing exultantly. He made no further attempt to have sex with me, but at least he enjoyed the fight. And perhaps I did, too. I remember that I felt different afterwards. Though I wasn't conscious of an awakening physical interest, there did seem to be a fresh and agreeably flirtatious edge to our verbal battles. If Sophie had not turned up at that point, there might have been, for a time, a new zest between us.

I had expected a middle-aged woman, tanned leathery by the fierce sun. Instead there was Sophie, blonde, frail and pretty – an exquisite nymphet princess out of an old fairy tale. It was hard to believe (as Pete kept repeating) that such a delicate creature could have survived this rough country. This was before the French left Morocco, and there had been riots, attacks on Europeans. Sophie smiled when Pete expressed his amazement. There were plenty of Berbers with light skins and light eyes; she had been safe with them, she had never been frightened. She spoke in a small, breathy voice and Pete had to lean close to catch what she said. 'So shy,' he marvelled. 'Like a shy little bird!'

There was no reason why Pete should not have invited her to stay with us when she came back to England. After all, as he argued (though I had raised no objection), we had had Hilde staying with us for months! Almost a year! If old Miss Loomis had not died so fortuitously and left her enough money to buy the lease of a flat, Hilde might still be with us. I said that I was quite happy for Sophie to come, but I didn't see what Hilde had to do with it, and Pete gave a sharp, incredulous laugh and looked at me strangely.

Tit-For-Tat was what he thought he was playing, though it took me some time to put a name to the game. Sophie came to England six months after we had met in Morocco, and I moved out six months later. Not because (or not only because) Pete was sleeping with her. He was discreet, going to her room late at night and always back in my bed by the time the children woke up in the morning. Apart from a certain social discomfort (I was afraid our nice daily woman would guess what was going on and spread gossip about our *ménage à trois* round the village) this arrangement did not trouble me much.

Or I pretended it didn't. I am not sure how I really felt, even now. I see that six months through a mist of grim greyness, like a damp, autumn mist, as a kind of endurance test. My natural prurience helped me to turn a blind eye to the details – Pete smelling of sex in the early mornings, Sophie's powdered diaphragm on the bathroom shelf. And fairness compelled me to see that I had no right to be angry. Indeed (so I told myself as I walked the children, shopped, dug the garden, fed my fat rabbits), I should be grateful to Sophie for taking over my unwanted duties so tactfully, for not making scenes and assuming other rights, a wife's privileges, just because she was being screwed by my husband. When we were asked out to dinner, she was happy to stay with the children; she never kissed Pete in my presence or showed, by a word or a look, that she had any claim on him when his parents, my parents, our friends, came to see us.

Perhaps it was being an anthropologist, used to strange tribal customs, that enabled her to disregard ordinary social conventions with such cheerful ease. Listening to her typing away in our spare room in the day time, I wondered about marriage customs among the Berbers, but did not like to ask. I imagined that sooner or later she would grow bored with Pete, as I had grown bored with him. When she had finished her book? Maybe she saw sex with Pete as a way of paying her rent while she wrote it. In the meantime, there seemed to be nothing I could do that would not make life disagreeable for all of us. To make a fuss would upset the children. It might even bring the situation out into the open. Our neighbours might get to know; Pete's mother and father; my mother and father. The thought of this made me sweat. It was as if the years had fallen away and I was back with Aunt Milly, listening to her hoarse and coarse whispers, trapped and humiliated. I would put up with anything to avoid this kind of exposure . . .

My acceptance hurt Pete. He was affronted by what he called my 'unnatural' behaviour. A 'real woman' would be putting up a fight, yelling and screaming. How could I be so cold and unfeeling? He had always known I was frigid, but had been 'decent enough' not to mention it. But could I not see that my calmness, my lack of concern, was the ultimate insult? He had treated me rottenly, he was prepared to admit it, ask my forgiveness, even send Sophie away and live with me 'sexless as a slug' for the rest of his days, but why should he bother when I obviously didn't care one way or the other?

These attacks were usually delivered in the early hours of the morning when he had returned to our bed. I would wake and find him beside me, propped up on one elbow, staring with smouldering eyes. I could see that he really was deeply bewildered, and sometimes I wished I could help him, ease his offended pride by some suitable demonstration of jealousy. The trouble was, he began to sound more and more absurd to me. None of his poses and protestations had any real meaning. When I asked, finally, 'Would you really send Sophie away?' feeling that I should test out this offer for the sake of the children, I knew, in my heart, that he had never intended any such thing, that it had just been a cunning move to make me 'fight back', play the game as he wanted.

He didn't answer for a moment. Then he smiled slowly. 'If you were prepared to be a real wife to me, I suppose I should have to consider it. But you never could be. I've said you were frigid, but that was politeness. I was being a gentleman! The truth is, you don't like men at all, do you? I don't know if you and Hilde were technically lovers, and I don't want to know, the idea disgusts me. But you brought her into my house and that drove the first wedge between us. A rift deeper and wider than my poor little Sophie!'

'Oh, poor Pete,' Hilde said, when she had stopped laughing.
  'Poor?'
'So keen to be taken seriously. He couldn't guess, could he, that you'd stick it out for so long, and then take umbrage over something so silly?'
'He called me a lesbian. That isn't silly.'
'Well, you're not. So it is. You don't think you're a lez, do you?'
'No. I love you more than I love Pete, but that's different. I mean, I don't want . . .'
'Of course not. Laura, darling, don't look so *worried*! It was just the worst thing a man like Pete could possibly think of. He must have been desperate.'
'To get rid of me?'
'No. That is, I don't *think* so, but then all I know is what you have told me.' She looked at me gravely, her dark, bright eyes steady. Then she said, 'I imagine, on his side, it was the only way he could explain why you were resistant to his irresistible charms. And on yours, that you wanted out. Only you didn't like to admit it, and couldn't see *how*! I mean, to leave your husband because he is being unfaithful, is so painfully obvious. You couldn't bring yourself to leave just for *that*, particularly since you weren't willing to oblige him yourself. You know how funny you are about sex. So you just sat tight and suffered in gloomy silence, waiting for him to produce something really outrageous that would give you the little extra shove that you needed.'
'Hilde! Am I really so awful?'
'Just devious, darling. Innocently and unselfconsciously devious!'
Her smile mocked me kindly. She looked so well, so rested and beautiful, it was hard to believe she had ever been ill. Young, too – as young as when we were schoolgirls together. It was as if the strong, capable Hilde who had rescued me from Aunt Milly, the Hilde I felt closest to and loved best, had been

returned to me; as if we had both been returned, by some strange trick, to our girlhood . . .

Though not so strange, really. The lease of Hilde's apartment – two floors in a converted house looking over a green square in Pimlico – had been paid for out of Miss Loomis's legacy. She had left Hilde her house and its contents and a small income from gilt-edged securities. The chairs we were sitting in, as we drank a bottle of Yugoslav Riesling, were Miss Loomis's chairs. We were surrounded by Miss Loomis's furniture. I recognised an ancient, high-backed sofa with silk tasselled corners, a slender, Regency bookcase, the big oak table beneath which we had slept during air raids, the Persian rugs on the floor, and felt that I was at home. Had *come* home. My children were sleeping upstairs, but Hilde and I were girls again, safe with Miss Loomis.

I said, 'I don't know what happened. I expect that you're right. I was bored with Pete. I didn't love him and I wanted to leave, but I was too scared. I was afraid everyone would think I was wicked. After all, I had married him for better or worse, and Sophie wasn't so very much *worse*. I mean, not in the context of the terrible things that do happen. Wars and earthquakes and people dying of cancer. I kept thinking – *What will Rosie say?* And – *My mother will be so angry*! This sounds terribly childish, but I'm being honest. My trouble is that I mind too much what people think of me.'

This seemed a craven confession, but the wine was making me brave. Hilde said cheerfully, 'Then you've done all right, haven't you? You've left your husband because he's treated you shamefully. Bringing his mistress into the same house as his wife and his children. That's straightforward, clear cut, *bad behaviour*, and everyone will be on your side, without question. *I* may know, and *you* may know that in fact you've come off best really, that you've got what you wanted, but no one else will know that unless you choose to be stupid and tell them. So you're in the clear, aren't you? Free as air!'

Although I laughed at Hilde's robust declaration, there were times, later on, when it made me wince inwardly. When Pete's father, that generous and courteous man, took me to lunch at Wheelers, ostensibly to see how I was going to manage financially, but really to apologise for his son, shame overtook me while I was eating my oysters and I felt impelled to point out that marriages were rarely broken by one partner alone and that Pete 'must have' some cause for complaint against me. But since delicacy (care for my father-in-law's feelings as much as my own) prevented me from explaining what I thought that cause might be, this attempt at a modified honesty merely increased, in his kindly eyes, my moral advantage. He touched my hand and said, gruff with emotion, 'I must say you are very magnanimous, Laura. I only wish I could get Pete's mother to see it.' He sighed and asked if I would like Lobster Thermidor to follow the oysters. I would have preferred Dover Sole, but I accepted the richer dish in the spirit in which it was offered: as compensation not only for Pete's treatment of me, but for his mother's behaviour.

Since I had left Pete, she had completely ignored me. This was not unexpected; in her view I had never been more than an appendage of her darling son, and so once we had separated I had ceased to exist for her. Or almost ceased to exist. Over lunch at Boulestin, just before our divorce became absolute, Pete told me that his mother never mentioned my name now. When she had to refer to me, she called me 'that woman'. Pretending to tell me this as a joke, Pete meant to hurt me; when I laughed he looked aggrieved and said that I had grown 'hard'. In answer, I smiled and ordered *foie gras*, and Partridge in Grapes as my main course. Meaner than his father, but not liking to admit it, Pete raised his eyebrows. Hard *and* greedy, too, his expression implied. I said that good food was a comfort in these otherwise uncomfortable circumstances but I would choose something cheaper if he preferred. Pained, he shook his head and changed his tactics. 'Poor sweet,' he breathed softly. 'How like you to try and put a good face on it! But don't be too brave! Not with me. Oh, I know I have been abominable to you, but I'm not an *absolute* monster! Don't you know how much it hurts me to know that my mother has hurt you?'

'I'm sorry,' I said, knowing that it was pointless to argue, to tell Pete that his mother had not hurt me at all, *could* not hurt me, since I was as indifferent to her as she was to me. (If I had once hoped, when Pete and I were first married, that she might come to like me, I had been disabused long ago.)

But, apart from Hilde, it seemed that no one would allow me to say this – or, indeed, to tell the truth about anything.

Not even Rosie and William.

'You would think,' Rosie cried, expressing her shock and dismay about Pete's 'frightful' mother, 'that she would at least think of her *grandchildren*. If she cares for them at all, how *dare* she behave so disgracefully to you! It would just about serve her right if you chose to turn nasty and prevented her seeing them.'

'Why on earth should I?' I said. 'In a way, it's an advantage to me when Pete takes them to his parents at weekends. She may not like me very much, but she's a sensible woman, she doesn't stuff the kids up with ice cream and sweets as Pete is inclined to, and I get a rest from them.'

Looking at William, Rosie shook her head sadly. They both looked at me with concerned admiration. 'Oh, Laura, you really are generous,' Rosie said. 'William and I have been so impressed, honestly! You've had a dreadful time, but you aren't vindictive, you haven't said even *one* bad thing about Pete!'

'I don't want to. I don't hate him. I don't feel vindictive.'

Rosie sighed softly. 'That's what so *good*, darling, so incredibly generous. Especially as you must feel, deep down, such *pain*.'

'No,' I said. 'No, I don't, really.' But Rosie sighed again, with such knowing pity, that I felt forced to qualify this honest statement to please her. She and William were being so kind, asking me to dinner alone so that I could talk over my troubles, making a fuss of me, even laying the table with candles and wine, as if for a party. The least I could do in return was accept the conventional wisdom, my role as the betrayed wife. I said, meekly, 'Well, perhaps, just a little,' sounding so false to myself that I was surprised to see Rosie's brisk, satisfied nod.

'Of *course* you do, you mustn't be ashamed of it. In fact, psychologically speaking, it could do you serious harm to bottle it up. William, my darling, give this poor girl some more gin!'

If there seemed to be a general conspiracy abroad at this time of my life to make me assume virtues I did not possess and deny those I had, my parents did not belong to it. Living in Kent, on my father's small pension, and fearing, perhaps, that they might have to support me, they believed what I told them but were unsympathetic.

'I hope you know what you're doing,' my mother wrote. 'Your father and I are afraid that having that little book published has gone to your head. You'll find that it isn't so easy to be independent. It's a hard world for a woman alone with two babies. You say, very grandly, that you have found you don't "love" Pete and want to be "free", that you feel as if you had escaped from some stifling prison into clean, open air, but it will be your fatherless children who will pay the price, poor Jeremy and poor little Claudia. Did you think of them when you flounced out of your husband's house? After all, whatever Pete had done to upset you, as long as you stayed with him at least they had a safe roof over their heads!'

This touched a raw nerve. I wrote furiously back. How dare she say, *whatever Pete had done*, when she knew the truth of the matter! Did she really think that being a mother meant you had to give up all your own human rights? Become a kind of serf, a bond slave who had to put up with anything? Well, I wasn't prepared to abandon my own life at twenty-six, and I was shocked that she seemed to expect me to. *It was, after all, the life she had given me!* (I was pleased with this argument, underlining it heavily, in case she should miss it.) And did she really think me so weak and incapable? Naturally, Pete would help keep his children, but I had already decided that I would only take the minimum for them, and nothing at all for myself. The money I had earned from the 'little book' she appeared to despise wasn't perhaps enough to support me entirely, but I had started another, and, in the meantime, I intended to find a job soon. Jeremy was old enough to go to a nursery school, and Hilde was not only prepared to look after Claudia, since she wasn't working herself at the moment, but she had provided the 'roof' my mother was so anxious about.

I was astonished by the fever of rage I felt, writing this letter. My mother's protests had not been so terrible, only showed a natural concern, why was I so angry? The emotion I felt was too strong to be mere childish pique because she had not backed me up without question, had not admired and encouraged me like Rosie and William. Had she, perhaps, frightened me, stirred up the dark terrors that were beginning to wake me up in the night, listening to the rain on the roof, the wind in the old, blocked-up chimneys of the converted Pimlico house, worrying about money, new clothes for the children, adding up sums in my head? My mother used to worry about money. I could remember her sitting at the kitchen table with pencil and paper, reckoning, contriving, always short at the end of the week. But I hadn't lived with my mother for years. How could she have passed on her fears to me? And why should I care so much what she said? I had cut loose from Pete. Why should my mother still bind me?

'I can't tell you, can I?' Hilde said. 'My parents are dead.'

Hilde's father had fought in the 1914–1918 war and been decorated for gallantry. He had the Iron Cross. Because of this, in the thirties, he had been safe for longer than most. Although he was moved to a department where he did not come into contact with the public, he was still employed in the civil service. A mild, patient man in his forties, he saw himself as German, not Jewish, and was sure that the Nazi 'madness' would pass.

In November 1938, Hilde was ten years old. On her birthday, her father came home in the afternoon and said he had been warned by a colleague that 'something was going to happen'. They were coming for the Jewish men. He said he would go to his widowed sister. He would be safe with her because her husband was dead. He tried to telephone his sister at the shop where she worked but when he picked up the receiver nothing happened. The telephone lines had been cut. Hilde's mother began to weep, and he told her not to be frightened; they would not touch the women and children. He would go and hide in the city; wait until his sister finished work and went home.

He took Hilde with him. They went to a cemetery. There were other Jews there. Cemeteries were safe places. The Nazis left people alone there. They respected the dead. 'Look as if you are mourning,' Hilde's father told her. They stood by a grave, in the cold, their heads bowed.

Later, on the way to her aunt's apartment, Hilde saw a synagogue burning. A crowd of people were watching in silence. Caught up in this crowd, Hilde and her father were forced to stand, watching. There was no sound except the roar of the flames and the crash of the rafters. Then, behind them, a woman said to her companion, 'I don't think this is really necessary,' and Hilde's father pressed his daughter's hand and smiled. 'You see?' he said when they were able to leave. 'It is only these madmen. The good German people do not approve of their behaviour.'

All the same, he began to arrange exit permits. It was still possible to leave, even though by this time the only countries that would accept them as a family were Peru and Northern Rhodesia. Out of an unreasoning, unreasonable hope, Hilde's father procrastinated. Hilde went with her mother to the library to read up details about these two foreign countries. In the evenings she heard her parents discussing the choice they should make in the calm tones of people deciding where to go for a holiday. On balance, since they both spoke some English, Northern Rhodesia seemed best. From Lusaka, they might be able to get to America or to England. When Hilde was offered a place in a train load of Jewish children going to London, they promised to follow her soon, or, if that turned out to be difficult, to send for her when they were settled. She cried at the station, leaning out of her carriage window to wave goodbye to them, and saw their hopeful smiles through her tears.

*   *   *

Hilde told me this in Morocco. We were at the beginning of our journey over the Atlas Mountains, sitting in a pine forest, eating a picnic lunch. It was cool in the shade but beyond the trees, the heat shimmered.

Hilde said, 'You know, for a long time I was angry with them for cheating me like that; for sending me off and then dying and leaving me. Then, when I stopped being angry, I felt worse, somehow. Guilt, obviously, but not only that. As if when they died they had taken part of me with them and left me empty and flat, like a shadow. I suppose having parents gives you an extra dimension. The same way that children do. You exist because they exist. I mean, you're not just yourself, Laura. You can see your past and your future in your parents and children. I have no one to give me this kind of reality. What I felt, this last time I was ill, was that I was alone on a bridge without the strength to move forwards or backwards.'

She had spoken slowly, pausing between each sentence as if she were dictating a testament. She sounded so desolate that I was frightened. She had only been out of hospital for two weeks. Was she going to be ill again? What would I do if she fell ill in the desert?

I said, 'Don't *brood*, darling,' and laughed boisterously. A false, asinine bray.

'I don't think I'm brooding,' Hilde said. 'Just trying to find out what has happened to me.'

She sat on the piney slope, drinking thin red wine out of a paper cup. She was just over thirty, a young woman who, when she was smiling, was still in the flower of her beauty. Frowning, as she was now, she looked sadder and older. There were lines round her mouth and her eyes were blankly dark as if she looked ahead and saw nothing.

I said, alarmed, 'You mustn't let your illness become your life, Hilde,' and she smiled at me then, her mouth curving warmly and sweetly.

'But it is my life, Laura. So I have to try and understand it, don't I?'

*   *   *

Schizophrenia is an illness that is diagnosed more often in America than in Europe. There is an American psychiatrist's joke: *If you want to cure your schizophrenic patients, send them to England.*

Statistics suggest (if you believe them) that at least one per cent of the world's population is schizophrenic and the incidence is the same in remote African villages as in our 'civilised' cities. Symptoms vary from loss of concentration, withdrawal, and apparent apathy, to wilder disorders: catatonia, paranoia, the hearing of voices, delusions of grandeur. The acute sufferers are in one sense the more fortunate. Their illness is plain to see, is clearly not idleness, some mysterious failure of will. If you believe you are the President of the United States, the Queen of England, or Napoleon, no one will tell you to 'pull yourself together'. (Even Rosie, who should have known better, once said this to Hilde.)

The word means 'splitting' of mind and is commonly misunderstood to mean a dual personality, a Dr Jekyll and Mr Hyde character. But the 'splitting' is more subtle than that. It is fragmentation, confusion, a disturbance of perception. The kindly old external world that most of us see is full of pitfalls and dangers, its messages scrambled. (When Rosie offers her a glass of wine, Hilde sees a poisoned chalice.)

There is no one, obvious cause. Environment, diet, genetic pre-disposition, biological factors – all may be guilty. Once it was fashionable to lay the blame on the family. The schizophrenic was the scapegoat, the innocent victim. Now (at the time I am writing) it is thought there may be some fault in the body chemistry, perhaps in the brain, in the basal ganglia. A malfunction, like Parkinson's disease. (If you give old people with Parkinson's too much dopamene, they may develop some of the signs of schizophrenia.) There are new drugs that seem to help the worst cases but for those who are not grossly disordered they are painfully crude in their action. While they reduce the anguish in the mind, they numb its sensibilities. When she takes her pills, Hilde complains that she feels like a 'zombie'. Most of the time she doesn't take them, fights her demons in her own way, and mostly she manages. Most of the time she gets up in the morning. Sometimes she has a job.

Some schizophrenics get and keep jobs, marry, have children, cling to normal life with astonishing courage. Others land up in the back wards of hospitals, or, when discharged, drift downwards socially. Gentle and aimless, they slip through the inadequate net of what is ironically called 'community care' – the failure of outpatient clinics, social workers, welfare departments, to keep in touch, co-ordinate, communicate, is a wicked parody of the illness that plagues them – and land up in doss houses, on park benches, in prison.

Hilde is one of the lucky ones. She has money. Before Rosie's father died he set up a trust fund that William administers for her, and there is also the small legacy that Miss Loomis left her. And, though she has no family, no parents, no husband, no children, she has friends who love her. She is hard to love sometimes. She can be unresponsive, cold as an effigy. A Snow Queen, frozen in ice. But when she laughs, the ice cracks; the eyes that look through it are the eyes I remember. She is still there, my sweet Hilde, whole and intact; not 'diminished' as the foolish doctors say, only imprisoned.

I was standing with Andrew outside Wormwood Scrubs, waiting to be let into the prison. I said, 'It's the waste that I hate.'

'Waste? Come on, don't dramatise, love. He'll be out in a few months. Perhaps he'll even learn something.'

He put his arm round me, hugging me close. There was one other couple waiting with us outside the gate, an elderly pair with anxious, pale faces, and about a dozen women. Mothers and wives. A girl in a short, old-fashioned, tight skirt, hair teazed into a high, blond, dry beehive, had already rung the bell. Andrew looked at her legs, at the curve of her buttocks, and said, into my ear, 'Try and be positive, now.'

Preparing himself for this moment, this ordeal, he had changed his pale green silk shirt for a blue woollen one and put on his tweed jacket before we left Rosie and William. Now (after that brief glance at the young woman's legs) he put his shoulders back and held his head high. When the small door in the big gate was opened, I saw his lips move as if he were praying.

I said, 'Andy?' and he looked down, tensely smiling. 'It's all right,' I said. 'They won't lock you up. And I was thinking of Hilde, not that idiot boy.'

Jeremy said, 'Thank you so much for coming.' He looked at us shyly. 'I mean, such a *bore*, on a Saturday.'

'Oh, not at all,' Andrew said. 'It fitted in nicely. I played tennis at Hampton Court, then we went to Rosie and William. Their Boat Race party. We took you once, didn't we?'

'I think so. I can't really remember. Did you win your game, Andrew?'

'Just about. Not a spectacular victory.'

'Good. You won, anyway.'

We all smiled politely. At one end of the visitors' room, a warder sat behind a raised desk. There were tables, one for each prisoner and his one or two visitors, and a counter where another warder sold coffee and biscuits. The effect was that of a schoolroom temporarily turned into a café; a coffee morning conducted for some educational purpose under the teacher's eye. We had been here several minutes and some of the visitors had already run out of conversation and were glancing at adjacent tables with furtive curiosity as at fellow conspirators. The young woman with the beehive hair was smoking a cigarette and talking vivaciously. Her husband (or lover, or brother) sat opposite and looked at her with an expression of sullen hunger. While Andrew talked at tedious length about the game he had played against the American banker this morning, I wondered if she had done her hair in this out of date style because it was how she had worn it when her man had been sent to prison. Or was it that time had stopped for her then?

Andrew pressed his foot against mine, warning me to stop staring so rudely and talk to my son. He said, 'You look quite well, Jeremy. You've put on weight, haven't you?'

He was plumper, his hair was shorter, his beard neatly clipped. He was wearing a slightly shrunken check shirt and blue jeans. He looked unusually clean.

I said, 'What's the food like?'

'Well. Let me see.' He screwed his eyes up. 'Smoked salmon and venison last night. Gulls' eggs and pheasant for lunch. I haven't seen the menu for dinner yet.'

Andrew laughed.

I said, 'Seriously, now.'

He shook his head, smiling. 'How's your book going?'

'Not too badly. Three-quarters done.'

'Good. How are Henry and Isobel?'

'Fine. Isobel still teasing Henry. You know.'

'Is Beatrice looking after them?'

'She has a language class and she's going out afterwards. But Granny is there. Andrew's mother.'

'They'll be playing games, then.'

'All afternoon, I should think. A games *marathon*. You know what she is!'

'It's kind of her to come, though,' Jeremy said with a touch of severity, picking up my snide tone and rebuking me for it. A nice boy. Thinking how nice, how generous and courteous, made my throat tighten. How could I, envious by nature, grudging, mean-spirited, have produced this good, obliging, magnanimous young man who never expresses a spiteful opinion, is kind to old women, chivalrous to young ones. Always ready to help unknown girls carry their heavy bags through the customs . . .

I said, with an uncertain snigger, 'Yes. Yes, of course, she's very good, really.'

He rewarded this reluctant admission with a bright grin. 'How is Claudia? Have you heard from her lately?'

'Not since you – I mean, she knows where you are. She rang from New York and said she would write to you. But she was just off to Mexico.'

'That's nice. Perhaps she'll send me a post card. Lucky old Claudia.'

Andrew said in a bracing voice (on the watch for self pity?), 'Well, she's got a rich husband. But you've had your share of travelling, haven't you?'

Jeremy blinked at this sharp reminder of how his last journey had ended, and then, nervously, smiled.

Andrew said, 'Sorry.'

'That's all right.' Close to tears suddenly (or perhaps he had been on the edge all the time, only masking it out of brave concern for us), Jeremy made an obvious effort, swallowing, crinkling his eyes at the corners, flashing his shy, doubtful smile from one to the other, as he always does if he fears we are angry or critical. Not that we have often been angry. But although we are proud of his unboyish tenderness, his lack of hostility, his gentle acceptance of whatever happens to hurt him, we have frequently exhorted him to stand up for himself, refuse to be bullied, hit back, encouraging him to think we despise and reject the very qualities in him that we secretly love and admire. It is no defence to say that we have only done this out of love, because we want to save him from pain and defeat. Watching him on this sad occasion, so neat and clean in his cheap prison clothes, so pitifully vulnerable, I felt limp with remorse for every unkind, thoughtless, remotely critical word I had ever said to him, every cruel impulse or action, and longed to make some splendid, expansive, perfect apology that would reassure him, reel the film backwards, allow us all to start again from the beginning.

What I actually said was, 'Rosie and William sent their love to you.'

'Thank you. I mean, please thank *them*. How are they? I'm sorry, I should have asked when you said you'd been to their party.' He looked worried. 'Is there anyone else I've forgotten? Oh, of *course*! How are Granny and Grandpa?'

'How are *you* is more to the point,' Andrew said quickly. 'We do want to know. That is, we think of you, and naturally wonder. What are the others like in your cell, for example?'

I thought this seemed a bit tactless, even brutal, rather like asking a hospital patient for humiliatingly intimate details of his condition and treatment, but Jeremy answered at once, with composure. 'Well, they change, don't they? At the moment, there is an ex-Borstal boy who's an awful trial, really. So bloody *tidy*! Up in the morning, cell spotless, bed stripped, blankets folded. It's the way he's been trained, of course, but it's hard on me and the other man who haven't had his advantages. This other bloke is a first offender, like me. Not quite like me, maybe. He, well, he killed his wife, actually. He found her in bed with their landlord and so he was able to plead provocation and only got eighteen months.'

'Oh God,' Andrew said.

Jeremy smiled. 'He's very nice. We play chess together. He usually beats me. He says, my trouble is, I lack the competitive spirit.'

'Ah!' Andrew said. 'Does he? Does he really? Well, well!' He leaned back in his chair, the tips of his fingers together. 'Let me see, you play chess, you eat these rich meals. What else do you do?'

'I make seats for motor cars. Seat covers, that is. I machine bits together. What they call *over-locking*.'

'Industrial training,' Andrew said brightly.

'Of a sort.'

'You don't think you want to take it up, though?'

'It depends what else offers. Though I'm getting quite good at it.' His smile broadened; he beamed at us mischievously. 'I mean, it might not be too terribly bad. To be a *good* Over-Locker.'

'Not at all,' Andrew said. Though he was trying hard to keep up his jovial tone, he was beginning to show signs of strain. Pretending to adjust his shirt cuff under his jacket sleeve, he glanced at his watch. 'In fact,' he went on, over-heartily, 'that's just the right spirit, the right way to approach things! When it comes down to it, the only way, really.'

'Better a good plumber than a lousy archbishop?' Jeremy offered demurely.

'Well, yes. An odd choice of alternatives, though.'

'Oh, they just sprung to mind.'

'Would you really like to be a plumber?' I asked, eagerly seizing on this suggestion as I had seized on others over the years, whenever he had shown some slight interest in future employment. 'A good plumber is never out of a job. And, anyway, it's *who* you are that's important, not what you do.

After all, you can always do your own thing in your free time, listen to music, write poetry . . .'

He was still smiling, but with a desperate playfulness, and his eyes were resigned and sad. I thought – *Why can't I keep my silly mouth shut? Think before I speak, leave him alone to find his own way? I love him as he is, don't I?*

He said, to please me, 'I think I would really like to do something practical. Perhaps I could be an engineer, like Granpa.'

I looked at Andrew. He was looking at me with an enquiring expression. I nodded, and he sighed.

He said, 'You ought to know, Jeremy. I'm afraid Granpa is ill. He's had another heart attack. Cardiac asthma. A left ventricular failure. Something like that. They've brought him through but he's very weak. A tired old heart, the doctor says. We're going to see him.'

'Oh. Oh, I'm sorry.' Jeremy looked at us helplessly. He said, 'If he does die, I won't be able to see him,' and the blood came up in his face. He looked defeated and shamed and I saw that we had played this quite wrongly. Either we should not have told him, or we should have told him at the start of our visit. Now we were going to leave him unhappy. Would the chess-playing wife-murderer comfort him?

A prison officer with ruddy cheeks and a curling moustache that made him look like a Victorian villain had appeared at the end of the room with a hand bell. He clanged it briefly, with some thoughtful delicacy. We all rose like schoolchildren at the end of a lesson. The girl with the beehive hair began to sob. Her prisoner put his arms round her.

'Tell him,' Jeremy said. 'Tell him – oh, I don't know. When I was little, he made me a wheelbarrow.'

'He loves you,' I said. 'He always loved you the best. He was always so proud of you.'

He shook his head weakly. We kissed him goodbye. He said, 'Thank you for coming.'

He stood, watching us go. Outside, in the yard, I said, 'Why do I say these stupid things? Oh, I should be struck *dumb*.'

'I didn't think you were particularly stupid. You need

experience to be a good prison visitor. We didn't manage too badly, and I thought Jeremy did *very well*.'

Andrew spoke with pride and relief and I saw he was thinking, at this moment, in conventional, sportsmanlike terms. His stepson had behaved 'like a man', and we were 'over this hurdle'.

There are times when it is easy to see that Andrew is his mother's son.

PART FOUR

Going Home

In Amsterdam once, after a lecture, on the way to the airport with twenty minutes to spare, I went to the Van Gogh museum and wept at a pair of battered old boots, worn with hard work and rough weather, but still stout looking and serviceable.

Vincent Van Gogh painted these boots in 1886, which was the year my father was born. When I saw this date in the catalogue, I thought of my father and hot, salty tears stung my eyes.

Apart from the date, there is no obvious reason why this famous painting should have made me think of my father. He does not resemble a pair of old boots. He is (or was then) a slightly bent but still strong and quite handsome old man, able, in spite of his heart condition, to dig his garden, cut his hedges and lawn, paint his house, mend his gutters and fences. But I am always strung up when I am forced into travelling and my heart becomes tender. Homesick and lonely, I accost strangers in hotel bars late at night, have long, soul-searching conversations, start smoking again, drink too much, grow sentimental, weep easily, am seized with wild remorse, morbid fears. *Ladybird, ladybird, fly away home, your house is on fire and your children alone*. Why did I leave them? Oh, my sweet, piteous babies! What a lousy mother I am, what an uncaring daughter, what an unloving wife! *Mea culpa*! I vow to do better in future, visit my parents more often, play with Henry and Isobel patiently, tell Andrew how much I love him.

The further away I get, the more emotional I become. And more accident prone. I develop stomach pains, aches in the joints, sinus trouble from flying, lumbago from hefting my baggage at airports. In Australia, leaving a party given to welcome me by two charming teachers of English, I fall into a

177

pothole on their unmade drive, hurting my back and twisting my ankle. My hosts pick me up, apologise for their pothole, carry me back into their warm, bright, beautiful house, bandage my foot, insist that I stay the night. It is too late to protest. The taxi that was to take me to my hotel has been sent away; their oldest son has vacated his bed and moved in with a brother. I am given a hot whisky toddy, lent a nightgown, and helped to my room which is small and boyishly untidy. A pile of books is awkwardly placed on the floor, near the bed. Because of my painful back, I decide not to move these heavy books, and because my ankle has made me clumsy, I trip over them, burning my left wrist as I fall on the metal shade of the reading lamp. An angry red weal that should be attended to, but it is so late by now, after midnight, and this kindly couple have already done so much for me, providing entertainment, clean sheets, a walking stick, aspirin and bandages. Well, there is no need to disturb them, of course. I may be lame but I am not paralysed and I know how to deal with a minor burn. I wait, nursing my sore arm, giving them time to undress, get to bed, before hobbling into the bathroom. I sit on the edge of the bath – and, at once, the plumbing leaps into noisy, throbbing life, the pipes banging and thumping, turning the sleeping house into an engine room. Quickly – resourceful, considerate Laura! – I fill a jug, turn off the tap. I will dampen a handkerchief, bathe my burn, be a nuisance to no one. Jug in one hand, stick in the other, I return to my room, fall over the books again, soak the bed with the water . . .

I do not understand it. At home I am nimble and neat, healthy and strong. I may not always sleep well, but I seldom get headaches or rheumaticky twinges, and my digestion is perfect. Why do I do it, then? (*Why did I come here*, I thought, sitting on that wet bed in Australia with my burned arm, my aching back, my twisted ankle, pondering my next move.) I could stay in my comfortable house, quietly writing. No need to accept invitations to conferences, universities, educational establishments, literary lunches, stand trembling before swimming rows of strange faces, appear on chat shows, smile until my face cracks at parties, stuff myself with codein phosphate against loosening bowels, valium for the night terrors.

Well, I like the applause. I am flattered to be asked and I find it hard to say no. Not just out of weakness. A missed opportunity is bound to be golden, and money comes into it. Self-advertisement is not just an ego trip; I am a pedlar, shouting my wares. Andrew might be struck down by a crippling illness. Men in their forties are entering the danger zone. Even if he keeps fit, our way of life is expensive (children, au pair girls, good clothes, theatres and whisky) and the house is always needing attention; paint, defective flashings, blocked drains, new wiring. We might want to build an extension. William has his fine studio at the top of his house, why should I not make a new office in an attic conversion? And, of course, above all, I have this work ethic, drummed into me by Miss Loomis but inherited, first, from my father, who left school at eleven, studied at night, took examinations, went to sea, fought in two world wars, working his guts out for his country, his family, and the P and O Company, but proudly, not slavishly, never complaining. Between voyages he came home with presents; hammered brass trays and ebony elephants with ivory tusks, embroidered purses and lengths of raw silk, painted boxes with secret drawers, toy Koala bears with black leather noses. But he never stayed long. He didn't dare leave his ship to spend time with his family. There were too many engineers on the beach, in the thirties.

I went to Amsterdam on the way home from Australia, to give a lecture arranged by the British Council, saw a painting of worn, leather boots in the Van Gogh museum, and (in a state of sentimental exhaustion induced by jet lag) wept for my father.

Driving down to Kent on the motorway, I thought – it is now I should weep. Now he is dying, in his ninetieth year, and all I can remember of his young manhood and middle age, the prime of his proud, working life, are the presents he brought me. Otherwise only glimpses, the briefest of memories, some of them shameful. Like the time when I was very small, five or six, and my mother took me to Tilbury Dock to welcome him home and I saw a dead pig in the water, floating belly up, bobbing and squeaking as it was pushed into the side by the slowly moving passenger liner. My mother said, 'Look at the big ship, Laura. Look at Daddy's ship coming in.' I looked up reluctantly (I had seen ships before; a dead pig was new and more interesting) and saw people at the rails, waving. I knew my father would be wearing a uniform. I saw a man in a braided, dark jacket and waved my hand hopefully. My mother laughed and said, 'That's not him, silly girl, he's down in the engine room driving the ship, don't you know your own Daddy?'

I said, to Andrew, 'I wonder what he was like as a young man. I can remember my mother. But it seems that I hardly knew him until he was old.'

Andrew considered. 'Rather dashing. An eye for the ladies and a good man for a party.' He smiled with amused affection. 'After all, he still likes his gin.'

This was not quite the picture I had been building up in my mind. I said, reproachfully, 'He worked so hard all his life. I wonder if he thinks now it was worth it.'

'I shouldn't imagine he goes in for that kind of speculation,' Andrew said, sounding surprised. 'He had a job he enjoyed, a career to be proud of. It's something to have been a good engineer, particularly when you've pulled yourself up by your bootstraps. All those years at sea, and then a good, long retirement, reading and making a garden. I hope when I'm his age, I'll be able to look back with as much satisfaction.'

The last time we had seen my father he had been sitting in his chair by the fire, a beret on his head to keep off the draught from the window behind him, reading the last volume of *The War At Sea*. He had been unusually dispirited. The week before (the week of his eighty-ninth birthday) he had fallen off the ladder while he was fixing a slate on the roof and twisted his ankle. 'I'm too old for ladders, they tell me,' he grumbled. 'But it's worse than that, even!' He held up his red, swollen fist. 'There's no strength in this any longer. I can't bang in a nail with this hand!'

Andrew said, 'Don't be too sorry for your father, love. He's had a good run. I should think he's ready to go.'

A good life to look back on. A merciful release. R.I.P. The living comfort themselves with these platitudes. I said, 'I can see it's convenient to think that.'

'He's proud,' Andrew said. 'He'd hate you to pity him. Of course one can't know how he feels, but that's something I'm sure of.'

It wasn't pity I felt, but a vast, unspecified sadness. Sentiment and nostalgia. When Jeremy was small, my father made him a wheelbarrow, using the tools he had fashioned himself when he had been an apprentice. A loving present for his first grandson, for the eager baby who toddled after him round the garden, calling, 'Wait-a me, G'anpa!' It was a long time before Jeremy could say his r's. My mother, the teacher, was anxious to teach him. 'Use your *tongue*, Jeremy, make it tickle the top of your mouth! *R*ound and *r*ound the *r*ugged *r*ocks the *r*agged *r*ascals *r*an.' And the little boy would try, solemn-faced, while we all beamed encouragement from our seats round the table until his little sister, Claudia, banged the tray of her high chair with her silver christening spoon to get our attention and shouted, 'Ragged rascals, ragged rascals,' enunciating the consonant perfectly and then rocking backwards and forwards with glee as we turned delighted faces towards her. 'See, Jeremy,' my mother said, 'it isn't so difficult, your sister can do it!' (Was this his first defeat, the moment when life began to turn its thumbs down?) Who can tell. What I remember, the point of this anecdote, is the happy pride on my parents' faces as they looked at their grandchildren, and the protective way my father patted Jeremy's hand and said, 'Jeremy has worked very hard today. He helped me dig the potatoes.'

I said, 'If he does die, what shall we do with my mother?'

'Do?' Andrew looked startled. 'She'll be all right, won't she? Of course she'll be lonely at first, we'll have to go to see her more often, ring her up regularly. Make sure she's all right financially, though we'll have to be tactful about it . . .' Assessing the extent of this new responsibility, he sighed a little. 'One thing – we must try to persuade her to keep the house warm enough. You know what a fresh air fiend she is!'

One winter morning, after we had spent the night with my

parents, we had gone to their bedroom to say goodbye before we drove back to London, and found their bed powdered with snow that had drifted in through the wide open windows.

I smiled at this memory. 'You won't change her. I don't suppose she will actually die of hypothermia. I was really thinking about that big garden. Dad's always been so obsessional. She's marvellous for her age, of course, but she's bound to slow up a bit.'

'She's only in her seventies,' Andrew said. 'Much younger than your father, don't forget. She won't thank you for turning her into a problem.'

'I didn't think I was,' I said, hurt. 'I was just looking ahead. I'm more worried about *your* mother, really. I mean, that awkward old flat! Up three flights of stairs and no lift.'

'She's quite active still, isn't she? Look at the way she plays with the children.'

'Oh, she's got plenty of energy. Enough to play ludo and snap with her grandchildren and think of new ways to annoy her daughter-in-law.' I laughed to show that this was not a serious complaint. (Or, if it was, that I didn't blame Andrew.) 'But the time will come, won't it? She has these giddy spells . . .'

Giddy spells, varicose veins, bowel troubles, arthritis. Irreversible decline setting in – though that was not, of course, how she saw it, always speaking of her physical difficulties as mere minor irritants, not here to stay. 'It's just the damp weather,' she explained when she told me that to deal the cards at long bridge-playing sessions, she had begun to wear calipers.

Perhaps all old people see their old age as temporary. If they feel a bit tired today, legs and backs aching, it is only because they have had a bad night. Tomorrow, when they wake refreshed from a good sleep and look in the mirror, the blotches, the wrinkles, the hairs on the chin will have vanished. These disfigurements are not, after all, visible to the mind's eye that still sees the young man, the young woman. Once, when Andrew was showing my parents a cine film he had taken on the beach the previous summer, my father got up from his chair and went to the screen, peering closely at a sunny picture of himself and Henry and Isobel, building a sandcastle, and said, in a tone

182

of innocent enquiry, 'Who is that old man with the children?'

And when we laughed, he shook his head, frowning, still puzzled.

I was shamed by this memory. How could we have laughed, been so thoughtless, so callous? I said, to excuse myself, 'It's odd, isn't it, how remote old age seems to be? I mean, you can look back and remember how you once felt and make a stab at understanding your children. But I have no idea how my parents really feel. Or your mother.'

'Just as well, probably,' Andrew said. Then he sighed. 'I suppose you're right about her flat. Well, I know you're right. I've just been reluctant to face up to it. I don't suppose she will listen, you know how stubborn she is, but maybe we ought to try and persuade her to leave it.' He glanced at me. 'Not to move in with us – don't worry, I wouldn't dream of putting *that* on you – but somewhere a bit nearer, so we can keep an eye on her.'

'Do you think she would move? It would be a terrible job. All that clutter.'

Andrew shrugged his shoulders. 'God knows,' he said.

Old age is Indian country. Uncharted and dark. Even when we have parents still living to provide us with maps; show us, over the rising hill, the rest of the road, we don't want to look. Fear, perhaps. Not of death so much as of all the indignities lying in wait for us; hardening arteries, weakening bladders, senility . . .

Rosie's mother is senile. Her Brighton flat smells like a rubbish dump. She orders huge quantities of food, cooks vast meals, lays places at table for her dead husband, her two, long dead, sons. Rosie drives down to see her three times a week, throws the wasted food in the bin, tries to calm down her mother who is furious because her men folk have not come home for their dinner. She rages against them. They are so selfish, so inconsiderate. The venomous hatred she appears to feel seems extraordinary in a woman who was such a loving wife, so devoted a mother. Rosie anguishes over this change in her. I suggest that her mother has, secretly, always been bitter. Like Rosie, she had once been a good pianist; perhaps she has always felt that she sacrificed her career to her family and now, in her mad old age, is at last free to express her resentment. It hurts Rosie to think that this might be so; it destroys the happy picture she has of her childhood. She reproaches me for inventing what she calls 'novelist's reasons'. Senile people are often aggressive, she tells me; all you can do is accept it and deal with it as well as you can.

As Rosie does. She is 'wonderful' to her mother, visiting her regularly, cunningly working the system to get the best out of the local authority – District Nurses, Home Helps, Meals on Wheels, commodes, incontinence pads. Rosie could afford to pay for a housekeeper and a resident nurse but she says that these free (or almost free) services are more reliable than private arrangements. She would prefer her mother to come and live with her – the house on the river is big enough, and it would save all the travelling – but the old woman is obstinate. She prefers her own frowsty lair. Besides, it would damage her grand piano to move it. She plays this piano in the middle of the night, loudly and badly, and the neighbours (who have Rosie's telephone number in case of emergency) ring Rosie up and complain, threaten to take legal action.

This has been going on for a long time; the background to Rosie's life for eight years or so, and Rosie is becoming exhausted. She is middle-aged, has a large house to run, and her medical practice. William is anxious about her. If her mother won't come to live with them, she must be certified, put in a hospital. But Rosie refuses to let her go among strangers. 'Why shouldn't I look after her? At least I love her and remember what she was like.'

The first time I heard Rosie say this, I was startled and shaken. She seemed to be echoing Elizabeth in my Women's Lib novel, who insisted on caring for a helpless old aunt, bathing and dressing and clearing up after her, even though her husband protested that the burden would cripple their future. But I wrote the book long before Rosie's mother grew senile, and Elizabeth, *I am sure*, was not modelled on Rosie. Nor on me, either. When I think of age and decay I am frightened; I remember Aunt Milly.

Perhaps Elizabeth is my 'good self', the woman that I would like to be. Thinking of my invented heroine as we reached the end of the motorway, I slipped into her skin and spoke through her. 'Of course we'll have your mother to live with us if her arthritis gets worse. We'll manage somehow, Andy darling, and the children are fond of her.'

At least my own fictions have taught me to express proper sentiments, even if I don't always feel them.

Hypocrisy is not one of my mother's failings. 'You've had a wasted journey,' she said as she opened the door. 'He's up and about again. I did ring quite early this morning to say you needn't bother, but you'd already left. Gone to a party, that au pair girl said, which seemed a bit odd to me, when you thought your father was dying.'

'It was only Rosie and William,' I said. 'It was on the way, and we didn't stay long.'

'You must have driven down pretty slowly, then!'

'Well, it saves petrol. And, you know Mother, there's an energy crisis!'

Andrew said, 'I had a business appointment I couldn't put off, that was really what held us up.'

'Oh, well, that's different. Something to do with your *job*! Laura, why didn't you say? I wouldn't have worried.'

'I said we couldn't get here until about five o'clock. I'm sorry, I should have explained, but it was all a bit complicated.'

She sniffed. I kissed her cheek. 'Darling, I'm so *glad* Dad is better! It really is marvellous!'

She smiled reluctantly. 'Well, *he'll* be pleased you've come, anyway!'

First round, I thought, to my mother.

'I'm an old fraud, it seems,' my father said cheerfully. He was wearing his favourite sweater, his beret on his bald head. Although he sat close to the fire and the room was warmer than usual, his hands felt cold. I took them between mine and rubbed them. 'You gave us a fright.'

'It was his water pills,' my mother said. 'He wouldn't take

them because they were making him go to the toilet too often. He was drowning in his own fluid, that's what the doctor told us. It won't happen again, I can tell you. If I have to force those pills down his silly old throat.'

She was looking bright-eyed, pink-cheeked, and pretty. The crisis had put her in a good fighting mood. My father was more simply elated. 'I must say, I thought I'd come to the end of my journey. About time too, probably, but I'm not sorry just at the moment. In fact, if you'd like a drink, Andrew, you could broach one of those bottles of whisky I'd put by for my funeral. There's a good malt. I might even have one myself.'

'No, you won't,' my mother said. 'And they'll want their tea first, if they've been drinking already. I've got the kettle on, it won't take a minute.'

When she had gone to the kitchen, my father said, 'I was ready, mind. Papers in order, everything ship-shape.' He looked at Andrew with his blue, sailor's eyes. 'You won't have to worry. I increased the insurance when the pension went up, and there's quite a bit in the bank. Your mother-in-law won't have to skimp, or go running to Laura.'

For some years now he had been looking ahead to my mother's future without him. Several autumns in succession he had said, 'If I go off this winter, your mother will have enough bottled tomatoes to last until spring.' Planning for her widowhood, he always spoke in the same tone of quiet satisfaction. 'I've moved that shelf in the kitchen, put it lower down so she'll be able to reach it.' Or, 'This suit will see me out, I'm not leaving your mother a lot of brand new gear to hand over to Tom, Dick and Harry, she can cut my things up for polishing rags, that's all they'll be fit for.'

Sitting beside him, I was choked with love, suddenly. I touched the sleeve of his darned, ancient sweater. 'You'll need some new clothes, Dad, if you've decided to hang on a bit longer.'

He shook his head, grinning. He still had his own strong, yellow teeth. 'You know what nearly finished me this time? Your mother tried to make me put on a new pair of pyjamas. It was fighting her off that brought on the attack.'

'Are you really all right now?'

'Old bones,' he said. 'Old bones. Don't waste your breath asking. How are the children?'

'Isobel and Henry wanted to come. To see Seaside Granny and Grandad! They sent their love to you. So did Claudia when she rang from New York. That was last week sometime, so of course she doesn't know you've been ill. She's in Mexico, now.'

'Always gadding, that girl. Jeremy, too. Is he home yet? I don't know what's wrong with them, Laura. You were a hard worker, settled down, stuck to it. They don't stick at anything, do they? This generation. Well, Claudia's a married woman. But Jeremy's different.'

'You spent your life travelling, didn't you? Perhaps he inherited your itchy feet!'

A frivolous and provocative remark. My father's face darkened but before he could speak Andrew said, quickly and soothingly, 'Jeremy's just back. He told us to tell you how sorry he was you were ill, and to ask if you remember that wheelbarrow you made him.'

'Indeed I do. I'm surprised he does, though. That was a good bit of wood, you don't get wood like that now. I had it off the chippy, gave him a bottle of Scotch for it, kept it by me all through the war. What happened to it, Laura? Has Henry got it?'

My mother, coming in with a tray, answered for me. 'Oh, I shouldn't think so, children don't hand on toys now. Today it's all easy come, easy go.'

My father winked at me. 'Well, it wasn't an heirloom, exactly. He had a lot of use out of it, didn't he? Helping his Granpa. Pity you didn't bring him down with you, Laura. I'd have liked to see Jeremy. Still, he's young, isn't he. At his age, I daresay he's got better things to do with his time.'

Yes, I thought. Oh, well, yes. Like keeping his cell clean and playing chess with a murderer. I smiled at my father.

Andrew said, clearing his throat, 'Should you give your mother a hand, do you think? Or shall I?'

*　　*　　*

The kitchen was full of the scent of geraniums, massed in pots on the window sill, and of steam from the kettle. 'Don't get in my way now,' my mother said. 'I know I'm a bit slow but I like to do things my own way. If you really want to be useful, you could chop up that bit of parsley. It's not much at this time of year, but all right for decoration. Don't cut yourself, though, that knife's sharp!'

'Ham sandwiches,' I said. 'Lovely. Andrew likes ham.'

'I can cook something if you'd prefer it. Seems a long way to come, just for a cup of tea and a sandwich. I hope Andrew doesn't mind. All that petrol! As you said, so expensive!'

'I didn't say it was expensive. That is, the expense isn't relevant. I said there was an *energy crisis*. And of course Andrew doesn't mind.'

'Well, he wouldn't say if he did. He's a good man, Laura.' Measuring the tea into the pot, she looked at me sternly. 'I hope you know how lucky you are!'

She often makes this remark and I always resent it. Does she really hold me in such low regard? I said, laughing, 'Am I such a bad bargain?'

'Oh, come on now, don't pick me up!' Her colour rose, her eyes sparked; she was ready for battle. I thought – we shouldn't have this aggressive relationship, mothers and daughters should be kind to each other . . .

'I was only teasing, darling,' I said. 'I know what you mean.' I thought of something to say, a peace-offering. 'You know, once, before Claudia married, I saw her by chance – I was driving through London, and I stopped at a traffic light, and there she was, crossing the street, walking away, wearing a tiny black leather jacket with silver studs, and shiny black satin trousers so tight that she might just as well have been naked. No shoes on her feet, her lovely, long hair flying loose, and I thought – well, what came into my head, was that Meredith poem. *Would that this wild thing were wedded.* Old-fashioned, un-feminist – but somehow perfectly natural. I suppose all mothers feel their young girls are so vulnerable.'

She was looking perplexed. 'But you weren't a girl when you married Andrew, you were a divorced woman with children.

And drinking too much. That used to worry me. I was grateful to Andrew for putting a stop to it.' She poured boiling water into the tea pot, narrowing her eyes against the steam; then covered the pot with the bright woollen cosy that Isobel had knitted for her last Christmas. She said, 'Do tell Isobel that we're using her cosy.'

'Yes, of course. She'll be pleased.'

'She's a dear little girl. She reminds me of you at that age. So sharp and eager and loving.' She sighed (thinking of the drunken divorcée I had grown into?) and went on, 'I'm sorry if I was irritable when you arrived. I was in a silly state. I was afraid something might have happened to you, an accident on the motorway, and earlier on, last night, when Dad seemed so sick, I was afraid you wouldn't come at all . . .' She spoke in a soft, plaintive voice, and then, more crisply, with a little, sly, glancing smile, 'After all, you didn't come when Cora was dying!'

My head spun with shock. How long had she been hugging this grievance? I said, 'Mother! You know why I didn't! I was stuck with Aunt Milly!'

'Milly? What did she have to do with it?'

'She was ill. Don't you remember?'

She shook her head, pulling the corners of her mouth down.

I said, 'She was so ill, she had to go into *hospital*. That was why I went to live with Miss Loomis.'

My mother was watching me with her brows drawn together. I couldn't decipher her doubtful expression. Perhaps she really didn't remember. Had I told her? She had been ill. Cora had died. I was afraid to upset her. Why couldn't I say this? I had done nothing wrong; the rational thing, the sensible, obvious thing, would be to explain what had happened.

I shook my head ruefully. 'I really did have an awful time with Aunt Milly.'

'Oh, you do exaggerate, Laura. She was just a poor, sick old woman. I know it wasn't an ideal arrangement, leaving you with her, but it was the best I could make at the time. I had a lot on my plate. You were old enough to understand that, I'd have thought.'

Now she was looking indignant. I said, helplessly, 'I know. I'm not blaming you.'

'It sounds very much like it.'

'No. *Honestly*, Mother! The last time you saw her, before you went to the sanatorium, she was just old and spiteful and grouchy. But she got very much worse. She went *mad* . . .'

It was absurd to be having this conversation all these years afterwards. And absurd that I should feel so strung up and nervous because my mother had seemed to attack me. Poor soul, she must have had such a sad, anxious night, lying awake, afraid that my father was dying, thinking of that other death, her dead baby daughter, that pathetic little ghost from the past, old wounds and memories churning. I should be sympathetic; think of her, not myself. I was grown up, for God's sake!

I said, 'I'm so sorry, this is so stupid. Of course we are bound to remember things differently. It isn't worth quarrelling over.'

'I'm not quarrelling, Laura!'

'Well. Perhaps that's not the right way to put it. We just seem to get our wires crossed . . .' The reason for this was suddenly clear to me. Eagerly – *foolishly* – I hastened to tell her. 'Perhaps it's because we don't see enough of each other. Or didn't when I was growing up, anyway. After all, if I'd lived at home when I was adolescent we'd have had silly spats and got over them. Worked *through* them to a proper adult relationship!'

'I'm sure I don't know what you're talking about,' my mother said stiffly. 'It may be very clever, but it sounds like a load of old claptrap to me. As for poor Milly, if she did go off her head a bit at the end, I can't see why you should get so worked up about it. Madness isn't something that worries you all that much, is it? All those years you looked after Hilde, put her first, before your own husband, before your own children! Still, that's all past and gone, I don't want to discuss it. As you said, we see little enough of you. I'm sorry if you feel you had an unhappy, neglected childhood, but there was a war on, if you recall, and a lot of us had to put up with things that were not to our liking.'

'I didn't *say* that. And, Mother . . .'

She smiled. 'The tea will be getting cold, dear. If you would just bring the sandwiches, and the hot water jug. And, if you want to please me, put on a smile for your poor father!'

She picked up the tea pot and sailed out of the kitchen, a small, sprightly, straight-backed, victorious figure. Vanquished, I followed her, seething and muttering, longing to answer back, put the record straight.

I am still a child in my parents' house; a child seeking approval.

Someone had to 'put Hilde first'. The war had done her more harm than the rest of us. Sometimes at night she wept and banged her head against the wall. The partitions in the converted old house were thin and her weeping and banging woke up the children. 'Has Auntie Hilde got toothache?' Jeremy asked. 'Poor Auntie Hilde.' And, once or twice, crawling into my bed for comfort, 'Mummy, I don't like it here with Aunt Hilde crying.'

He was nervous of Hilde. She was nervous of him, too; watching him warily when he was in the same room, shrinking when he came near. She didn't like to be touched, fearing contamination of some kind, and a robust and bouncing small boy was a threat to her. Jeremy recognised her fear, though not, of course, the reason for it. He kept away from her, playing quietly with his toys in the bedroom, carefully placing himself on the opposite side of the table at meal times, eating in silence, occasionally glancing up timidly, shyly peeking at Hilde with a wide, troubled gaze. Athough I was sorry to see him so crushed, so apprehensive and docile, his lonely and bewildered air began to madden me.

'If you look like that all the time, as if you were scared someone was going to hit you, then someone might do just that,' I muttered in a low, savage voice, undressing him roughly one evening, hurling him into his bed. When he wept, I clasped him remorsefully, a lump in my own throat. 'Don't cry, darling, Mummy didn't mean to make you cry.' (Oh, but I did; tears allowed me to comfort him!) 'Hush,' I said, rocking him. 'Hush. Don't wake Claudia.' He whispered, warm lips on my neck, 'Why don't Aunt Hilde like me? Does she think I've got chicken pox? Is she afraid she will catch it?'

I was astounded by his perspicacity; his grave, childish logic. 'Something like that, my lovely. Aunt Hilde does like you, it's just that she's been ill and it's made her shy. You're shy sometimes, aren't you? So don't worry, be kind to poor Hilde, be Mummy's kind boy.'

And he answered bravely, lips quivering, 'I'll try to be, Mummy.'

Luckily, he was at school in the daytime, and Hilde seemed to find Claudia much less alarming. Though she handled her gingerly, never kissing or cuddling her, I was confident that she was capable of taking charge of her.

Perhaps I deceived myself because it suited my plans. Rosie thought so; she said I was 'ruthless' – softening this rebuke with a kindly laugh and saying that she could see I had to be, in the circumstances. All the same, she couldn't help feeling that to expect Hilde to look after Claudia while I worked at the sub-editor's job Pete's father had kindly found for me, was too much responsibility to put on her shoulders. 'Besides,' Rosie said, 'she should be starting to make a life of her own, not living in your shadow.'

Rosie needed a receptionist in her practice. Surely Hilde could manage that? It would be a part time job, just a few hours a day in sympathetic surroundings; much less arduous than a demanding small baby, and it would mean she got out, met new people.

'New people frighten her,' I said. 'Claudia doesn't. Babies don't expect conversation. And Hilde does go out, she wheels the pram round the park every afternoon.'

'Well, Hilde wants to help you, of course,' Rosie said. 'And I can see that it's convenient for you just at the moment. But don't you think, if she's capable of looking after a baby, that it would be better for her to have one of her own? Some nice, understanding man. Of course one would have to be careful to explain her background and history, but she's still very beautiful. A good marriage would give her security.'

I said, 'She's secure with me. Honestly, Rosie, I'm not making use of her, if that's what you're trying to tell me. I agree, it would be marvellous if she met someone she could fall in love with, but I don't think she's ready. Just at the moment, she's best as she is. And I believe she is happy.'

We were both happy, I thought. My job was unexciting but I had a reasonable salary, enough to pay a daily woman to clean the apartment and help Hilde with Claudia. After that conversation with Rosie, I asked the woman to stay two extra hours and watched Hilde closely. If she seemed tired, I had enough energy for both of us. I shopped in the lunch hour, left the office early enough to fetch Jeremy from his nursery school, cooked supper, put the children to bed. Most evenings I worked on my novel while Hilde sat, curled up in one of Miss Loomis's chairs, chain smoking and apparently dreaming. When I asked her if she would like to go out, she shook her head lazily. Sometimes she picked up a book but put it down after a page or two. She said, 'I don't want to read, or do anything, really. There's so much going on in my head. Lighted rooms and people talking.'

'Does it bother you, my sitting here typing?'

'No. It's like a friendly voice chattering. It keeps the lights on.'

'How do you mean?'

She looked at me. 'I don't have to tell you, do I?'

'No. No, darling, of course not. I'm sorry.'

She laughed. 'I mean, I don't have to tell you because you know, don't you? Outside this room where we are, the house is dark, isn't it?'

Sometimes, when I wake at four in the morning, alert to the dangers about me, cracking pipes, rotting floors, crumbling plaster; when I climb the stairs to the derelict attic and listen to the happy, unheeding voices in the safely lit room beneath me, I wonder if it is Hilde's 'dark house' I am visiting; if the locked room on the right of the hall, the room that I am so frightened of, is the one she withdraws to when she can no longer endure the light and the laughter.

My mother said she was mad. She accused me of 'making a choice between my children and a madwoman'. It seemed to me that I made the only decision I could; that I had no real choice at all.

Sophie had left Pete. One Saturday morning when he came for the children, I asked how she was and he said, 'Sophie?' in a bemused, incredulous voice as if he had no idea who I meant. (Or, if he did know, thought it cruelly indelicate of me to mention her.) A year later, eighteen months after our divorce, he married most suitably. Poppy was fresh out of drama school, a tall, handsome girl with a magnificent voice range, an upper class, wealthy background (Pete's mother, Pete told me, 'adored' her), an uncritical mind and an emotional nature. The first time we met she informed me in an awed, throbbing whisper that Pete was 'terribly sensitive'. She was not very bright but she was friendly and kind and good with the children. She bought a Labrador puppy for Claudia, a palomino pony for Jeremy, and though at first I was angry and jealous, it was clear that these gifts were not wicked devices to win their affection and wound me, nor the only reason they looked forward so eagerly to the weekends they spent with their father and cheerful young stepmother, and returned to the flat, to Hilde and me, so reluctantly.

When Hilde had to go into hospital, I was grateful to Poppy. 'Of course, sweetie,' she cried when I rang her, '*of course*, I would *love* to look after them for you, they are such dear little people, and it would be *super* for Pete to have a chance to be a real Daddy instead of a sort of luxury Uncle.' And, when Hilde was better, and we had come home from Morocco, and I went to fetch them, they looked so bright-eyed and happy, so healthily rosy with good food and clean, country air, that I was ashamed of my hurt, sullen heart. I watched them say goodbye to the puppy, to the pony, to Poppy. Claudia cuddled up to me in the train, singing little songs under her breath, but Jeremy sat apart, staring out of the window. He sighed, several times, very deeply, and later, back home, after supper, when I put him to bed, his tears fell. I put my arms round him and he twisted away from me. 'Poor Daddy and Poppy,' he said. 'They will miss us so badly.'

I spent most of that night writing to Pete. I took the letter to his office on my way to work the next morning. The moment he got in, he rang me. 'Laura, that was a beautiful letter. So touchingly, wonderfully generous, it almost made me fall in love with you all over again. I want you to know that I really do understand and appreciate the sacrifice you are making . . .'

He went on for some time, praising me in lush terms for my unselfishness, my fine, noble spirit, until I shouted at him, 'Bugger you, Pete, I can't give them what you can, that's *all*,' and slammed down the telephone.

I took them the next day. I packed their clothes and their toys, bundled everything into a taxi. It was a warm, late spring day; in the garden of the house where I had once lived with Pete, the lilac bushes I had planted were blooming. Poppy opened the door, her large, lovely eyes moist with pity, her voice sunk to a deep, tragic contralto. 'Oh, Laura, what can I say? I promise you, I'll do my best for them.' She gave me a drink (gin again – how I hate gin!) and left me in the sitting room while she carried the cases upstairs. Jeremy followed her. I could hear his feet scampering and his excited, shrill laughter. I smiled at Claudia who was standing beside me, her fat little thumb in her mouth, and she turned a deep, painful crimson, climbed on my lap and hooked her arm round my neck fiercely. I felt nothing. I was numb. I disengaged myself gently, kissed her and left her.

She was four years old then, a strong, healthy child, determined and wilful. I believe she was happy with Poppy and Pete who have loved and indulged her. But now she is twenty-three, married to a rich man in his late thirties who left his wife for her, she refuses to see his young son, his young daughter. She says, 'Children belong to their mother.'

I knew this would be the general view. But I had not expected Rosie to take it.

She said, 'Laura, how can you bear it? Your sweet, lovely children.'

'Pete's children, too. His turn, I thought. And they'll be better off, Rosie. A garden, dogs and ponies and bicycles, and a proper house, not a stuffy flat, cooped up with Hilde and me.'

'You don't have to live with Hilde.'

'I don't have to,' I said. 'But I do.'

'Suppose she gets married! Oh, Laura . . .'

'I don't understand you.'

'You'll have given up your children for nothing.'

'They don't belong to me.' I looked at Rosie, holding her first child, her baby girl, and thought about Claudia. The small, milky bundle of physical pleasure. My breasts ached with the memory. I said, 'It's only when they're tiny that you feel they are part of you. You'll find that out later. They become separate people.'

She shook her head, holding her baby protectively close. Over its downy skull, her sweet brown eyes reproached me. 'I'm not criticising you, Laura. It's just that you've always seemed such a warm, loving person, such a good mother, you know how much William and I have always admired you. But I can't understand you now. How could you let them go?'

'Pete let them go, didn't he?'

'That's different. Don't you see that it's different?'

'No. It's only social conditioning. Do you really think Pete didn't miss them? I know he's a frightful old moaner, but he does have some genuine feelings.'

'You didn't send them back to him for his sake, though, did you?'

'Not for mine, either, if that's what you mean. Not even for Hilde's. It was difficult when she was ill, of course, she worried the children, and they worried her, but she's better now, we could manage. But it's not a good life for *them*, Rosie!'

Why should I have to explain this, examine myself, when for once in my life I truly believed I had no murky motives?

I said angrily, 'Poppy is always there. She has time for them. I have to work, fit them in, take them to the dentist, buy shoes, get them to and from school, always hustling them backwards and forwards with an eye on the clock. It's a lousy life for them.'

'Is your work really more important than they are?'

'It's what we live on.'

'You could make Pete support you. Then you'd not only have time for your children, you'd have more time for your writing.'

'Why should he? I'm not his wife any longer. It's irrational to expect him to pay a wage for looking after his son and daughter when he has a better home for them than I can provide. And to suggest I should take his money so that I can get on with my novel is a kind of blackmail, isn't it?'

'I didn't mean it like that. I was just thinking of a way to persuade you.' She sighed. 'Poor little Jeremy. Poor little Claudia.'

'They are very fond of Poppy. She loves them, I think. Pete loves them, I *know*.'

'Nothing can replace a mother's love,' Rosie said.

Well, maybe. *My* mother said, 'I believe you think you are doing the right thing, but you can't expect anyone else to see it that way. So don't come to me expecting my sympathy. I'm sorry for you because I feel you have made a dreadful mistake, handing your children over to Pete like a couple of unwanted parcels, but that's as far as I'll go. In most people's opinion, I think you'll find, a woman who abandons her children has sunk very low. I know about Hilde, how responsible you feel for her, but I've already told you that I'm afraid you made the wrong choice, so I'll say no more now. I only hope, for your sake, that you'll feel it was worth it, that Hilde can comfort you.'

I wanted to say, *You don't hope that, you hope I'll be punished!* Or, *It was Hilde who came to my rescue when you abandoned me to Aunt Milly!* But both these remarks seemed unfair, below-the-belt blows, and so I said nothing.

The restraint (or the masochism) of my generation sometimes amazes me. Listening to friends and acquaintances (by which I mean not only Amanda and Rosie and William but many other friends and acquaintances of our age who do not, for the sake of narrative flow, appear in these pages) it seems we share the same common ground. Criticised by our parents, attacked by our children, we hold our fire, seldom fight back as we could do.

It has something to do with the pace of change. Our parents were disciplined into believing that you did what you had to, not what you wanted, that the future was worth waiting for, that you respected your parents and worked hard for your children. We have some of that discipline, though the strain is watered down, weaker, and in most of our children it has disappeared altogether. Trying to provide a frail bridge between the old and the young, protect the one from the other, we accept absurd handicaps in the family game.

Andrew's mother, my parents, have often run down the two older children. Jeremy's hair and beard are too long, he has no job, no degree, is an 'idler', a 'drifter'. Why don't we do something about it? Claudia, until she got married and became, in their view, her husband's responsibility, was 'lazy' or 'sulky' or 'wild'. Andrew and I have mostly sat, meekly listening, only occasionally and very gently defending. Why don't we shout back at them, tell them to mind their own bloody business? Do they think that because they are old, on the brink of the grave, they have special privileges, can say what they like? Are they trying to hurt us by insulting our children? Why don't we answer instead of bottling up anger, biting the bullet?

Oh, the old are so vulnerable. And perhaps we are cowardly. Once, when Andrew's mother was taunting Jeremy, rasping on about his dirty clothes, the smell of his feet, his generally unwashed appearance, Andrew lost his temper and turned on her. 'At least the boy is *polite*. He doesn't tell you that your wrinkled skin, the smell of your powder, are disgusting to *him*.' She burst into such a storm of shocked and pitiful weeping that although with part of my mind I was cruelly exultant, I put my arms round her with horrified sympathy and shouted at Andrew. How could he be so brutal to his poor mother!

Good-hearted, sensitive Laura! And yet, when my father (older than Andrew's mother, kinder, more reasonable) embarked on the subject of Jeremy while we ate our ham sandwiches, roaring rage suddenly filled me. I found myself thinking – *It would shut him up, wouldn't it, if I told him his long-haired layabout grandson was also a jail bird? Give him something real to agonise over!*

My father was saying – reflectively, mildly – 'I know you don't like to admit it, but he must be a disappointment. You get to an age when you look forward to handing on the torch to your children. As I see it, Jeremy is only too likely to chuck it away. It's a pity. I wish I understood. Why doesn't he get a job? I'd have thought any job would be better than nothing. You'd think he'd want to get off your backs, make you proud of him!'

Andrew's face was white. He said, 'Of course I wish Jeremy could find a job he enjoyed, but I'm not in the least disappointed in him because he hasn't found one yet. I happen to think we should value people for what they are, their personal qualities, not for what they do. It's the only way if you want a decent society. If you reflect for a minute about how we treat our old people, you'll see what I mean. Once they're retired, no longer working, we disregard them, pay them a pittance. They are no longer profitable, they don't produce anything, so they can be thrown on the scrap heap.'

My mother sat indignantly straight in her chair. 'I know old age is a sin, but I never expected to hear you say it, Andrew!'

I said, 'Oh, mother, don't be *ridiculous*! Andrew didn't mean that. In fact, he meant just the opposite! He was just trying to show you what Dad's argument really *meant*! Jeremy isn't a useful *machine*, any more than you are. We don't attack you for not working!'

'I should hope not. I should think we have earned our retirement. Certainly your father has. It's a fine thing, I must say, to know you despise him for doing his duty! When he was Jeremy's age, he had been at sea for eight years! He knew what work was! Jeremy has never done a hand's turn, and listening to you and Andrew, I can begin to see why. You should be proud of your father, not set him down in this thoughtless way, just because you don't like what he tells you. After all, if what you are saying is that everyone is entitled to be treated with dignity, then *we* have a right to speak our minds and be listened to, haven't we?'

Andrew smiled at her. He has a special, sweet, flirtatious smile for my mother. 'Of course you have, love. I'm sorry if I upset you. Perhaps we are a bit over-protective of Jeremy.'

I said, 'If we are, we haven't exactly been over-successful!'

My heart was pounding. In my mind, sometimes, I have calm, controlled conversations with my mother and father. We sit round the table in a warm, lighted room, eating and drinking and talking. I smile at them and they smile back lovingly. There is no tension between us, no hidden anger, no secrets. I speak of my worries unguardedly – I have nothing to conceal from these two kindly, beaming old people, whose role in my self-centred fantasy is to listen, advise and console me.

Instead, when I am with them, my pulse thuds unevenly, my skin prickles. I brood over slights, real or imagined, burn with silly frustrations, say foolish things, cheat them by lying to them. As I was lying then, hiding the truth about Jeremy. But how could I have told them? My father was too ill, too near to his death.

He said, sounding tired, 'It's because I do value the boy that I don't like to see him muck his life up. I expect he'll find his feet sooner or later. Only it needs to be sooner if I am to see it.'

I said, laughing, 'Oh, Dad, don't be *morbid*!'

No one answered me. My father raised one of his bushy eyebrows that used to be wholly black but now had long, stiff white hairs bristling out, like prawn's whiskers. My mother was frowning, seeking, it appeared, some happier topic. She gave a little cough, to mark the transition. 'What are you working on at the moment, dear?'

I laughed again, awkwardly. 'Well, you know, a novel . . .'

Her mouth pursed. What else would I be working on? She said brightly, 'Is it going all right? What's it about this time?'

'Oh. People. A married couple. Their children, their parents, a day in their lives. How people keep going. I'm sorry, I'm bad at explaining.'

Andrew came to my rescue. 'She doesn't like talking about work in progress. She's superstitious about it.'

'You mean I shouldn't ask?'

I said, quickly, 'No, mother. It's only that until it's actually *there*, down on paper, I'm nervous. Afraid that it won't work out as I want it to. Or that if I talk about it too much it will slip away somehow. Perhaps that's superstition. I don't know.'

'It's going to be quite good, I think,' Andrew said kindly.

They all smiled at me encouragingly; my kind husband, my mother, my father.

My mother said, 'Well, it keeps you busy, that's the main thing. And there aren't many careers that fit in so conveniently with running a house, looking after the children. Not like teaching.'

'No. It's a nice occupation for a married woman.'

My mother looked at me suspiciously. My father said, 'There aren't many who'd stick at it as you have done, Laura. I admire you for that. It must take some discipline. Though sometimes I think you should branch out a bit. Write a book like *The Caine Mutiny*.'

Since *The Caine Mutiny* was the only novel he had ever read with real enjoyment, this advice was seriously offered.

Andrew's eyes lit with tender amusement. 'Unfortunately it's been written already.'

'Well, I suppose she hasn't the background,' my father said thoughtfully.

He yawned, leaned back in his chair, closed his eyes. We watched him, for a moment, in silence. Then my mother gave the little cough that heralded a change of subject, but before she could speak, the telephone rang in the hall. She started to struggle up (when she has been sitting a while, her knees stiffen) and Andrew said, 'Shall I answer it for you?'

She sank gratefully back. 'If you would, dear. It's bound to be Arthur. He rang last night when the doctor was here. Just tell him all's well and say that I'll ring him tomorrow.' As Andrew left, closing the door after him, she smiled at me. 'Oh, the telephone! A blessing in one way, a curse in another!'

'Who's Arthur?'

'Dad's cousin. Well, second cousin. You won't remember him, Laura, he used to keep a fish shop in Hackney. We never saw much of him when we were young, it's only just lately, since his wife died, that he's been getting in touch. She was a great big bullying woman, led him a frightful dance, but of course now she's gone he's busy re-writing history. Poor old chap, he's a bit of a nuisance, the way he runs on, extolling her virtues. Always when you're busy, in the middle of something. I have to keep telling myself it must be hard to find yourself alone after a lifetime . . .' She looked at my father who appeared to be fast asleep now, beret crooked, mouth slightly open, and gave a little, sad sigh.

I whispered, 'Is he all right?'

'Oh yes, dear. He often drops off like that for a cat nap. In fact he sleeps more peacefully in that old chair than he does in his bed. Sometimes I hope . . .'

She stopped and sighed again, watching my father sleep, massaging her knees under her woollen skirt.

I knew what she hoped. I was afraid she would tell me. I said, 'Are your knees hurting?'

'Just a twinge now and then, nothing worth talking about. I was going to ask you something when Arthur telephoned. What was it? Oh, memory, memory!' She gave the side of her head a sharp tap and laughed. 'There! I know now. Funny how a bit of a knock often works. Shakes the brain up, gets the rusty cogs working. I was going to ask – how is Hilde?'

The question, and the conciliatory tone in which she asked it, was an olive branch. I accepted it cautiously. 'She's very well at the moment.'

'Still in the same flat?'

'Yes. She's got a lodger now, a music student. A young man who plays the French horn. They get on very well, go to concerts together. She cooks a bit for him when she's in the mood for cooking, but he doesn't mind when she isn't. He's very nice to her.'

'Good.' She nodded approval. 'That must be a relief to you, knowing she isn't alone. Though you see a lot of her still, I suppose? What about Rosie? I mean, I know she's a forgiving girl, one of the best, but after that terrible thing Hilde did to her . . .'

'Oh, Rosie still sees her. It wasn't *so* terrible!'

'Really, Laura! I should think to have a cup of boiling coffee flung in your face . . .!'

'It wasn't actually boiling.' My mother arched her eyebrows. *She* knew better! I said despairingly, 'Honestly, mother, Rosie was shocked at the time. But it was such a long time ago. Ages. Before Andrew and I were married.'

'Time doesn't heal all things,' my mother said. 'But I suppose you think you know best. You always have to see things your way, don't you?' She put her hands on the sides of her chair and heaved herself up with a faint grimace of pain. 'Put a bit more coal on the fire, dear. I think I had better go and rescue your poor husband from Arthur.'

Of course I see things my own way. What other way can I see them?

But I am a novelist, I thought, as I sat on the hearth rug and built up the fire, gently placing small lumps of coal, and hoping that the creeping whisper of falling ash would not waken my father. I should be able to project my imagination, see my mother's point of view. After all, I had a grown up daughter! How would I feel if Claudia were to leave her rich husband, give up her children to look after a dotty and demanding friend, take to *drink*! Not an alcoholic, perhaps, but a steady, routine drinker, never quite sober, a reserve whisky bottle always packed in her suitcase whenever she came to stay? (Even if I washed out the glass before I went to sleep, my mother must have smelled my drunkard's breath when she brought me a cup of tea in the morning. I can remember her little frown, her pursed lips, as her eyes darted stealthily round, in search of the hidden bottle.) Was it surprising that she was grateful to Andrew, galloping to the rescue of her wild-eyed lush of a daughter? Or that she blamed Hilde for my condition? 'I suppose *she* drinks, does she?' she asked on several occasions. And when I denied it, refused to believe me. 'If you're not careful, she'll drag you down with her.'

Poor Hilde, who needed me to love and support her. My mother saw her innocent need as destructive. Even Rosie thought it 'unnatural', though her concern was more for Hilde than me. She would have liked to find her a husband (the more I think about it, the more convinced I become that she had intended Andrew for Hilde) and did her best to find work for her.

But love without understanding is dangerous. Rosie said that Hilde was managing 'marvellously', but I knew the effort it cost her to be Rosie's receptionist; sitting behind the desk in the waiting room, looking so calm and so beautiful, but inwardly splintered with terror. When I fetched her, as I always tried to do at the end of the surgery, she was broken in pieces; unable even to speak to me, huddling silent and shaking in the passenger seat of my little car. Why didn't I tell Rosie this? Why didn't I *warn* her?

Well, of course, this is hindsight. At the time, I thought that perhaps Rosie was right; it would 'do Hilde good' to be independent. I had no idea that she might, in despair, turn on Rosie. And, in fact, the situation was convenient for me. Andrew was living with his mother; most weekends I spent with my children. Hilde's flat was the only place we could be alone. On the days she was working for Rosie, at evening surgery, Andrew came straight from the office. I opened the door to him naked; I was weak with love for him, but I was ashamed and afraid to tell Hilde. Though it was partly embarrassment (my old prurience still at work in me) I was also nervous of hurting her. She had so little; to speak of my happiness might look like a betrayal of what she did have, a blow in the face. Andrew was puzzled – Hilde would have to know sometime, what was the point of keeping it secret, I didn't think, *did I*, that we would grow bored with each other? – but he was patient, and, mistaking his patience for tolerance, I thought I had found a way to live that harmed no one. I was happy to keep my life in separate compartments – my friend, my lover, my whisky bottle, my typewriter. Until the day I went to fetch Hilde and found Rosie alone in the surgery with a livid burn on her cheek, bathing it, weeping . . .

That is something I could tell my mother, I thought, sitting back on my heels, looking into the blue and yellow flames licking round the small coals and privately smiling. If Hilde had not thrown that hot cup of coffee, Andrew and I might never have married each other . . .

My mother said, 'Laura!' Her face, bending over me, sagged from her cheek bones and jaw line in soft, pale little pouches. Seen from this angle she looked very much older and so pitiably weary that I had a moment of crude, selfish panic (if she dies first, what will we do with my father?) and then, at once, a rush of painfully guilty affection. How much this frail, gallant woman had suffered through me! I stood up and said, 'Darling, you look so tired. Sit down by the fire and I'll clear the dishes.'

She shook her head. Her eyes were flushed with tiny burst blood vessels. 'I'm sorry. My poor child. There's trouble . . .'

She glanced at my father who was stirring in his chair but still sleeping, making little whimpering sounds, deep in some dream.

I said, 'Arthur? Trouble with *Arthur*?'

'No, no.' She was holding my arm above the elbow, digging her nails in, plucking my sleeve impatiently. 'Andrew will tell you. It's better . . .'

He was in the cold hall. I looked at his face and saw death and destruction written there plain. I thought, *Ladybird, ladybird, fly away home*. Hollow sound filled my head; a roll of drums booming.

Andrew was making me sit on the bentwood chair by the telephone. 'Put her head down,' my mother cried. 'I'll get some cold water.' Andrew's hand was on the back of my neck, hurting me. I forced my head up, snorting hysterically, almost laughing. 'Andy, don't! What is it? The *children* . . .'

'They're all right. All right now, anyway. It's my mother. She's been taken to hospital.'

'Your *mother*?'

'Yes.'

'Who telephoned?'

'William.'

'But I thought, I thought it was *Arthur*.'

Andrew gave me a strange, spluttering giggle.

'My mother *said* it was Arthur!'

'I was wrong, dear.' My mother was beside me now, holding a glass of water to my lips. The water was cloudy from the tap. I took a sip and choked. She said, 'There, dear, try and drink slowly.' She held the glass in one hand; with the other, she was stroking my forehead. I peered past her at Andrew, a giant figure, looming above us. There was barely room for three people in the tiny hall.

He said, 'They telephoned us. Rosie and William. I mean, what happened, you see, they rang our house to find out how we'd got on. They didn't know, or hadn't hoisted it in, anyway, that we were coming here to visit your father. They'd assumed we were going straight home after we'd been to the prison.'

He stopped and coughed loudly. I gave a wild, strangled yelp. 'The bank, you mean, don't you? You had to go to the bank!'

Andrew nodded. Beneath the dim, overhead light, his face looked like a wax model's; shiny yellow skin, eyes fixed and glassy. He said. 'Yes. Yes, of course. What a curious Freudian slip! I had to look in at the *bank*.'

My mother appeared to have paid no attention to this exchange. She was regarding me anxiously, still stroking my forehead, still offering water. I said, 'Thank you, mother, I'm quite all right now. Andy, *please tell me . . .*'

'Hush, dear, don't shout,' my mother said. 'Remember your father.'

'I'm trying to tell you,' Andrew said in an aggrieved tone. 'If you would just *listen*. William rang our house, or it may have been Rosie, and Isobel answered. She said her Granny was hurt, she had blood on her face and she wouldn't wake up, would someone come quickly. She was upset, obviously, but perfectly sensible. So they rang the police and the ambulance service and drove over themselves. Quicker in the end than trying to get hold of some neighbour. And they didn't know where we were until they got there and Isobel told them. It's more or less sorted out now. Rosie and William are at home with the children and they'll stay till we come.'

I heard myself moaning.

Andrew said, '*Listen*. They were playing a game in the kitchen. My mother heard someone upstairs. Or thought she heard someone – you know what she is. She told the children to keep quiet and stay where they were. She went up to investigate, and, well, it's not clear what happened. William says there was a bit of a mess in our bedroom, but no more than we might have left, going off in a hurry this morning. The window was open. So I suppose there could have been a burglar and my mother surprised him. But Isobel didn't see anyone. She heard my mother cry out and found her on the floor with blood on her face.'

'Perhaps she had a heart attack. Hurt herself falling.'

'I suppose so.'

'If there had been a burglar, the dog would have barked. Did he bark?'

'I don't know. I didn't ask William.'

My mother said, 'Poor little Isobel. Oh, that poor baby!'

'William said she was marvellous. Stayed with her granny, cleaned her face up, tried to give her some water. She sent Henry to get the woman next door, but he didn't. William found him hiding in the outside lavatory.' Andrew grinned weakly. 'Fingers over his eyes, thumbs in his ears . . .'

I snorted. 'Typical Henry!'

'He is only a tiny boy,' my mother said sternly. 'Of course he was frightened.'

'Isobel must have been, too . . .' Kneeling beside her unconscious grandmother, wiping the blood away, trying to wake her up, waiting for help to come. My veins ran with ice. I said, shivering, 'How long was she there on her own?'

'God knows.' Andrew sighed; spread his hands.

I thought – We both seem to be *acting*. I shook my head dolefully. 'How is your mother? I mean, when Rosie and William arrived . . .'

'They were carrying her into the ambulance. Rosie didn't have time to examine her. Isobel was yelling blue murder because no one would help her find Henry. There was a police-woman with her, but she didn't seem to understand, or believe, there was another child there. So Rosie had her hands full.' He looked at his watch. 'It's a bit soon to ring the hospital. Better not waste the time, anyway. We can call in on the way home. Or not. See how it goes.' He smiled at me. 'Are you ready, love? All right? We'd better say goodbye to your father.'

'Be careful what you say, dear,' my mother warned me.

I got up from the bentwood chair. My limbs felt heavy and thick, as if I were pushing through water. As I went into the room, my mother was whispering to Andrew. I heard my own name, then the door closed behind me.

My father was waking and blinking. I said we were leaving now, and kissed him goodbye. His warm cheek was bristly. He mumbled, 'Give my love to the children, to Jeremy. Fancy him remembering that old wheelbarrow . . .'

Andrew driving. Changing gear round the tight bends of small lanes, headlamps full beam, hands steady on the wheel, concentrating, grunting under his breath. Swinging into the approach road to the motorway, tyres screeching, roaring full throttle into the straight, in the fast lane, passing long container trucks exceeding the speed limit for heavy vehicles, swaying motor caravans, elderly vans. Cross winds thud against the side of our car, rocking it. Frightened of the road ahead, streaming towards us, vanishing under our wheels like black water, I stare out of the side window. At this speed, the passing country becomes a toy landscape. Secret, small woods, dark, handkerchief fields with tiny sheep glimmering white, the flash of a river, the lights of a town spread along the horizon, a miniature train rattling out of a cutting. Two hours driving. Longer, if the traffic is heavy on the outskirts of London. Have we ever done this drive in two hours? Before the motorway was finished, it had taken three. When Henry and Isobel were small, and we drove to my parents' house, we used to stop at a transport café, a wooden shack built into the side of a hill, for buttered toast and strong tea. Earlier still, before Henry was born, when Isobel was a few months old, I had fed her in the car. Re-fuelling in flight, Andrew called it, amused by this silly joke, driving carefully (more carefully than he has ever done since), flinging his arm out to protect us if he had to brake on a corner.

Isobel had been an ugly baby, plump-chinned, beady-eyed, an owlish, hooked nose. A little old woman; a strong resemblance to the old Queen Victoria. Andrew had been hurt when I said this. He feared I was disappointed because she wasn't as pretty as Claudia. Once, when Isobel was about six months old, I found him looking through an album of photographs that Pete had taken of me and our daughter. When I came into the room,

Andrew closed the album, looking defensive. Isobel was his first child, so important to him; he was afraid I might think she came first with him, before his stepchildren. He said, in an innocently thoughtful tone, 'She really was amazingly beautiful, wasn't she?' And I answered, disingenuously, squinting at the closed album with affected bewilderment, choking back laughter at my own slyness, 'Who?' Oh, I see, you mean *Claudia*. Well, she takes after Pete. Classical features. Her face will get heavier as she gets older.'

Isobel is like me, my mother says. Loving and eager. (Short and plump, too. And jealous. Demanding. Glaring at Henry when I pick him up, cuddle him, hiding her bitter resentment behind a tight and furious smile.)

Looking at Isobel, I can see my young self, meet myself going back. (I can remember the feel of that tight smile on my own face when my mother held Cora.) Perhaps it is because I understand Isobel better that I have never been as worried for her as I have been for her brother. Henry's fears trouble me; they seem so numerous, so huge and so nameless. He holds his breath, listening to the footsteps of approaching disaster, the slither of monsters under the bed. I try to cheer him up, jolly him out of his panic, but it is so difficult. He can't speak of what frightens him, simply stands quivering, watching me mutely. 'Silly Henry,' I cry, 'silly baby. There's nothing to be scared of. If you don't believe me, you can ask Isobel!'

Isobel isn't fearless, but her terrors are out in the open; she meets them head-on. 'Why do you sing hymns when you go to the bathroom?' Andrew once asked her, and she stuck out that plump, jaunty chin. 'Oh, just to keep off the bogeys in the lavatory cistern. Keep them off me.'

Now something terrible has happened to her, and I wasn't there to prevent it. Well, you can't be in two places at once. I thought – If I had known this terrible thing was going to happen, would I have stayed at home today? Abandoned my father and Jeremy?

Tears rolled down the side of my nose. That poor little girl! Hearing the scream from the bedroom, going bravely upstairs, banging heart, leaden feet. Eight years old. Did she sing as she sat on the floor by her grandmother and waited for Henry to come back with our neighbour? Waiting and waiting. I couldn't bear this pathetic picture alone. I gave a loud sob, to attract Andrew's attention.

He said, in a grim, even voice, 'I am driving as fast as I safely can. You don't want me to crash the car, do you? That wouldn't help anyone.'

I was astonished. What had I done to deserve this attack? 'Don't be a bloody fool. I was thinking of Isobel.'

'Of Henry, too, I should hope,' Andrew said. 'Poor little chap. Hiding in the outside lavatory, scared to death of the spiders.'

'*Spiders?*'

'There was one the other day. A big web in the corner. He told me and I meant to do something about it. Bloody *hell*. He'll be so ashamed, he so badly wants to be brave. Don't take it out on him, will you?'

'*Andy!*'

'Well, you know what you are. You wish Henry was different. Bolder. More boy like. And, you know, he's aware of it.'

'He wants to be different,' I said. 'Am I supposed to pretend that what he wants *himself* doesn't matter? Of course I try to encourage him. I don't think that's wrong of me.' I tried to be crisp but tears made my voice wobble.

Andrew said, 'For God's sake stop snivelling. You've got nothing to worry about. It's just self-indulgence. The children are safe. Rosie's there.'

A vengeful rage rose up in me. In answer to Andrew's hostility? Or from some deeper source. I said, 'Good old Rosie. Always in at the death.'

As soon as I had spoken I saw that in the circumstances this could have been better phrased. If Andrew's mother was dying.

I said, lightly, trying to make a joke of it, 'What I mean is, Rosie scents trouble. Sniffs it from a distance like a forest fire. I don't mean I'm not glad of her talents on this occasion. But they used to burn witches.'

Andrew said, 'How unkind.' He gave a short laugh, but he was still on the war path. 'Witch yourself, Laura! You put people in books. That's as bad as casting spells or making wax models and sticking pins in them. Worse, really. You're always selling people short. Getting your own back. D'you think they don't notice?'

'Now *you're* being unkind.'

'Maybe. But you shock me. The way you always sink your teeth into Rosie, particularly. As if you couldn't bear to admit you might have some cause to be grateful.'

I said, mutinously, 'I always have to be grateful to Rosie.'

'What's wrong with that? So you bloody well ought to be.' Andrew clamped his mouth shut.

I looked at his tight-mouthed profile. He was pressing his upper lip against his top teeth, working his jaw muscles nervously. Approaching headlamps licked his face like yellow flames. I could see the damp shine of one eye, the sweat on his forehead.

I said, 'I'll drive if you like. If you're tired . . .'

'Shut up.'

'What do you mean, I should be grateful to Rosie? Apart from today . . .'

'If you don't know, I can't tell you.'

'Are you sure you don't want me to drive?'

'Absolutely. Please don't be patronising.'

'I didn't mean to be. Darling, are you very frightened about your mother? Oh, of course you are, how silly of me, how appallingly clumsy. I'm sorry. I do hope she's all right.'

'Do you? Do you *really*?'

'You know I do. Don't be so unfair, Andy. I know it's awful for you not knowing. But please don't let's quarrel.'

I was beginning to admire my magnanimous temper, though no doubt it was partly fear that restrained me. Andrew was driving so fast. He was so angry.

He said, with a hiss, 'Christ! I'm not quarrelling.'

The sweat was running into his eye. He shook his head, blinking. He said, in a gentler tone, 'What I keep thinking of is that story about the man who met Death in the market place and fled to Samara. I mean, there we were, belting down to your father, and all the time, back at the ranch, that poor, stupid old woman . . .! Oh, God, Laura! It's like some frightful, circular nightmare.'

I said, 'I know. Everything beginning again. There was a film, an old film, years ago. *Dead of Night*. I didn't see it, but Hilde told me . . .'

He nodded absently, wiping the sweat away with the back of his hand. I thought of something to say to amuse him. I was so relieved he seemed friendly again. 'You know, it's ridiculous, all those foolish house dreams I have, fire and flood, the roof falling in, gas pipes leaking, the floors giving way, and the staircase . . .'

'Yes. That is, I ought to know, oughtn't I? You've told me often enough. What is it, *exactly*, that you now find ridiculous?'

His tone should have warned me. But I was too charmed by my own sweet and innocent folly to pay attention. I said, with a little laugh, 'Only that I never once thought of burglars!'

Andrew sighed.

'What's the matter?'

'Oh.' Another sigh. Full of pained indignation. 'Nothing.'

'Come on,' I said. 'Tell me.'

He said, slowly and heavily, 'Has it ever occurred to you that I might resent all that nonsense? That I might, just occasionally, when my defences were down, find it *hurtful*? After all, I don't any longer have any private ambitions. Creative ambitions. All I do, all there *is* for me, really, apart from a game of tennis sometimes, is work to keep that roof you're so nervous about safe and mended over your ungrateful head. And you don't recognise this, you just go on and on, moaning. It never strikes you, apparently, that it's a bloody insult to me.'

I said, 'I can't help my dreams.'

'You could keep quiet about them.'

'I'm sorry. In future I will. I only mentioned them now because, well, it seemed so perverse. The way it's always something you never thought of that leaps up and clobbers you. It was just an example . . .'

'Oh, I daresay you'll make good use of it. You have this advantage over the rest of us, don't you? We're just raw material to you, grist to your mill. I don't say I'm not fascinated by the fictional process, but there are times when it chills me. Your mother put her finger on it when you were saying goodbye to your father. You seemed so shocked, I was worried about you, and your mother said not to be! She said, don't worry about Laura, it's all meat and drink to her. She'll take it into herself and spew it out later.'

'My mother said *that*?'

Andrew laughed, rather unpleasantly. 'I thought that would hit the spot! More than anything I could say. But it isn't true, actually.'

I said, amazed, 'Then why did you say it?'

'God knows. I suppose I wanted to hurt you. Get through that carapace of self-regard somehow. Oh, that's not true, either. It was just that it suddenly seemed, when this awful thing happened, after the telephone call, that all the concern was for you and the children. Nothing for me, or my mother. No one cares about the old trout, it seems. With good reason, perhaps, but it made me want to lash out, and you were convenient . . .'

He laughed again. This was not an apology.

He said, '*In fact*, what your mother said was that she was sorry, she was afraid she'd upset you, said something about your sister Cora that wasn't fair and she wanted me to tell you that, put it right with you. It was all she seemed to be able to think of, and it started me off. I thought – Lucky Laura, loved by all, fussed over. Even the heroine of her own novels. Why the heroine, always, I ask myself. Explaining and justifying, inventing, distorting. Dressing up . . .'

'*Dressing up*? What do you mean, Andy?'

'Just that I think you ought to look at yourself more honestly sometimes. Branch out as your father said. Though not *The Caine Mutiny*. Just have a go at the truth. Try walking naked. There might be more enterprise in it.'

I said, 'That's a quotation.'

He didn't answer. We were coming off the motorway on to a narrower road, two way traffic, approaching the lit tower blocks of East London. We stopped at a traffic light. A sign said POLICE EXPERIMENT.

I said, 'Well, at least I know what you think of me. Self-regarding, dishonest, ungrateful. Anything else while you're at it? I mean, we might as well clear the decks. I suppose I ought to be grateful that you've had the courage to come out at last. But I feel too much of a fool at the moment. I was stupid enough to believe that you loved me and that we were happy. And all the time, all these years, all this *poison* has been bubbling away like some horrible cauldron . . .'

'Rubbish,' he said. 'You know that it's rubbish, you know that I love you, cut it out, Laura.' Purged and cleansed by this outburst, drumming his fingers on the steering wheel, waiting for the lights to change, he grinned at me almost cheerfully. 'Do you think we had better stop at the next petrol station? Fill the tank, ring the hospital?'

But I was still swollen and throbbing with acrimony. I said, virtuously destructive, eyes burning, 'I should never have married you. It was all a mistake. You forced me into it, but I'm not going to blame you. The guilt is entirely mine. I made the wrong choice.'

As my mother had done. She had left her baby, come with me to London for my sake, and caught the cruel illness that was to kill Cora. Ever since, pain and guilt had been growing inside her. Not because she had made the wrong choice – though what must have looked to her, sometimes, like my rake's progress, may have tightened up a few screws. The pain is having to choose at all.

I never thought I would have to. There was no conflict between my love for Hilde, my love for Andrew. Two innocent passions, different, but complementary. No reason why one should exclude the other; these two sides of my life, beautifully balanced, made one, harmonious whole. In bed with Andrew, that early evening, I thought only of him; all that concerned me, when we arrived at the surgery and found Rosie alone, bathing her scarlet cheek, her eyes puffy with weeping, was to find Hilde and comfort her.

I was angry with Rosie. 'You shouldn't have offered her

anything. You know she's frightened of being poisoned, always has been, she can't *help* it. Even in the flat, she keeps her plates and cups and things separate, pours her own drinks, cooks her own food. I never touch what she uses, not even a saucepan.'

They were both looking at me. My old friend, my new lover. Andrew's expression was startled. I had told him about Hilde, of course I had told him, but this was the first time I had been so explicit.

Rosie's astonishment, on the other hand, seemed perverse to me. As did her shocked cry, 'But you can't live like that, Laura!'

'We have, for a long time. Don't pretend, Rosie. You've been to dinner with us, you and William. And you know she won't come to you.'

Rosie shook her head. A puzzled disclaimer.

I said, 'You only see what you want to see, don't you? I know that you've tried to help her. But, for Christ's sake, she lives on the edge of a *pit*! One push and she's over. She knows, at least, *part* of her knows that it isn't true, that no one is trying to harm her, but she can't escape from it. It's the terrible shadow she has to live with. You have to accept that it's there, that it's real to her, even though you don't believe it. It's not much to put up with, to save her.'

Rosie said, 'And you're the only one who can, is that it?'

'No. No, of course not. Oh, Rosie, stop playing *doctor*. If you say *medically speaking*, I think I shall hit you! I love her, that's the important thing. No one else *loves* her . . .'

She said, very sharply, 'No one else has a chance to!'

'That's not fair.'

'Isn't it? You pander to her delusions. Exaggerate them, I sometimes think, to keep hold of her. She's had coffee here other times, I always make coffee when we've finished surgery. And she's drunk it . . .'

'She may have done. She *tries*, Rosie. Tries to act normally – oh, so pitifully hard. But sometimes it's harder than others. When she's tired, over-worked, under strain, she can't always manage . . .' Rosie's small, pensive smile infuriated me. I yelled at her, shrewishly screaming, 'I told you the job was too much for her!'

215

Rosie stopped smiling. She said, in a grave voice, 'Does she – forgive me – does she know about you and Andrew?'

I felt as if I were falling. A flying dream, just before waking. Although I don't think I can have moved, Andrew put his arm round me, holding me steady. He said, answering Rosie, 'We haven't told her, but yes, I think she must know.' And to me, 'We ought to look for her. Where do you think she will have gone, Laura?'

He usually called me *dearest*, or *love*, or *my baby*. And other small, silly, private names. Never plain *Laura*. It sounded cold. I trembled in his embrace, deliberately playing the scared little girl, put my head on his shoulder. I said, 'Some pub or other. She'll have picked up some man and be drinking, probably.'

This seemed to surprise him. 'Aren't you worried?'

'No, why should I be?' I looked at his face and saw why. 'Oh, she won't *kill* herself, Andy! Nor even threaten to, there's no need! Throwing that coffee at Rosie was enough to explain to me how she was feeling. Hurt and rejected – if you're right and she's guessed about us. But she'll just settle down in a pub, have a drink or two and wait till I fetch her. She knows I'll always come running.'

Andrew said, 'How appalling!' He gave a short unamused laugh and looked beyond me, at Rosie. 'Did you know it was like this?'

And she said, watching me sadly, speaking reluctantly, 'No, not really. Oh, Laura, I'm sorry. It can't go on, can it?'

I knew what she meant. That is, I think now that I must have known what she meant, even though at the time I refused to admit it. I widened my eyes, playing innocent, and said, 'What can't go on, Rosie?'

Irritated by my mother-in-law's passion for bridge, I once said to her, spitefully, that it seemed excessively foolish to me to devote so much time and attention to a game in which you only had to stand up and look at your opponent's cards in order to win. And she answered, with one of her occasional sparks of angry intelligence (or intelligence sharpened by anger) that she couldn't see it was any different from reading a novel. 'After all,

Laura, I only have to skip a few pages, and all your work's gone for nothing. All the energy you put into your little stories, deceiving people, keeping the suspense going, is just a game, isn't it? You're assuming your readers will play it your way, but if they don't want to, they only have to look at the end.'

She delivered this home truth with a proud thrust of her powerful jaw, a triumphant spark in her pale and prominent eyes. And although this was only a minor scuffle in the long running battle between us, it impressed me, affected me. When I think of 'my readers' I envisage my mother-in-law, an adversary to be outwitted if I can manage it. So I write as I have done in this story, signalling events ahead, hoping that the interest will lie not in what happened, but how, when, and why . . .

As we sat in the back of Rosie's car, Rosie driving, Andrew's arm was confidently protective about me. The brief coldness I had sensed earlier (that had really been doubt) had quite gone. He had chosen his role and was drawing it round him. Becoming Andrew, my husband – even though, at that moment, I didn't yet know it.

There were seven pubs Hilde was accustomed to visit, where she hid when something had hurt or disturbed her and she wished me to find her. The old Hide-and-Seek game – only now I was always the Seeker, the Comforter.

We found her in the fourth pub. She was in the corner, at a small table, a man sitting opposite her. The back of his head looked young; short, thick hair, a smooth neck above his dark jacket collar. Hilde was smiling, eyes black in her pale face, holding a glass of red wine. She looked up and saw us; the three of us coming towards her. She looked at me, at Andrew, at Rosie, and then, still smiling, that bright, sweet, thoughtful smile, crushed her glass in her fingers.

Glass tinkled. A small sound, but it was quiet in the pub, half a dozen people perhaps, softly talking. Heads turned. Remained turned. No one stirred; the scene was fixed for a moment, a still frame from a film. I tried to move but Andrew was holding me. I heard Rosie whisper, 'Let her go, Andrew.'

The man had vacated his chair. I saw his face for a second, before I sat down, a young, pink-and-white, surprised, guileless face, young, gleaming lips beneath a small, neat moustache. Then there was no one but Hilde. She had stopped smiling. Her eyes regarded me earnestly; questioning, troubled. I said, 'You've cut yourself, darling, let me see, will you?' But before I could stop her she lifted her hand – both hands now – and ground the broken glass into her cheeks, pulling her eyes down, until they showed red at the corners.

I took her hands, pulled them away, towards me; held them down, between mine, on the table. They were warm, trembling, and strong. As I held them, using all my strength, the glass cut me. Blood oozed like rubies between our joined fingers. She looked down at them and started to cry, to weep helplessly, a hopeless passion of grief. Tears ran down her beautiful face, mingling with blood, and red wine, and small, savage splinters of glass. I wept with her, blinded. I said, 'Hilde, Hilde . . .'

I don't know how long we sat there. Only minutes, perhaps. I didn't dare let her hands go, and after the first shock of pain from the glass that seemed to stab up through my wrists, through my whole body, I felt nothing. Then Andrew said, in my ear, 'Hang on, love, the ambulance will be here very soon.'

Hilde heard him. She began to struggle and shriek, throwing her head back, up and down like a horse, wrenching her hands free, tearing at her cheeks, at her mouth, at her forehead. I shouted, 'Andy – her eyes, her *eyes* – mind her eyes!' But Rosie was already there, pushing round the table in this crowded corner, knocking a chair flying, seizing Hilde, pinioning her arms back behind her, a practised doctor's hold, thrusting Hilde's head forward.

I moaned, 'Rosie, be careful, don't hurt her . . .'

Rosie's face was drained and expressionless. She said, looking at Andrew behind me, 'I can manage. Get Laura away, out of this . . .'

Andrew was pulling me, dragging me off my chair, turning me round to face him, my back to Hilde. I beat at his chest with my fists. I wailed, loud as Hilde was wailing, 'Let me go, *let me go*, I can't leave her.'

And he said, 'You can't help her. You can go if you like. Only you have to choose, Laura. Her or me. I'm not sharing you.'

Did he *really* say this? Considered objectively, it seems somewhat unlikely. Such a clear statement – or threat – in that confused moment. I don't know. All I know is what I remember. What I told myself afterwards. Only force could have kept me from Hilde, made me abandon my friend. I said, 'Please let me go, Andy, at least let me go in the ambulance with her.' But though I struggled against him, pushing and sobbing, smearing his shirt front with the blood on my hands, it was only for show, for my own vindication. The truth, the naked truth, is that I had chosen already.

And a bloody rotten choice, too, I thought glumly, waiting in the car at the petrol station while Andrew was telephoning the hospital. He doesn't love me, in fact he despises me, or he would never have said all those cruel and horrible things. *The heroine of my own novels*, indeed! Looking at him as he stood at the pay phone in the shop, between two conical stands of cheap, packaged sweets, stroking his upper lip as he listened, then scratching his ear as he answered, I thought, 'Well, I'll *show* him.'

But, of course, as he left the shop and came running towards me, this childish vindictiveness vanished. (Or sank away temporarily, along with a lot of other shaming but lively and useful resentments into the slime and the mud, the creative sediment of the mind.) I leaned across and opened the door for him.

He got into the car. He fastened his seat belt; switched on the ignition. He said, not looking at me, in a controlled, steady voice, 'We're going straight home.'

I put out my hand. He took it and squeezed it and handed it back to me. He said, 'She's unconscious.'

'Then we ought to go to the hospital.'

He shook his head. 'She won't come round. Well, one doesn't know, naturally, but what they said was, *we are not very hopeful*, and you know what that means in hospital jargon. She's had a massive stroke, she must have hit her head when she fell, as you said. On the bedstead, or the side table. Some sharp corner.' He made an odd, involuntary sound with his mouth open; half a gasp, half a groan. He started the engine and said, 'So no drama, no burglars.'

'If there had been a burglar, the dog would have barked.'

'Yes, indeed. But since we don't know if he barked or not, why keep on about it? She thought she heard someone, that's all that matters. It was brave of her to go up to see. Protecting the children. Are you trying to diminish that, in some way?'

'No. No, of course not. It's just, I was thinking – all those rapists and murderers she was always afraid of, up on the common. And there was no one there, after all.'

He started to cry. He put his head down on the steering wheel. The engine was throbbing; the whole car vibrating. I could see his neck shuddering.

I said, 'Darling.'

He sat up and looked at me. Tears had left shiny lines like snail tracks on his cheeks. His eyes were washed clear. He said, 'Sorry. So stupid. I mean, I was expecting it. That's why I was so filthy tempered. Do you mind driving?'

He unfastened his seat belt and got out of the car. I wriggled across the gear lever, banging my knee on the dash, adjusted the driver's seat forward. Andrew opened the passenger door and sat beside me, blowing his nose.

He said, 'Poor old thing. That's all I feel, really. I wish I felt more.'

'I think we should go to her. Even if she's unconscious.'

'They'll ring us. She could hang on for days.'

'Darling, I know that . . .'

'Look,' he said, 'Listen. We both need some sleep. Rest, anyway. Food. I don't know about you but I could do with a drink. Lucky it's Sunday tomorrow, I don't have to go to work, all the same, we'll be busy. I imagine the police will want to see us, since they were called in. Make some routine check, whatever they do to keep their files tidy. We can split the duties between us. I'll visit the hospital. You can receive the Law, comfort the children.'

He was smiling. Actually *smiling*. To reassure me; to show me, in all this confusion, the smooth curve of life. Dear, considerate Andrew, who tries so hard to understand, and perhaps understands more than I think he does about some things, and worries more than he need about others. My dream, for example. The locked door. The desolate attic. The innocent, heartbreaking laughter from the safe room beneath. But it is only a dream. A dark warning.

'Don't,' I said, perturbed by his smile that was meant to console me, 'don't make a joke of it.'

'I'm not,' he said. 'Our house is still standing.'